Praise for Beth Wiseman

"Beth Wiseman writes with a masterful hand
that reaches the recesses of the soul. Her capability for
understanding the human condition exceeds traditional
empathy and moves the reader to both introspection
and exhilaration. Characters connect, transform, and
redeem, making for a must 'one sit' read. Wiseman's
comprehension of grace and redemption plays out
in the subtle confines of the everyday and
teaches the reality that new life is possible for all."
—Kelly Long, bestselling author of *Sarah's Garden*

"Wiseman's voice is consistently compassionate
and her words flow smoothly."
—*Publishers Weekly* on *Seek Me With All Your Heart*

"In *Seek Me With All Your Heart*,
Beth Wiseman offers readers a heartwarming story
filled with complex characters and deep emotion.
I instantly loved Emily and eagerly turned each page,
anxious to learn more about her past—
and what future the Lord had in store for her."
—Shelley Shepard Gray, bestselling author
of the Seasons of Sugarcreek series

The Wonder
of Your Love

The Wonder of Your Love

BETH WISEMAN

Love Inspired

Recycling programs for this product may not exist in your area.

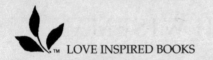

ISBN-13: 978-0-373-78704-3

THE WONDER OF YOUR LOVE

First published by Thomas Nelson, Inc. 2011

Copyright © 2011 by Beth Wiseman

Scripture quotations are from the King James Version of the Bible.

www.LoveInspiredBooks.com

Printed in U.S.A.

To Sherry Gregg

Glossary

ab im kopp—crazy, off in the head

ach—oh

aenti—aunt

boppli—baby or babies

bruder—brother

daed—dad

danki—thank you

Deitsch—Dutch

dochder—daughter

eck—special place for bride and groom at the corner of the wedding table

Englisch—non-Amish person

fraa—wife

grossmammi—grandmother

guder mariye—good morning

gut—good

haus—house

kaffi—coffee

kapp—prayer covering or cap

kinner—children or grandchildren

lieb—love

maedel—girl

mamm—mom

mariyefrieh—tomorrow morning

mei—my

mudder—mother

nee—no

onkel—uncle

roascht—roast

rumschpringe—running-around period when a teenager
turns sixteen years old

schee—pretty

sohn—son

Wie bischt?—How are you?

wunderbaar—wonderful

ya—yes

Chapter One

Katie Ann reached into the drawer of the end table next to the couch and pulled out the letter she'd received two weeks ago. She knew it would upset her stomach to read it—as it had a dozen times already—but she unfolded it anyway. She couldn't imagine why her husband's mistress, Lucy Turner, was planning to travel all the way to Colorado to see her. She took a deep breath and read the letter again.

> *Dear Katie Ann,*
> *I hope this letter finds you well. I heard from some of our mutual acquaintances here in Lancaster County that you had a healthy baby boy and named him Jonas. Congratulations to you. A baby is such a miracle from God.*

Katie Ann rolled her eyes, the way she always did at Lucy's mention of God. *A good, godly woman wouldn't get involved with another woman's hus-band.* Although she knew good and well that it took two for such deception. She let out a heavy sigh and continued reading.

> *I'm sure that I am the last person you want to hear from, and I'm sorry to bother you, but I need to meet with you. I know it is awkward, but I have something important to discuss, and it's too much to say in a letter, or even over the phone. As soon as I can arrange to be off work, I will be traveling to Colorado. I hope that you can find time to meet with me to discuss this urgent matter. I thought it might be easiest for you if you knew in advance that I'm coming. All the best to you and your new little one, Lucy Turner*

Katie Ann folded the piece of paper and put it back in the drawer, determined not to let thoughts of Lucy ruin this day. But as she crossed through the living room toward the kitchen, she couldn't help but wonder exactly when Lucy was going to show up on her doorstep. And what she wanted.

Katie Ann poured a large bag of M&M's into a Tupperware bowl, then put the container next to the other food she would be carting to the Detweilers' house. Both the candy and container were a gift for the bride and groom. It was traditional to place a fun and edible gift on the *eck*, something that held special meaning between the giver and the recipient. Katie Ann guessed that lots of people would choose M&M's, though. It was no secret that the candy was Emily's favorite.

She couldn't believe that the wedding was tomorrow. It seemed like just yesterday her husband's nephew David was a young boy, but tomorrow he would marry Emily in front of a hundred friends and family. A small crowd for an Amish wedding. She recalled the nearly four hundred guests at her own wedding, but she quickly brushed the memory aside as she snapped the lid closed on the bowl.

"Martha! Are you ready? Is the baby ready?" She walked back through the living room, turned the corner, and strolled into little Jonas's bedroom. It was a beautiful room, painted in powder blue and trimmed with a lively, multicolored border of dancing ponies. Matching curtains covered the two windows facing the Sangre de Cristo Mountains. The fancy décor would be frowned upon by the bishop if he were to visit, but it was all Martha's doing, and Katie Ann didn't have the heart to change it. Martha was a widow and didn't have any children of her own.

"This little one needs a real nursery," her *Englisch* friend had said with a huff before Jonas was even born.

Martha would be upset if she knew that Katie Ann had heard from Lucy.

Katie Ann stood quietly in the doorway for a moment, savoring the view of her little miracle in Martha's arms and the contented expression on the older woman's face. Martha was as much a grandmother to Jonas as Katie Ann's own mother would have been if she were still living. Katie Ann smiled as Martha gently cradled Jonas in her arms, pushing the oak rocking chair into motion with her foot.

"Why don't you let me stay with the baby while you go on over to the Detweilers' house? No need to drag this young one into the cold, plus he's finally stopped crying and is sleeping soundly." Martha touched her finger to Jonas's cheek as her lips curved into a smile. After a moment, she looked back up at Katie Ann. "Unless it's too cold for you to take the buggy. We can bundle him up real good and take my car."

Katie Ann shook her head. "No, no, I don't mind the buggy ride. It's crisp outside, but sunny. It would be *gut* if you could stay with Jonas. Are you sure you don't mind?"

Katie Ann had been up more than usual during the night with Jonas. He just wouldn't stop crying, and nothing she did seemed to calm him.

Martha looked up at her and scowled. "Now where else on the planet do you think I'd rather be than with this baby?" She raised one hand out from under Jonas and tucked a piece of brownish-gray hair behind her ear, a strand that had fallen from beneath the butterfly clip on the top of her head.

Katie Ann pushed a loose tendril of her own hair beneath her *kapp* as she moved toward the rocker. "Just checking." She leaned down and kissed her precious bundle on the cheek. "See you soon, my darling."

Martha raised her chin as she spoke in a whisper. "You tell Vera Detweiler that I'm expecting creamed celery tomorrow. Lots of it."

Katie Ann nodded as she moved toward the door. "You know there's always lots of celery at weddings." She pulled her heavy black coat, gloves, and bonnet on. Once she was bundled up, she came back to the bedroom door and glanced in at Martha. "I'll be back soon. You'll check on him often, right?"

Martha nodded. "Yes, I will. Now, you go." She waved a hand at Katie Ann.

Martha hadn't missed a day since Jonas was born. Sometimes she stayed for hours, and she often spent the night. Katie Ann was grateful to have the older woman in her life. Being a single mother was challenging.

As she closed the door behind her, she thought about Ivan. Despite her husband's infidelity, she was sorry that he would never see his son. She still mourned Ivan's untimely death, but with each passing day, her sorrow became less as her anger grew stronger. She was thankful to God for blessing her with Jonas so late in life, but even her relationship with Him had suffered. Maybe it was all the sleepless nights she'd been up with Jonas, too tired even to pray. That's what she kept telling herself.

She climbed into the buggy and turned on the battery-operated heater on the seat next to her. The thermometer outside her window showed thirty-three degrees, but as was usually the case here in the San Luis Valley, the sun shone brightly, making it seem much warmer than it was. Clicking her tongue, she set the buggy in motion and breathed in the fresh country air, wondering if it would snow later. She'd read in the newspaper that morning that there might be a flurry, but no hard weather was forecast. She wondered if the Detweilers' relatives had arrived safely. Vera was doubtless beside herself, busy with preparations for her daughter's wedding. Katie Ann was disappointed that the weather back in Lancaster County would prevent Ivan's side of the family from attending. She'd always been close to her in-laws, and she was sure David must be disappointed as well.

Once again, recollections of her own wedding swirled in Katie Ann's head, and her eyes filled with tears as she thought about the good years she'd had with Ivan. And the bad. But she never could have predicted that Ivan would leave her—for the likes of Lucy Turner—and take up residence with the *Englisch* woman back in Lancaster County. She still struggled to forgive her dead husband's choices…and Lucy Turner.

Eli Detweiler thanked the cabdriver and whistled a tune as he walked across the snow to his cousin's house. He blocked the sun's glare with his hand; he'd never seen a more beautiful day. His spirits were high, and he felt like he had his entire life ahead of him—even though he'd already lived at least half of it. But at forty-three he had a new sense of freedom, the kind that comes from being a new empty nester, as the *Englisch* called it. He'd married off the youngest of his *kinner* two weeks ago, and with Maureen out of the house, he was on his own. After Sarah died, he'd managed to raise six young children by himself, and he couldn't recall a moment's peace.

Five of the six were girls, and he never could have predicted the challenges of raising daughters. Thankfully, he had one ally in Jake, his only son and the oldest of the bunch. He grinned as he knocked on the door, knowing he wouldn't have changed anything about his children or his life— except for that one dreary day in November seventeen years ago, the day he lost his beloved Sarah. She'd been his one and only true love, and not a day went by that he didn't think about her. No woman had even sparked his interest since then, despite the many attempts by family and friends to fix him up. It was the Amish way to remarry quickly following the death of a spouse, and he had to admit he could have used the help. He'd had a few random dates, but there hadn't been anyone who could hold a candle to his Sarah.

"Eli! It's so *gut* to see you." His cousin's wife wrapped her arms around his neck.

"*Gut* to be here, Vera," he said as he returned her embrace. "Hard to believe it's been over a year."

Vera stepped aside so he could enter, and the warmth of a glowing fire met him as he stepped into their living room. His eyes scanned the room. He saw his cousin Elam and two of their four children, Betsy and Levi. He knew Elam and Vera's third child, Jacob, had married last fall and was living in his own home with his wife, Beth Ann. Eli regretted not being able to attend the boy's wedding, but the weather had kept his family away last year. After he said his hellos to all of them, they all turned their attention to the stairs and watched Emily come down. A year had made quite a difference. Elam and Vera's daughter looked…happy. And as her face lit up, Eli recalled everything that the girl had been through. It was a true blessing to be here for her wedding.

"You look so *schee*, Emily," he said as he hugged her.

"*Danki* so much for coming, *Onkel* Eli."

Elam's *kinner* had always called him uncle, even though he was really their cousin.

"I wouldn't have missed it, *mei maedel.*" He eased away and found Vera. "Now, Vera, don't let me be in the way. I remember with *mei dochders'* weddings, it's a busy time. So you just put me to work wherever I'm needed."

Vera dismissed his comment with a wave of her hand. "You must be tired from your travels, and really, I think everything is about ready. We've had people helping us all day. We'll be up early in the morning to start warming food and to finish setting up the chairs. You can help then."

She sat down in one of the rocking chairs facing a tan couch on the opposite wall, motioning for him to sit as well. "Everyone else from Middlefield is staying at the local bed-and-breakfasts since this house isn't nearly as big as we were used to back home. They were all here earlier helping, but you probably won't see them all until *mariyefrieh.*"

Tomorrow morning was fine by Eli. He was weary from travel, and just chatting with his cousin's family would be plenty for this evening. He nodded, and a moment later Betsy walked up to him, toting a book under her arm. "Hello, Betsy. You've turned eight years old since moving here, haven't you?"

A strand of curly blond hair fell from beneath her *kapp* as she nodded. *"Ya."* She cocked her head to one side and stared at him.

Eli knew from past experience that there was no telling what might come out of Betsy's mouth. He braced himself.

"*Mamm* doesn't understand why a handsome man like you doesn't have a *fraa*."

"Betsy!" Vera covered her eyes with her hand as a rosy blush filled her cheeks. "Excuse Betsy, Eli." Then she glared at her daughter, but Eli just grinned.

"Because I just haven't found anyone as pretty as you," he said. Then he tickled her, and she squealed until he released her.

When someone knocked at the door, Vera stood up and eased her way across the living room. Cousin Elam moseyed to the fireplace and stoked the dwindling fire until orange sparks shimmied upward, then he gave the logs a few more pokes until the flames stretched high.

Eli leaned back against the couch and crossed one ankle over his knee. He stroked his beard as he thought about how long he might stay in Colorado. This was his first trip, there'd be much to see, and he didn't have to rush home to tend to one single thing. *A vacation*. His daughters had all married fine men who took good care of them and the five grandchildren they'd given him, and his son's wife was expecting number seven, the second for the couple. Yes, all was well in Eli's world. Freedom to do as he pleased. He stroked his beard, feeling giddy as a young man in his *rumschpringe*. His musings were interrupted by the return of Vera and another woman.

"Eli, this is Katie Ann. She's soon to be Emily's *aenti*." Vera motioned toward the woman on her right. "She's David's *aenti* on his father's side."

Eli uncrossed his ankle from atop his knee, stood up, and extended his hand to the woman. "Nice to meet you."

She latched onto his hand, nodded, then followed Vera to the kitchen.

Elam waited until the ladies were out of the room before he spoke in a whisper. "Pretty, isn't she?"

Eli narrowed his brows, wondering why his cousin would make the comment about another man's wife, and not sure how to respond. "*Ya*, I suppose so." He tried to sound casual. "What's her name again?"

"Katie Ann." Elam told Betsy to go help in the kitchen, and his young cousin pouted a bit before padding out of the room. "And she is a widow." He kept his voice low. "But she hasn't been a widow for long. Her husband was killed only a few months ago in a car accident." Elam stepped closer and lowered his voice even more. "He'd left her before that, though, for an *Englisch* woman. He'd moved back to Lancaster County and was living with that woman when he died."

Eli glanced toward the kitchen for a moment before he looked back at Elam. "That's terrible."

"*Ya*." Elam shook his head. "A real shame."

Eli stroked his beard again, and the two men were quiet as the ladies reentered the room.

"It was nice to meet you, Eli." Katie Ann waved briefly in Eli's direction as she moved toward the door. "See you all tomorrow."

Eli returned the gesture, watching her as she crossed the threshold. As the door closed behind her, Eli scratched his chest. Not that it itched. He just wasn't sure why his heart was beating so fast.

Katie Ann drove home and tethered her buggy, then waved to Lillian as she walked toward her own house. She was blessed to have Ivan's brother and sister-in-law living right next door on the same property. The two households shared a barn and phone, and Samuel and Lillian were as much her family as they were before Ivan left her.

She slipped quietly into her living room, where Martha was sitting on the couch reading a magazine, bare feet propped up on the coffee table.

"Did Jonas sleep the whole time I was gone?"

"Yep. I kept checking on him, but the little fella is sleeping soundly." Martha didn't look up as she flipped a page.

"When did you last check on him?" Without waiting for an answer, Katie Ann hurried to Jonas's room. She stared down into his crib. As his tiny chest rose and fell, she breathed a sigh of relief.

After a few moments, she walked back into the

living room. Martha's arms were folded across her chest, and Katie Ann quickly pulled her eyes from the older woman's glare.

"I told you that I have been checking on him. He's just fine, isn't he?"

Katie Ann fluffed a throw pillow on the couch beside Martha and slowly sat down. "*Ya.* He is." She crossed one leg over the other and nervously kicked her foot into motion. It had taken her a long time to leave Jonas with anyone, and the only ones she trusted with her baby were Martha and Lillian. And that hadn't come easily.

They were quiet for a few moments, and Martha resumed turning the pages of her magazine.

"I'm doing better," Katie Ann finally said as she fingered the string on her prayer covering. "You know, about checking on him."

Martha twisted her mouth to one side and grunted. "How many times did you get up to check on him last night?"

Katie Ann thought about all the nights she'd just watched Jonas sleeping. Martha would be shocked if she knew the real amount of sleep Katie Ann had lost hovering over the baby, fear consuming every inch of her being. "Not that many."

Martha faced her. "How many, Katie Ann? Once to feed him? Three times? A dozen times?"

The last was probably most accurate, but Katie Ann just shrugged. "I don't know. But he has been crying during the night, and I don't know what's wrong with him."

It was true. The past week she'd been up with him even more than usual. And not just to watch him breathe. He would wail, and Katie Ann wasn't sure what was wrong, which just added to the fear that he would die before he reached his first birthday. The way Annie did.

"You're a good mother, Katie Ann, and Jonas is a healthy little bundle." Martha patted Katie Ann on the knee and returned to her reading. "Babies cry sometimes."

Katie Ann had never told anyone but Ivan about Annie. It happened so long ago…

They were quiet again, and after a few moments Katie Ann glanced at Martha and frowned. "I don't know why you read that garbage. It has nothing to do with us or our community."

"I'm not Amish. It's allowed." Martha didn't look up this time.

Katie Ann gently elbowed her. "I think you should be baptized and become one of us." She'd had this conversation with Martha many times, and the answer was always the same. "You attend worship with us every other Sunday, you love the Lord, and you are always doing for folks in our community."

Katie Ann thought back almost a year, to when she'd become close to Martha. It was an unlikely friendship—a pregnant Amish woman whose husband had left her…and an older *Englisch* widow who was gruff, outspoken, and set in her ways. But it didn't take Katie Ann long to realize that beneath Martha's crotchety temperament was a woman who just wanted to love and be loved—to have a family. And that's what Katie Ann, Jonas, and Martha had become. Family.

Martha closed the magazine slowly, pressed her lips together, and squinted her eyes as she glared at Katie Ann. "I'll tell ya *again*…I'm not wearing those clothes of yours, and especially not those prayer coverings. Anything on my head makes my scalp itch. And I am not giving up my television." She tossed her head back, grunted, and went back to her magazine.

Katie Ann took note of Martha's red-and-white-striped pants outfit, her mismanaged curls beneath the butterfly clip, and her bright red fingernails, and grinned. Converting would indeed require a large makeover for Martha. But Martha often visited the bishop, and Katie Ann wondered what they talked about.

All of a sudden Martha gasped, slammed the magazine closed, and twisted to face Katie Ann. Her eyes were round as saucers. "Did you meet *him*?"

"Who?" She leaned her head back against the couch as she yawned.

"Eli Detweiler, Elam's cousin."

Katie Ann uncrossed her legs and shifted her weight. "As a matter of fact, yes. Why do you ask?"

Martha pinched her face together until her wrinkles looked like they were all connected. "Is he as handsome as Vera says?"

"What?" Katie Ann turned her head to face her.

Martha cackled. "Vera's got good taste. That Elam of hers is quite a looker. If she says Eli is handsome, I bet he's a hunk."

Katie Ann shrugged. "I didn't notice."

"Did she tell you that he's a single man? Lost his wife seventeen years ago, and—"

Katie Ann bolted from the couch, slammed her hands to her hips, and glared at her friend. "I am in mourning, Martha. My husband has only been gone for a few months. How could you possibly think—"

"Oh, stop it." Martha stood up. "That scoundrel cheated on you and left you for another woman. I'd get to know that handsome Eli Detweiler while he's in town."

Katie Ann blinked back tears, determined that there would be no more crying where Ivan was concerned. "You are being inappropriate, Martha."

Martha placed her hands on Katie Ann's arms. "Katie Ann, I couldn't love you any more if you were my own daughter. It's your people's way to marry soon after a spouse dies, and Vera said that Eli is a fine fellow."

"If he's such a fine fellow, then why has he been single for the past seventeen years?" She freed herself of Martha's hold and walked to the fireplace.

She poked the glowing embers several times until a spark eased up between the logs.

"Apparently he's been raising six kids, and the last one just got married. Maybe he was dedicated to his family? An admirable quality, wouldn'tcha say?"

Katie Ann didn't look up as she gave the fire another poke. "Maybe."

Martha chuckled. "Or maybe he's just been waiting for *you* for the past seventeen years."

Katie Ann put the fire tool in its holder and faced off with Martha. "*Ya.* I'm sure that's it." She rolled her eyes.

Martha clomped across the wooden floor, grabbed her red purse from the couch, and slipped on her black slippers by the door. "I'm heading to my house. I need a nap."

Katie Ann followed and wondered if she'd have time for a little shut-eye before Jonas woke up. "Martha, why do you wear your slippers when there is snow on the ground?"

Martha raised her foot and flashed the sole of her shoe upward, giving it a pat. "These aren't regular slippers, dear. I ordered these on the Internet, and they weren't cheap. They're water resistant and easy on my corns." She put her foot down before she lost her balance. Her brows shifted upward. "Another thing I couldn't give up to join your people. My Internet!" She pulled Katie Ann into a hug. "You get some rest. Gonna be a long day tomorrow." Then she winked.

Katie Ann stepped onto the porch as Martha eased her way down the porch steps. "Martha?"

Martha looked over her shoulder. "What?"

Katie Ann wagged a finger in her direction, recalling the time Martha tried to fix her up with an Amish fellow at the hardware store barely a month after Ivan died. "No funny business tomorrow. No matchmaking. Do you hear me?"

Martha flashed a broad toothy smile. "Of course, dear."

Katie Ann closed the door and went to check on her precious baby. She tiptoed into his room, lightly touched his head, and spoke to him in a whisper. "You are all that I need, my little miracle."

She and Ivan had tried to have a baby for most of their twenty years of marriage. It was bittersweet the way it all turned out, and again she wished Ivan could have held his child. He died three months before Jonas arrived, and never even knew Katie Ann was pregnant. She wondered if she'd done right by Ivan not to tell him, but at the time she hadn't wanted him returning to her out of obligation, and she wasn't sure he even deserved to know.

It was quiet in the house. She considered taking a nap, but sure as she laid her head down, her baby boy would wake up. Instead, she let her mind drift to a place she often went during quiet times. As visions of her early years with Ivan danced in her head, she tried to stay focused on those happy memories, but as usual, it wasn't long before images of Ivan and Lucy bombarded her thoughts. She shook her head and anger wrapped around her heart in the familiar way.

In the beginning she'd blamed herself for not being a better wife. Later she'd faulted Lucy for seducing her husband away from her. Most recently she'd decided that Ivan was a weak, dishonest coward—and he was the one responsible for ruining her life.

How could Martha even suggest that she open her heart to another man? *Even good Amish men lie and leave their wives.*

Chapter Two

Eli slipped on his shoes, surprised at how well he'd slept in the extra bedroom upstairs. He couldn't remember the last time he'd awakened anywhere besides his own bed. After he pulled his suspenders up on his shoulders, he lifted his arms high above his head and stretched. It was five thirty, still completely dark outside. Only the light from his lantern flickered nearby. But he could hear folks bustling about downstairs. It was a fine day for a wedding, and he was looking forward to all that life had to offer him in this new stage.

He walked casually down the stairs, fighting the urge to whistle. When he reached the bottom of the stairs, he hugged several of his cousins who had arrived early to help. He spotted Katie Ann among the women scurrying around in the kitchen. She smiled, and he found himself holding her gaze for longer than he should have. She looked away and went back to buttering loaves of bread. Eli wondered if she knew that Elam was trying to play matchmaker.

Elam walked in then, followed by Jacob and Levi. They were carting chairs, and Eli figured that was his job for the moment. "More chairs in the barn?"

Elam nodded. "*Ya. Danki*, Eli."

Eli recognized the tense lines running across Elam's forehead. It wasn't just a busy day for the father of the bride—in a way, he was losing his little girl, sending her off into adulthood, trusting that her husband would always take care of her. Eli had felt the rush of panic on the wedding day of each of his daughters.

After he retrieved four more chairs, he met up with Elam in the living room. "David seems like a *gut* man, from all I've heard."

Elam unfolded one of the metal chairs and placed it in a row with the others. "*Ya*. David is a fine fellow."

There was nothing he could say to alleviate his cousin's anxiety. Eli glanced up to see Katie Ann walking into the living room, and he nodded at her, knowing he was flirting, yet unable to take his gaze from her. Her deep brown eyes drew him in, but she looked away as she leaned down into a playpen and scooped up a baby.

He eased his way slowly toward her. "What a fine-looking *boppli*."

Katie Ann's face lit with pride. Her eyes softened and her cheeks glowed as she looked down on the little one. Nothing like a baby to warm a woman's heart—or a man's, for that matter. Every time someone commented about one of his grandchildren, Eli's heart swelled with pride. Even though it wasn't the Amish way, Eli was pretty sure God allowed it for grandparents.

"*Danki.* This is Jonas." She twisted so that Eli could see the child she was cradling in her arms. Eli leaned closer to the baby—and to her. His arm barely brushed against hers, causing her to step back a bit, but not before the sweet smell of lavender filled his nostrils. He wasn't sure if the scent came from her or the baby, but he drew in a deep breath as he gazed upon the child.

"He looks to be about two months, no?" Eli forced himself to stand tall and give the woman some space.

"*Ya.* He is two months old this week."

Eli remembered when his first grandchild was born. His daughter-in-law, Laura Jane, had gone into labor early. Scared them all to death, but little Leah fought her way into the world at four pounds, and today she was a healthy, beautiful four-year-old. "He has the same deep brown eyes as you," he said after a moment.

Katie Ann's cheeks took on a pink flush. "He's everything to me." She eased the baby up in her arms and kissed him on the forehead.

"Your first one?"

She lifted her head to face him. "*Mei only* one."

Eli nodded. "I have six…and one on the way."

Katie Ann narrowed her brows as she squinted, and Eli could almost feel the prick from her piercing eyes. "Did you say…one on the way?"

"*Ya*. Due next month."

She bit her lip. "I see."

Eli looped his thumbs beneath his suspenders, knowing he should be carting more chairs in. He chuckled. "I'm guessing I'll have a dozen or so more when it's all said and done."

Her eyes grew round as she stared at him. *"Really?"*

"Sure. Aren't you hoping for lots more?" He stroked his beard as he wondered how many children she had.

She raised her chin and gave him an icy stare. "I'm quite sure this will be my only one."

Eli scratched his forehead, unsure what to make of her comment. "*Ach*, you never know. We can't control how many grandchildren we'll end up with."

Katie Ann gasped as she took a step back from him. "*Grand*children?"

Oops. He'd made a big mistake. He took off his hat, pressed it against his chest, and cringed for a moment. "That's not your grandchild, is it?"

She shifted the baby in her arms and stiffened.

"No. Jonas is *mei boppli*." Katie Ann's cheeks were red as her eyes avoided his.

Eli felt like a heel. "I'm sorry. I guess I just figured that—"

"—a woman *my* age would be a grandmother and not a new *mudder*?"

"Nee, nee." Eli's mind searched for a way to mend the situation. "Of course that's not what I thought. I know lots of Amish women who've had *kinner* into their forties, but Elam told me that you were a widow, so I guess I just assumed the child must be a grandchild."

She smiled politely, but the damage was done. Then Eli recalled the way the rest of the conversation had gone, and gave a laugh.

Katie Ann pulled the baby closer to her, cradling him with one arm as she cupped her free hand to her hip. "This is funny?"

"Ya. It is." He took a deep breath. "I must have sounded *ab im kopp* when I said I'd probably have a dozen or so more. Of course I meant grandchildren, not children, and…" Eli shrugged, hoping for a smile, but she brought the baby to her shoulder and frowned.

"I have to go now."

She hurried across the living room before Eli could get her to see the humor in the situation, and a moment later she headed up the stairs and drifted out of sight.

He put his hands on his hips and sighed. He had embarrassed her. He'd just assumed her children were grown, like his, and that maybe she'd be interested in getting to know him better as they both started the second half of their lives. But she was starting the second half of her life with a baby. *No way.*

Eli had raised all the *kinner* he was going to. There was no point in getting to know this woman, however attractive she might be.

Too bad.

Katie Ann had intrigued him for sure.

Katie Ann finished changing Jonas's diaper on Vera's bed atop a small blanket she'd brought with her. She picked up her baby and kissed him on the cheek. "Is that better?"

She packed her supplies back into the diaper bag, depositing the wet cloth diaper in a plastic bag. Martha thought she was crazy for not using disposable diapers, but she didn't mind washing the cottony linens for Jonas. They were softer on his behind and caused less chafing.

She walked to the mirror in Vera's room and almost gasped. Her eyes were puffy, with dark circles underneath. No wonder the man had thought she was a grandma. She leaned closer to the mirror and took a better look.

She'd gotten even less sleep the night before than

usual. Jonas had cried on and off, and although she'd tried everything to make him happy, nothing had worked. She was thankful that he seemed content so far this morning.

So much for Martha thinking that perhaps a romance would develop—not that she would have considered such a thing. Even if she weren't recently widowed and hadn't lost all trust in men, Eli was a chatty fellow, not at all her type. And was it really necessary for him to get such a chuckle out of their misunderstanding?

She let out a huff before nuzzling her nose to Jonas's neck. "We don't need anyone else, do we?"

An hour into the wedding ceremony, most of the congregation was focused on Katie Ann and her little one, who was wailing at the top of his lungs. Even from across the room, Eli could see her bottom lip trembling as she tried to comfort the child, rocking him back and forth. She'd already left the room twice, and both times when she returned, little Jonas was quiet for about a minute before he started up again. An older *Englisch* woman sitting next to her—dressed rather brightly in a pink and white dress—had tried to comfort the child as well, but ultimately handed him back to his mother, shaking her head.

Katie Ann had circles under her puffy eyes, and he sympathized with her. He remembered when

Maureen was that age. She'd cried constantly. At first Eli had assumed it was because the poor child didn't have her mother and that he was failing miserably, but it turned out to be something entirely different. And there had been an easy fix.

He watched Katie Ann maneuver her way past a row of women, then slip out the back and into the mudroom. Eli tapped his foot as he tried to focus on what the bishop was saying. He glanced at the clock on the wall. It would be at least another hour before Emily and David actually said their wedding vows. And that poor child was still wailing. He shifted his weight, knowing that what he was about to do was irregular for an Amish man. Children were women's work.

Unless your spouse died and left you six of them to raise.

"Excuse me," he whispered to his nephew Jacob as he stood up and eased by him. He hoped everyone would think he was heading to the bathroom. His black dress shoes clicked against the wooden floor in the Detweilers' living room, and he was glad when he rounded the corner and the bishop's voice faded. His heart sank, though, when he saw Katie Ann sitting on a chair in the far corner of the mudroom crying right along with her child. She looked up at him with teary desperation as he walked toward her, but quickly swiped at her eyes.

"What are you doing back here?" she asked in a loud whisper.

"I thought I might be able to help."

She cut her eyes at him. "I assure you, I've tried everything."

Eli sighed, unsure what to say. Katie Ann started to cry again.

"I don't know what to do." She dabbed at her eyes with a tissue. "He just won't stop crying." She shook her head as she continued to rock Jonas. "He did this most of the night too, and I'm so"—she closed her eyes for a moment, then looked down at the screaming child—"tired."

Eli squatted down beside her. "May I?" He reached his hands out toward the baby, but Katie Ann stiffened and sat taller.

"No. I'm sure you won't be able to help." She sniffled as she shook her head.

Eli couldn't help but notice how pretty she was, even with her eyes swollen from little sleep and tiny lines that feathered from the corner of each eye.

He kept his arms out as he spoke, easing into a chair beside her. "I've raised six children on my own for the past seventeen years. I've learned a thing or two." He raised his brows, and Katie Ann reluctantly handed over the unhappy little fellow.

"There, there," Eli whispered, lowering the little one onto his lap, faceup…and still screaming. He slipped one hand under the baby's neck, and with his other hand, he took two fingers and traced them from below Jonas's breastbone all the way down his tummy, applying a small amount of pressure. When he could feel the top of the child's diaper beneath his blue onesie, he moved his hand in a circular motion back and forth across the child's abdomen. In less than a minute, Jonas had stopped crying.

Eli smiled at Katie Ann, whose jaw hung low.

"How did you know to do that?" Her eyes held a glint of wonder.

Eli was surprised at how nice it felt to hold a newborn. He thought about his son's wife, Laura Jane, who would be delivering next month. It would be nice to have another baby around. On a part-time basis, of course.

He handed Jonas to his mother, then shrugged. "A little something I learned when my daughter Maureen was that age. She struggled with a gassy tummy too." He swallowed, recalling the hardship of losing his wife while she was delivering Maureen.

Katie Ann cuddled her child in her arms, smiling down at the little one. After a few moments, she looked at Eli. Her eyes grew sharp and assessing, and with what seemed like resistance, she thanked him.

"You're welcome. Does he get fussy like that a lot?"

"*Ya*. He does."

Eli stood up and rubbed his hands together. "Rub some baby oil in your hands like this, until it gets warm. Then do what I just did with your palm against the baby's bare skin." He grinned. "Works every time."

Katie Ann stiffened. "I should have known that, I suppose." She pressed her lips together as she stood up, and Eli wished he hadn't boasted.

"You learn these things with experience." He smiled again, but she did not. Eli reprimanded himself for being prideful, but there was no denying that experience played a big hand when he'd raised his children, and sometimes he *was* proud of what he'd accomplished on his own. Jake and Hannah were already six- and five-years-old when Sarah died, but he still had a three-year-old, two-year-old, one-year-old, and baby Maureen to raise.

"I should get back to the wedding." She placed the baby up on her shoulder. "*Danki* again."

"You're welcome." He wasn't sure he was winning any points with this woman. No matter, he decided. He waited a minute, then rejoined the service.

Katie Ann dabbed at her eyes when Emily and David took their vows. She couldn't think of a couple more deserving of such happiness, and she knew that everyone in the room was thinking the same. They might be young, but they had both lived through much. David had nearly died six years earlier, his life saved only through a kidney transplant. And before Emily's family moved from Middlefield to Canaan last year, Emily had suffered a rape and had to endure the trial of her assailant.

Katie Ann was glad that they had fallen in love and had each other to lean on. *Be good to each other*, she said silently.

Ivan's faced flashed in her mind's eye, and memories of their own wedding danced in her head. She never would have imagined that he would run off with another woman, leaving her to raise a baby on her own. A baby he didn't even know about. She dabbed at another tear before it made its way down her cheek. Again she wondered if she'd been fair to her husband by not telling him she was pregnant. As the bishop blessed the union, Katie Ann wondered if visions of her life with Ivan would ever stop haunting her. She had believed that her marriage was sacred, a union blessed by God. Where had it gone wrong?

She bowed her head along with the rest of the congregation, but her communion with God was as it had been for the past several months—limited. Something had gone amiss after Ivan left her, and she was struggling to get it back. She missed God. The way it used to be. And no matter what the circumstances of their separation, she missed Ivan.

"Amen!" Martha said loudly beside her.

Katie Ann gently elbowed her friend.

"Don't nudge me, Katie Ann." Martha raised her brows. "You know how these long services hurt my back. Thank goodness you people have added some chairs to your worship services. I don't know who started that whole backless bench thing, but it's ridiculous." She pointed a few rows in front of them. "Look at poor Lillian up there on the front row. She's half my age, but I watched the poor girl rubbing her back on and off throughout the service. I say you should ban all those backless benches."

Katie Ann sighed as she and Martha stood up. "Time to serve the bridal party." She glanced down at Jonas, who was sleeping soundly in his baby carrier.

"How'd you get him to stop screaming earlier?" Martha now nudged Katie Ann. "I saw the Detweiler fella follow you out of the room. What was that about?"

"Keep your voice down," Katie Ann whispered as she picked up the baby carrier. They followed some of the other women toward the kitchen. "As you pointed out, he's raised six children, so he was helping me with Jonas."

"Now that's a good man, I tell ya." Martha grinned. "You need to get to know him."

"We talked about this. I'm in mourning." Katie Ann frowned in Martha's direction. "Besides, the man is a bit…prideful."

"With his good looks, he's got plenty to be proud of." Martha cackled.

"That is not our way, Martha, and you know it." Katie Ann moved toward the stairs. "I'm going to go lay Jonas down in Vera's room."

"Did you bring the baby monitor?"

"*Ya.* Tell Vera I'll be back to help serve in just a minute."

Martha rubbed her hands together. "Can't wait to dig into that creamed celery."

Katie Ann wound her way around the others in the room and went upstairs. After she had Jonas settled in the playpen in Vera's room, she quietly made her way back down.

Martha was busily chatting with Eli in the living room. They both looked up at her, and Katie Ann could tell that Martha was up to no good.

Chapter Three

Martha quizzed Eli about his life back in Middle-field, and she listened intently as he told her about his children and grandchildren. He was certainly qualified to take care of little Jonas, so she mentally checked that off her list.

"And what kind of work did you say you do?" Martha batted her lashes at him. If only she were a little younger, she'd convert and snag this fine Amish man for herself.

"I worked construction for many years—and farmed, of course. But right now I'm just farming."

A hard worker. Good. Katie Ann stayed busy, and like most of her people, she believed in hard work and love of the land. "How long will you be staying in Canaan?"

"I'm not sure." He smiled, and Martha decided she was going to slap Katie Ann upside the head if she didn't latch onto this handsome fellow.

"I've never been here before," he added. "Since I was raising six children on my own, there was no time for travel. I guess you could say that this is like a vacation for me. Vera and Elam told me to stay as long as I like, but I don't want to wear out my welcome. And my son, Jake, is tending to my farm. I don't want to burden him for too long."

The wheels in Martha's head were spinning at full capacity when she saw Katie Ann heading her way. Katie Ann was so suspicious of men now, Martha feared she'd never give this nice man a chance. "Vera needs you, Katie Ann," she said quickly and waved her away.

Katie Ann hesitated but then headed toward the kitchen.

"She's like my daughter," Martha said as she raised her chin. "And that little one is like my grandson. I figure he'll call me Granny when he gets older." She sighed. "But I won't always be around to take care of Katie Ann and Jonas. I have my own life to lead, don'tcha know?"

He nodded, and Martha decided she'd better not travel along that road just yet. She didn't want the guy to feel pressured. He'd fall in love with Katie Ann on his own, and the rest would come together.

"I'm making chicken lasagna Saturday night at Katie Ann's house. You should come for supper." Martha grinned. "I'm not much of a cook, but Katie Ann has taught me how to whip up a few things, so every Saturday I cook for her. Easier for me to bring supper to her house so she doesn't have to get the baby out in the weather."

"I, uh…should you check with Katie Ann first?"

Has manners too. He's too good to be true. Martha waved her hand. "Nah, she'll be fine with it. Seven o'clock?" She raised one palm toward him. "I know your people normally eat at five o'clock, but my stomach isn't on that schedule." She lifted one brow and waited.

"*Ya.* Seven o'clock then."

"*Wunderbaar gut!*" Martha slapped him on the arm and went to help the ladies in the kitchen.

Eli watched the funny *Englisch* woman walk away, and grinned. Only tourists said *wunderbaar gut.* The Amish folks poked fun at it.

Martha was a character, though, and she was certainly playing the matchmaker. But Eli didn't mind playing along. Katie Ann was sure pretty, and he loved lasagna.

He stroked his beard as he walked out the door to join some of the men on the porch. He was already looking forward to Saturday night.

Katie Ann wrapped Jonas in an extra blanket before she eased him out of his car seat in the back of Martha's car. "I'm glad you wanted to come home early. I'm so tired."

"Bundle that little one up good." Martha looked over her shoulder from the driver's seat.

Katie Ann shut the back door, then leaned in the front window on the passenger side. "*Danki* again for driving. See you tomorrow?"

"No. I have a doctor's appointment in town."

Katie Ann's chest tightened. "What for?"

"Don't look so worried. Routine tests. But it's gonna take most of the day, so I won't see you until Saturday."

Katie Ann nodded.

"I'm bringing lasagna, a nice salad, and garlic bread."

Katie Ann grinned. "*Ach*, that sounds very fancy."

"That's 'cause company is coming."

Katie Ann squinted her eyes. "Who might that be?"

"That nice Eli Detweiler is coming for supper." Martha held up a crooked finger before Katie Ann could speak. "And don't you dare be mad. He is a fine man, and it wouldn't hurt you to get to know him."

"Martha! You shouldn't have done that. You know how I feel about dating. I'm still in mourning."

Martha rolled her eyes. "Well, I'll give you until Saturday night to get done with mourning that scoundrel husband of yours."

Katie Ann's eyes started to tear. She knew that Martha loved her, but she still couldn't stand it when Martha talked badly about Ivan. Only *she* could talk badly about him. "I've told you before how upsetting it is to me when you talk like that. I loved Ivan, and—"

"Okay," Martha said loudly. "I'll try to do better. Now get that baby out of this cool air."

Katie Ann narrowed her brows. "I know what you're doing, and you should not have invited Eli for supper. I can tell by our short interaction that we are nothing alike. He is...I don't know...so..."

"*Happy*, Katie Ann. That's the word you're looking for. The man smiles a lot. Something you should do more of."

Martha rolled up the window, and Katie Ann watched her pull away. She pulled Jonas closer to her and walked up the steps to her house. *Martha's wrong. I am happy.*

After she fed the baby and tucked him into his crib, she ran a bath and climbed into the tub. As she sat in the warm water, she leaned her head back and cried. She'd waited to have a baby and a real family her entire life. She only had half the equation. Even though she loved Martha, it wasn't the same. She missed Ivan with all her heart. *Why, Lord, did You take him from me? And why did Lucy Turner have him when You decided to call him home?*

She laid the warm washrag across her face as she thought about what Martha said. *I am happy.* She was happy about being a mother and thankful that the Lord had blessed her with Jonas. But she wasn't fulfilled. And it was no mystery to her as to why. Her relationship with the Lord had changed since Ivan's death. She just couldn't understand why everything had to happen the way it did, and through no rhyme or reason could she understand what God's plan for her might be. She'd been taught her entire life not to question the Lord's will, and the more she did so…the further away she felt from Him.

After allowing herself another fifteen minutes of self-pity, Katie Ann pulled herself from the tub, dressed in a clean blue dress, and went into the living room. It was too early to change into her nightclothes and go to bed. Jonas would be up for another feeding, plus she didn't want to get caught in her nightclothes if Lillian or Samuel came calling after the wedding.

She sat down on the couch, crossed her legs, and opened up a book she'd bought in town about being a new mother. *That is all I need to concentrate on… being the best mother I can to Jonas.*

Saturday morning, Katie Ann bundled up Jonas and herself and walked next door to her sister-in-law's house. She knew Lillian would be baking, and Katie Ann often visited with her this time on Saturdays.

She lifted her tall black boots and picked her way

carefully across the snow as she toted Jonas in his carrier. She was thankful to have gotten more sleep the past two nights. Thursday night after the wedding she'd been exhausted, and both she and Jonas had slept much better. She'd only gotten up once to feed him and once to soothe his gassy tummy by using Eli's technique with the baby oil, which had worked—and twice she'd tiptoed into his room to make sure he was breathing. Friday she'd gone back to help Vera with cleanup, and again she and Jonas had gone to bed early and followed the same routine as the night before.

Martha had overstepped her bounds by inviting Eli to supper, but she'd worry about that later. This morning she needed to talk to Lillian about something else. As she eased up the porch steps to the old farmhouse, she marveled at all of Lillian's and Samuel's hard work. In a year they'd taken this run-down old house with no bathroom, no insulation, in need of an entire overhaul, and turned it into a beautiful home. She knocked on the door.

"Hi, *Aenti* Katie Ann."

Katie Ann smiled at her youngest niece, Elizabeth. The five-year-old was Jonas's biggest fan and loved to keep him company while Katie Ann chatted with Lillian.

"Hello, Elizabeth." Katie Ann moved past the little girl and into the living room. "Is your *mamm* in the kitchen?"

"*Ya*. She's making peanut blossoms!" Elizabeth bounced on her toes.

Katie Ann let out an exaggerated gasp. "Really! That's special, Elizabeth. We usually make those only at Christmastime."

"I know, I know!"

Katie Ann followed Elizabeth across the living room and into the spacious kitchen. Katie Ann recalled the chipping blue paint on the cabinets when Lillian and Samuel had first moved in, now shimmering with shiny white paint and gold knobs that bordered on being fancy…but Lillian said she deserved the knobs after having to live in that house prior to the overhaul.

Lillian hadn't always been Amish. She'd married Ivan's brother, Samuel, eight years ago and converted. Most of the time, you'd never know that she hadn't been Amish her entire life, but occasionally she'd bend a certain rule based on her own way of thinking, and no one faulted her for it. Lillian was bubbly, happy, and kindhearted, and Katie Ann didn't know of a soul who didn't adore her.

"You are just in time for peanut blossoms," Lillian announced.

Lillian's older daughter, Anna, was sitting in a chair at the kitchen table mashing chocolate kisses on top of the warm peanut butter cookies. "*Guder mariye, Aenti* Katie Ann."

Katie Ann placed Jonas's carrier on the table. "*Guder mariye* to you, too, Anna."

She was glad to hear Anna using their native dialect this morning. She'd worried about the girls when they were younger, because they didn't know much Pennsylvania *Deitsch*. Normally, children didn't learn English until they started school, but since English was Lillian's native language, she'd raised the girls by speaking that to them. Samuel said it didn't matter what language they spoke, only the meaning behind the words they said. And Elizabeth and Anna were good girls. Lillian and Samuel were doing a fine job with them. Katie Ann hoped she would do as well with Jonas.

Lillian wiped her hands on her apron, approached the table, and leaned down to kiss Jonas on the forehead. "Hello, my precious Jonas."

Lillian looked up, and Katie Ann knew what she was going to say. She said it daily, and it had just become a "thing" between the women.

"Have I told you how glad I am that you named this baby Jonas?"

Anna spoke up before Katie Ann had a chance to. "*Mamm!* You say that all the time."

Lillian cupped her daughter's chin. "I know I do, and you'd know why if you had known your great-grandpa Jonas. The best man who ever lived, I believe."

"I thought *Daed* was the best man who ever lived," Elizabeth said.

Lillian smiled. "Well, besides your *daed*!"

Katie Ann sat down beside Anna. "So what's the occasion? Why are you making peanut blossoms today?"

Lillian walked to the stove and pulled out a fresh batch of cookies. Without turning around she said, "Whatever do you mean?"

Katie Ann heard the playfulness in Lillian's tone. "*Ach*, so there *is* a reason."

Elizabeth skipped to Katie Ann's side. "Martha asked *Mamm* to make them to have tonight for your date."

Katie Ann stiffened. She took a deep breath. "Elizabeth, I don't have a date tonight. Martha is just having a friend over to have supper with us."

"That's not what *Mamm* said. She said—"

"Elizabeth!" Lillian spun around. "Take your sister and go play in your room for a while so I can visit with *Aenti* Katie Ann." She took a step forward. "Scoot now. After I chat with your *aenti*, you can both come back downstairs and have a double helping of cookies."

Both girls nodded, then scurried upstairs. Katie Ann waited until they were out of earshot before she spoke. "Lillian…"

"*Ya*, dear sister-in-law." Lillian grinned from ear to ear as she eased into a chair beside Katie Ann.

Katie Ann stifled a grin. She needed Lillian to understand that there was no chance of courtship with Eli Detweiler. "This is not a date tonight, but I am well aware that everyone is trying to play matchmaker between me and Eli." She shrugged. "I suppose in some ways that makes sense. We are both alone, without spouses. But..." She held up one finger. "That does not mean that we are anything alike. And besides, Lillian, I am still mourning Ivan."

Lillian reached over and patted Katie Ann's hand. "I know, sweetie." Lillian quickly sat taller and grinned. "But he sure is handsome, and Vera said Elam's cousin would be a great catch. Did you know his wife died seventeen years ago and he raised his six children alone since then?"

Katie Ann stiffened again. "*Ya.* I know. And he is very proud of his accomplishments."

Lillian put her elbows on the table and laid her chin in her hands. She spoke softly. "Don't you think he should be a tad bit proud?"

"I don't mean to sound harsh, Lillian. I'm sure he did a wonderful job, but I'm not ready to date anyone, and if I was, I don't think it would be Eli."

"I wouldn't rule him out so quickly, *mei* sister."

Katie Ann waved her hand in the air. "Never mind about Eli. I need to talk to you about something else."

Lillian's eyes widened. "What is it?"

Katie Ann took a deep breath. "It's about Lucy Turner."

Lillian grimaced. "What about her?"

"She sent me a letter a couple of weeks ago." Katie Ann watched Lillian's left eyebrow lift. "And she is coming to visit me."

"What *for*?" Lillian placed her palms flat on the table. "She doesn't need to come here for anything. I'd like to get my hands on that woman and—"

"Lillian!"

"I know, I know. It's not our way. But I'd still like to rough her up a bit." It was endearing the way Lillian had always been protective of Katie Ann, even if sometimes her old *Englisch* ways rose to the surface. "Did she say in the letter why she's coming?"

"To discuss an urgent matter." Katie Ann shrugged. "I have no idea what could be so pressing. And, Lillian…I haven't told anyone about the letter. Not even Martha."

"Can't blame you there. Martha would camp out at your house, and I wouldn't put it past her to follow through and take that—that *woman* to the woodshed for a *gut* licking!"

They were both quiet for a moment as Jonas squirmed, but he quickly grew still, sleeping soundly.

"Anyway, it's just bothering me. I don't want

Lucy coming here, but I'm so curious about why she'd even want to."

"It's bound to be driving you crazy."

Katie Ann sniffed. "Lillian, is something burning?"

"*Ach! Mei* cookies!" She jumped up, and Katie Ann waited while she pulled a fresh batch of cookies from the oven and set them on a cooling rack. "There, that was the last batch," she said as she sat back down. "Wow. You have a lot to think about. First the letter from Lucy, and now your *date* tonight."

"Lillian, what did I say?" Katie Ann shook her head. "I'm sorry to disappoint everyone, but nothing is going to develop between me and Eli."

"We shall see."

Katie Ann loved to be around Lillian. Her sister-in-law was always cheerful and happy. She recalled what Martha had said about Eli. *"Happy, Katie Ann. That's the word you're looking for. The man smiles a lot."*

Well, good for Eli Detweiler. I'm happy too.

"Do you think you could watch Jonas for a few minutes?" Katie Ann leaned over her baby, who was still sleeping soundly. "I want to carry a few logs to the *haus*."

Lillian put her hands on her hips. "I'm always ready to watch my little nephew, but you should let Samuel haul that wood for you."

Katie Ann waved a hand at Lillian. "*Nee*, I will do it. I can use the exercise, and besides, Samuel probably feels like he has two *fraas* half the time, the way he's always doing extra chores for me."

"He loves you, Katie Ann. He doesn't mind at all."

"He's a *gut* man, but I need to stretch my legs." She kissed Jonas on the forehead as she stood up. "I'll be back shortly. I just want to make sure we have plenty of logs tonight."

"*Ya*, for sure." Lillian winked. "For your *date*."

Katie Ann playfully swatted Lillian before she left the room through the door in the kitchen.

Pulling the barn door open, she was surprised to see that Samuel had split even more wood since the last time she was out here, and her brother-in-law made sure the logs were small enough that both she and Lillian could carry them inside. Katie Ann liked to keep several in her rack by the fireplace and a few more in her small mudroom at the back of the house. She lifted two logs, cradling them in front of her, and turned to leave, but was startled by a movement to her left. The three horses didn't seem bothered, nor did the laying hens or four pigs farther down the way. She stood perfectly still and silently prayed that it wasn't a skunk.

She was getting ready to head out when she heard a tiny cry from the far corner of the barn, back behind where the shovels leaned in the corner.

She eased the logs onto Samuel's workbench, then headed toward the pitiful meow.

"Hello," she said softly as she reached her hand out toward a small black cat. The little fellow cowered back even farther against the wall, his fur standing on end and his ears pulled back as if taped to his head. "It's all right." She squatted down until she was at eye level with the animal. Poor thing was shivering.

She stood up, picked up her logs, and went toward the house. When she returned, she brought an old blanket. She laid it in the far corner on the other side of the workbench atop a pile of hay. "There. You have your own bed now."

Ivan had never liked cats, said all they were good for was keeping mice away. Barn cats, he called them. So Katie Ann had never had one for a pet. But Ivan wasn't here anymore.

Katie Ann jumped when the cat dashed out from behind the shovel, then ran across the barn like its tail was on fire. She'd barely focused on the animal when it took off again down the aisle, horses on one side, pigs on the other. One of the hogs let out a snort, but otherwise, the cat went unnoticed. Katie Ann tiptoed down the aisle, but the cat had either gone out a stall window or was hiding. Either way, she decided, she was going to name her cat Dash.

It was six thirty when Eli readied his cousin's buggy to travel to Katie Ann's for supper. He'd spent most of the previous day helping with cleanup after the wedding. Katie Ann had come to help, too, but the woman seemed to steer clear of him all day. But tonight there would be no avoiding each other. He'd thought about canceling, but he hadn't been able to come up with a good excuse, plus Vera would have been awfully disappointed. She'd made reference to his supper plans several times throughout the day.

Everyone was playing matchmaker, but none of them knew that it was all in vain. Eli and Katie Ann were moving in different directions in life, and he wasn't about to step onto a different path.

By the time he arrived at her house, it was straight up seven o'clock.

Martha answered the door. "Come in, Eli."

Eli took note of her bright green britches, matching blouse, and big gold earrings. Her hair was bundled atop her head in a mass of brownish-gray curls, and bright red lipstick matched her fingernails. Clearly Katie Ann was close to this woman, but it seemed an unusual friendship.

"Danki," Eli said as he moved into the living room, which he found instantly inviting. As with most Amish homes, the walls were white and there were no pictures hanging, but the focal point in Katie Ann's living room was a large bookcase that spanned one wall. In addition to books, she had several potted ivies on the shelves, two candles, a

lantern, and a basket full of yarn and knitting needles. A light brown couch faced two finely crafted rocking chairs, and there was a small coffee table in front of the couch. A propane lamp lit the area, and Eli breathed in the aroma of what must be the chicken lasagna.

"Hello, Eli." Katie Ann stopped a few feet in front of him. "Can I get you some iced tea or *kaffi*?"

"Tea, please." He smiled, suddenly wondering what he was doing here. She was bound to know this was a setup, and he had no business leading her on.

"Let me take your coat." Martha held out a hand, and Eli removed his long black coat and black felt hat. She hung them on a rack by the door, then pointed to the couch. "You have yourself a seat, and I'll go see if Katie Ann has everything ready."

Martha disappeared around the corner, too, but instead of sitting down, Eli found his way to the bookshelves and gingerly ran his hand along the titles. In addition to novels, she had a large collection of books on parenting. He turned when he heard footsteps.

Katie Ann handed him a glass of tea.

"Danki." He nodded toward his left. "You have a fine collection of books."

"I like to read when I have time."

A slow smile trembled over her lips, and Eli

could tell that she was nervous. He stroked his beard, studying her.

Martha's voice broke the trance. "Supper's ready! Come and get it!"

Eli couldn't help but grin at the woman's loud voice booming from the other room. But Katie Ann laughed, and it was everything he could do not to tell her how pretty she was when she smiled.

"Forgive Martha." Katie Ann scratched her forehead, grinning. "She's the best friend I have, but we are working on her manners."

Eli just smiled, and Katie Ann motioned with her hand for him to follow her. Martha was already seated at the table.

After they were seated, and following silent prayer, Martha scooped a generous portion of lasagna onto Eli's plate first, then Katie Ann's.

"Help yourself to some salad and bread, Eli." Martha pushed the serving bowl closer to Eli from where she was seated across the table.

"Little Jonas in bed for the night?" Eli scooped some salad from the bowl.

Katie Ann sighed. "He doesn't sleep through the night, but his tummy troubles have been better."

Eli nodded but didn't say anything. He already felt he'd been a bit boastful.

"This lasagna is very *gut*, Martha," Eli said after he swallowed his first bite.

"Yeah, it's not bad." Martha grinned. "Our Katie Ann is the real cook around here."

Eli glanced to his right at Katie Ann, whose cheeks flushed slightly.

He'd almost cleaned his plate and was considering a second helping when someone knocked at the door.

Katie Ann excused herself.

After several long minutes of silence with Martha, the older woman finished her lasagna. "I'd better go see who's here and what's taking our girl so long." She flashed a toothy smile and pushed back her chair.

Our girl? Eli wondered again if this was a mistake. But the lasagna was excellent. He piled another helping on his plate but stopped cold when Martha bellowed from the next room.

"I don't care why you need to talk to Katie Ann. You have no business coming here!"

Chapter Four

"Stop it, Martha." Katie Ann clenched her hands into fists at her sides and wished Martha hadn't overheard her call her visitor by name. Even though Martha had never met the woman, she'd certainly heard a lot about her. Katie Ann wasn't sure what was worse—Lucy Turner on the doorstep, Martha yelling, or the fact that Eli Detweiler could hear everything from the kitchen.

"You got a lot of nerve showing up here unannounced." Martha leaned around Katie Ann, her face twisted, her voice loud.

Katie Ann, holding a lantern, could barely see Lucy's face by the dim light. But even in the darkness, she recognized the deceitful blue eyes of the woman who'd stolen her husband. "Now is not a *gut* time, Lucy."

Lucy pulled her black jacket snug. "Didn't you get my letter telling you I was coming?"

"What letter?" Martha glared at Katie Ann. "Did you get a letter from this tramp?"

"Martha! Stop it." Katie Ann heard footsteps and briefly wondered if this situation could get any worse.

"Everything all right in here?" Eli eased up to the door and peered through the screen.

"This woman was just leaving," Martha said with force as her hands landed on her hips.

Katie Ann gently pushed Martha back. "*Ya*, Lucy. I received your letter. Please come back Monday morning. As I said, now is not a *gut* time, and tomorrow is the Sabbath. Please come back on Monday."

Lucy nodded. "I'm sorry, Katie Ann. I wouldn't have come if—"

"You're sorry?" Martha huffed. "Little late for that, don'tcha think?"

Katie Ann took a deep breath as she recalled the way Martha often talked about Lucy. *"No excuse for infidelity,"* she always said. Katie Ann had reminded Martha several times that Ivan was not an innocent bystander.

"Again, I'm sorry." Lucy took a step backward. "Katie Ann, I'll see you on Monday morning."

Martha slammed the heavy wooden door before anyone could say another word. Katie Ann wished the floor would open up and swallow her. Her cheeks burned, and she wondered if Eli knew about her past—about Lucy.

"You're not really going to meet with her, are you?" Martha demanded. "And what's this about a letter?"

"Martha, let's finish our supper. We'll talk about this later." She finally looked at Eli. He was stroking his beard with one hand and glancing back and forth between Katie Ann and Martha.

"I'm not hungry anymore." Martha pulled a brown overcoat from the rack by the door. "I'm going home."

Again Katie Ann wondered which was worse—that Martha was mad at her for not telling her about the letter, or that she was about to be left alone with Eli.

"No, Martha. Don't go." She reached out to touch her arm, but her friend pulled away and put her coat on.

"I ate too much anyway." Martha buttoned her coat as she held her chin high. "You kids have fun."

"But—"

As the wooden door slammed for the second time, Katie Ann briefly wondered if Martha would go hunt Lucy down, and the thought touched her as much as it frightened her. She took a deep breath but couldn't look Eli in the eyes. "I'm so sorry."

Eli slowly walked closer and put a hand on her arm, which was unsettling. "Don't be."

Katie Ann pulled away and stepped back. "I'm—I'm just very embarrassed." She could feel

Eli's eyes on her, and when she finally looked up at him, she could see the pity in his expression.

Don't you dare feel sorry for me.

She stood taller, folding her hands in front of her. "Should we finish eating?"

"Sure." He nodded, and Katie Ann didn't think this night could end soon enough.

Eli followed her back to the kitchen, and they both finished eating without conversation, except for an occasional comment from Eli about how much he was enjoying the meal. Katie Ann felt obliged to offer him coffee and some peanut blossoms.

"*Kaffi* would be *gut*." Eli stood from the table. "I saw you shivering. Should we have *kaffi* in the living room, in front of the fire? I can add a log."

For a moment Katie Ann reflected fondly about how nice it would be to have a man to take care of such things, no matter how small. *"Ya. Danki."*

Eli went into the living room, and Katie Ann started the percolator on top of the stove, then set to clearing the table. She was sure Martha would be over first thing in the morning to find out about Lucy's letter, and then her friend would most likely camp out here on Monday, waiting for Lucy to arrive. She wondered how she would handle Lucy and Martha in the same room at the same time. She knew Martha's angry attitude was propelled by love, but her ranting and raving were only going to make things harder. She'd just finished cleaning the kitchen and pulled two coffee cups from the cupboard when Eli walked into the kitchen.

"I think I hear the *boppli* stirring."

Katie Ann wiped her hands on her apron. "He's probably hungry. I'm sorry, the *kaffi* is almost ready. I'll be right back."

Eli walked toward her and reached for the coffee cups. "I can ready our *kaffi* if you'd like."

His fingers brushed against hers as he took the mugs in his hands, and a tingle raced up her arms. It took her a few moments before she nodded.

When Katie Ann walked into the living room with Jonas a short while later, Eli was sitting on the couch and asked if he could hold the baby. She leaned down and eased Jonas into Eli's arms, then stepped back. It usually made her nervous for a stranger to hold Jonas, but the warmth of the freshly stoked fire hit her, and the sight of Jonas in Eli's arms caused a lump to swell in her throat. She could almost see Ivan sitting on the couch holding his son. She shook her head to clear the thought.

She sat down on the couch next to Eli and had to admit it was touching, the way he cradled Jonas and made funny little baby talk. She'd never seen a man do that, and she lifted her hand to her mouth as she stifled a grin.

"He is a beautiful child." Eli glanced over at Katie Ann. "Like his—"

"If you say *grossmammi*, I'll smack you." Katie Ann was shocked at her own playful comment, but Eli's face lit up, and a certain amount of tension between them seemed to melt away.

"I was going to say, like his *mudder*."

Katie Ann felt the flush filling her cheeks. His smooth, gentle voice sounded almost seductive, and she became very aware of how intimate this scene was. But as he returned his gaze to Jonas, Katie Ann let her eyes scan the stranger sitting next to her. He was handsome, no doubt. Even beneath his long-sleeved blue shirt, she could see the strength in his arms, and she'd already noticed the tall, confident way he carried himself. A trace of gray at his temple and speckled discreetly through his beard lent him a sophistication that was attractive. His hazel eyes were soft, and when he smiled, laugh lines filled his face. Martha's voice rang in her mind. *"Happy, Katie Ann."*

"Danki," she finally managed to say. She watched as Eli lifted Jonas to his shoulder, patting him on the back. She wondered if Ivan would have been as involved with Jonas as this visitor in her living room. "Tell me about your *kinner*," she said.

Eli lowered Jonas, placed him faceup in his lap, and rubbed his tummy as though he'd done it a million times. "Jake is my oldest. He's twenty-three. Then there are all my girls—Hannah, Ida Mae, Karen, Frieda, and my youngest, Maureen."

He leaned down, smiling at Jonas. "And I've been blessed with six grandchildren." He glanced up at Katie. "And one on the way. Laura Jane is expecting in a couple of weeks. She's Jake's *fraa*."

"When did your…" Katie Ann wondered if she was being too personal.

"When did *mei fraa* die?" Eli looked up, but his eyes drifted somewhere else as he spoke. "She died giving birth to Maureen. Seventeen years ago."

"I'm so sorry," Katie Ann said. "I can't imagine how hard that must have been on you. And the *kinner*."

Eli turned to face her, and a different kind of expression filled his face, one Katie Ann couldn't quite interpret. "I had lots of help in the beginning, but over time I realized that I was somehow going to have to be both parents, and be *gut* at it, if I wanted *mei kinner* to have a *gut* upbringing." He chuckled. "Everyone tried to match me up with women in our district, but no one could compare to my Sarah." Eli's face brightened as he mentioned his wife's name.

Katie Ann bit her bottom lip. *Why couldn't Ivan have loved me like that?* "I'm sure you did a wonderful job raising them all. Jonas has sure taken a fancy to you."

Eli gently lifted the baby and handed him to Katie Ann. "*Ach*, I don't know about that." He avoided meeting her eyes.

He took a deep breath, then let it out slowly. "I do feel like I've earned a bit of a vacation, so to speak. All *mei kinner* have made fine homes for themselves, and I plan to travel some." He raised his brows. "Of course, I'll still farm. My love of the land won't change. But I plan to enjoy some time to myself." He looked hard into Katie Ann's eyes. "Do you think that's selfish?"

She was surprised by the question. "*Nee.* I don't. I know how much time and energy it takes to take care of one small *boppli.* I can't imagine you raising six *kinner* on your own. Very admirable." She smiled. "I think you've earned some time to yourself. Where do you plan to travel?"

Eli stood up, walked to the fire, and gave it a poke. "*Ach*, I have a long list." He turned to her and smiled as he stowed the fireplace tool. "But I'm starting here in Colorado. Maybe you can tell me some nice spots to visit while I'm here?"

Katie Ann cradled Jonas in her arms and rocked him back and forth. "I'm probably not a *gut* person to ask. Since we've lived here, I've either been pregnant or with a newborn. I'm afraid I haven't had a chance to travel much farther than Monte Vista, the nearest town."

Eli sat down beside her, took a sip of his coffee, and stared at her for a moment. "You do know that several of the folks around here are trying to play matchmaker between us, no?"

Katie Ann pulled her eyes from his, again feeling a blush in her cheeks. "I—I, uh…"

"I'm sorry. I didn't mean to embarrass you. I just felt it was best to clear the air. I'm planning to stay for a short while to do some sightseeing, so I'm sure we will be seeing each other, but I don't want you to feel uncomfortable around me."

She lowered her head and rubbed her forehead. "I'm in mourning, and it would be inappropriate to…to…"

Eli ran a hand the length of his beard and shook his head. "No worries. I know you recently lost your husband, and we…well, we're in two different places in life." He shrugged. "But we could sure give them all something to talk about." He grinned. "You said you haven't seen much of the area. Would you and Jonas like to spend the day doing some sightseeing with me?"

Katie Ann was shaking her head before he even finished his sentence. "*Nee, nee.* I'm not going to fuel gossip. And besides, it's much too cold for Jonas to take a buggy trip anywhere."

Eli chuckled. "It must be different here than where I come from. Gossip might be frowned upon, but it's plentiful just the same."

Katie Ann started to agree, but Eli went on. "And no buggy ride for me. I'm going to hire a driver. You should take advantage of my offer and see some sights while I'm here visiting." He grinned. "And providing a ride with a heater."

It was a tempting offer, but inappropriate. "*Danki*. But I think not."

"Why?"

Katie adjusted Jonas in her arms and stiffened. "Because I just can't shuck my chores around here and go on a frivolous outing with you."

"Why?"

She narrowed her brows. "Because I just can't."

Eli drank up the last of his coffee. "Okay. I just thought it might be nice for two friends to share a sightseeing trip together."

He stood up as if preparing to leave. *Finally.* She rose from the couch, too, and allowed herself a few moments to dream about seeing more of the San Luis Valley, maybe even the sand dunes. She'd heard about the massive mounds just an hour away. "Where are you planning to go?"

Eli chuckled. "Aha. You are interested, just a little?"

Katie Ann shrugged one shoulder. "Maybe." She had felt a bit claustrophobic as of late. And she'd never admit it, but it would be fun to see Vera, Lillian, and especially Martha's reaction to her spending time with Eli. And besides, Eli's plans for his future were so completely opposite of her own that he suddenly seemed *safe*. Maybe even someone she could be friends with.

"Tomorrow there isn't worship service, so I thought I would spend the day with Elam, Vera, and the *kinner*. Monday I was planning to travel to the Great Sand Dunes. Have you heard of them?"

Katie Ann's heart leaped as she considered the possibility. "*Ya.* I have. David took Emily there before they were married, and they said it is quite the sight."

"I can be here with a driver on Monday at nine o'clock. How does that sound? You, me, and Jonas can have a nice lunch somewhere and see some things neither of us has seen before." He raised a brow. "Always more fun to sightsee with a friend."

Suddenly she remembered Lucy. "I'm sorry. I forgot that, um…the woman you saw earlier…she'll be here Monday morning."

Eli walked toward the front door. Katie Ann followed, watching him pull his hat and coat from the rack.

"I'm wide open on Tuesday too."

She took a deep breath and wondered if spending time with Eli would be acceptable. It wasn't like they were teenagers. And Eli had made it clear that he sought nothing from her but friendship. Before she could answer, Eli spoke.

"I hope that you and the woman named Lucy have a nice conversation."

It was a strange thing to say, in light of what he had seen, and it was clearly an invitation for Katie

Ann to share about Lucy, which was not going to happen. *"Danki,"* she said smoothly.

He looked at her, waiting.

"I'm sorry about the display earlier. Lucy is someone I knew in Lancaster County, and as you could see, Martha is not fond of her."

Eli grinned. "I noticed that. I hope I don't ever get on Martha's bad side."

Katie Ann couldn't help but smile as she propped Jonas up on her shoulder. "It's not a *gut* place to be."

"See you on Tuesday?" Eli adjusted his hat.

Katie Ann bit her bottom lip for a moment. "I would like to see the sand dunes." Then she shook her head. "But I don't know, Eli—about Jonas. Maybe I shouldn't have him out in the weather."

Eli leaned close and touched Jonas on the cheek. "We will keep this little one bundled up well."

Jonas puckered with delight at Eli's touch, but Katie Ann went weak in the knees as Eli's hand brushed against hers. She wondered if she was making the right choice about going with him. But she just nodded.

Eli fought the night chill all the way to his cousin's house, and by the time he got home everyone had retired for the evening. He went straight to bathe, then propped himself up on the bed. After he adjusted the lantern, he read from the Bible for a while, but eventually his thoughts about Katie

Ann won over, and he closed the book. He sighed as he made a mental note to do a little extra reading from the Good Book in the morning. Right now he couldn't seem to shake the vision of Katie Ann playfully teasing him about not calling her a grandmother. She didn't smile a lot, but when she did, it stirred things in Eli that had long been dormant. A thought that was both exhilarating and frightening.

He snuffed the lantern, lay back, and closed his eyes, wishing that things were different. Katie Ann was the first woman since Sarah who had lit a spark inside of him, but she was not anyone he'd ever pursue. Although she was lovely, and Jonas was a cute little *boppli*. He smiled, thinking about his time holding the child.

Rolling on his side, he knew those days were behind him. All he had to take care of was himself, and it had been a long time coming. But surely it was safe to spend time with Katie Ann. The woman was mourning her husband, and Eli had been deliberate in his use of the word *friend* in their conversations.

He rolled onto his back, then back onto his side. *So why am I having so much trouble falling asleep?*

Katie Ann finished nursing Jonas, laid him back down, and watched him until he fell asleep. Normally she'd eat a bowl of homemade granola for breakfast, but this morning she'd made herself some scrambled eggs. She couldn't wait until Jonas was old enough to sit at the table. Lillian often invited her to take dinner with her family, since they lived right next door, and Martha came for most suppers, but breakfast time was lonely.

After checking on Jonas, she carried her leftover eggs out to the barn. Maybe Dash would eat scrambled eggs. She opened the barn door and was pleased to see that the cat was using the blanket she'd laid out for him. "I have a treat for you," she said softly as she walked across the barn. She hadn't taken three steps when the cat dashed around the corner and out of sight. "I'll leave this for you anyway."

She set the plate down, then headed back up to the house. A few minutes later there was a knock at the door. She looked at the clock on the wall. As Katie Ann predicted, Martha had arrived early.

"*Guder mariye*, Martha."

Martha squirmed out of a black jacket and stocking cap and hung them on the rack by the door. She grunted before she asked if Katie Ann had coffee ready.

"*Ya*. A fresh pot in the kitchen. I knew you'd be here early." She grinned as she closed the front door.

Martha didn't say anything as she padded across the room in a black velour sweat suit, her brownish-gray hair matted in the back of her head as it rested in a crumpled mess above her shoulders.

"Yes, I know. My hair is a mess." Martha glanced over her shoulder and frowned. "But that wool head covering is warm, and I don't care."

Katie Ann followed her friend to the kitchen, where Martha was already helping herself to a cup from the cabinet.

"I didn't say a thing about your hair." Katie Ann found her own cup that she'd used earlier for coffee, and she poured herself some after Martha was done.

Martha sat down at the kitchen table, crossed her legs, and leaned back in the chair. "Now I want to hear about your time with that handsome Eli, but first things first. Tell me about this letter from Lucy."

Katie Ann pulled out a chair across the table and sat down. "She sent me a letter a couple of weeks ago, saying she needed to talk to me about an urgent matter."

Martha uncrossed her legs, leaned forward, and placed her palms on the table. "What urgent matter could that woman possibly need to talk to you about?"

"I don't know." Katie Ann shrugged. "But you don't need to be here when she comes tomorrow."

Martha folded her arms across her chest. Scowling, she said, "I thought I was your best friend. But you didn't even tell me about this letter."

"Martha…" Katie Ann spoke gently. "You are my best friend, but I knew you would react like this."

Martha snapped her fingers. "A woman like that only wants one thing. Money! I bet that tramp is coming to ask for money."

"I am not going to have you use such language in my house. Do you hear me?" Katie Ann cut her eyes at Martha across the table.

"Fine. But I'm sure she must be trying to get some money out of you. That's got to be it."

Katie Ann searched her heart and soul for a moment. "Maybe she's coming to say she's sorry?"

Martha grunted. "I doubt it." She pointed a crooked finger at Katie Ann. "And I know it's your people's way to forgive and forget, but the woman had an affair with your husband."

"I don't need to be reminded, Martha, and yes… we do try hard to forgive." She sighed. "Forgetting is not always so easy. Don't you think I'm nervous about Lucy coming here tomorrow? But she's traveled a very long way to talk to me."

"I don't care if she took a rocket from the moon. She's got no business here."

Katie Ann stood up, one arm folded across her churning stomach and her coffee cup in her other hand. She paced the kitchen. "I don't want you here tomorrow morning, Martha. It will be hard enough just having Lucy here."

"Don't worry. I won't be here."

Katie Ann breathed a sigh of relief. She had expected resistance. *"Gut,"* she said as she smoothed wrinkles from her apron. "It will be best that way."

Martha scratched her nose, then pulled a handkerchief from her pocket and blew her nose. Then she blew it again, and again, and again.

"Are you sick?" Katie Ann sat back down across from Martha.

"Yes, I'm sick. I'm not well at all." Martha squeezed her nose with the handkerchief and blew with force. "I feel like poop, but I'm forced to come over here in this weather this morning to find out about a letter from that…" She looked up at Katie Ann and huffed. "That *woman.*"

"I was going to tell you. After my visit with Lucy."

Martha shook her head as her face shriveled into a frown. "I don't even like to hear her name."

"Well, it doesn't please me to say her name either." Katie Ann decided to try to change the subject. "You said you went to the doctor the other day. Did you have this cold then?"

"I don't have a cold. I'm much sicker." Martha pinched her lips together.

Katie Ann knew that Martha often exaggerated her aches, pains, and illnesses. Sometimes her friend even faked ill health for attention. When the women first became friends, Martha often complained of a backache. Katie Ann was never sure of the extent of the ailment, but Martha's backaches always manifested when she needed something from Katie Ann, even if it was just companionship. And when Martha showed the slightest sign of a cold, she was worse than a child. But Katie Ann always showered Martha with sympathy and affection—sick or not sick. Because the woman truly was her best friend.

However, Martha disliked doctors. For all her aches and pains, Katie Ann couldn't recall one single time Martha had visited a physician.

"I'm sorry you feel poorly. What's wrong with you?" Katie Ann tapped her finger to her chin. "And what type of routine tests did you have?"

Martha stood up from the table, straightening the collar of her black velour pullover. "Once a year I force myself to visit that idiot doctor in Alamosa, and I let him run all those stupid tests on me. And every year, I'm fine."

"Did you mention your cold?"

Martha slammed her hands to her hips. "Did you not hear me? I don't have a cold." She raised her chin. "I'm very ill." She lowered her gaze. "I have to go for more tests tomorrow."

Katie Ann eased closer to her friend. "What kind of tests?"

"Lung tests."

That sounded serious to Katie Ann, but she tried to speak as though she wasn't concerned. "I'm sure everything will be fine."

Martha sighed. "I doubt it. But we all gotta go sometime." She didn't say anything more as she turned and walked toward the living room.

"Martha…" Katie Ann caught up to Martha by the front door. "Do you want me to go with you to the doctor?"

"And cancel that fine visit with Lucy you have scheduled?" She grunted, rolling her eyes. "I wouldn't dream of asking you to do that."

Katie Ann grinned as she stuffed her hands in the pockets of her apron. "Martha, now you stop it. You know I'll cancel with Lucy to be with you."

"Do you even know where she's staying?"

"Well, no…but…"

"Don't worry about it. I'll give you a full report tomorrow evening." Martha frowned. "Kiss Jonas for me. I don't think I should be too close to him until the doctor finds out what's wrong with me."

"I will. But please come over tomorrow evening and let me know what the doctor said."

Martha cut her eyes at Katie Ann. "Only if you tell me what that horrible Lucy had to say." She pulled on her gloves, then pointed a finger at Katie Ann. "I still say she's here for money."

Money was something Katie Ann had plenty of,

thanks to a mysterious box of cash that had been left on her doorstep last year—money she suspected had originated from Martha, even though the woman denied it. But she couldn't imagine Lucy coming all the way to Colorado to ask for money from Katie Ann, the woman whose husband she'd stolen.

"I don't think she's coming to ask for money."

"No, you wouldn't think that. You see the good in everyone."

Katie Ann didn't say anything, but she certainly didn't see the good in what Lucy Turner had done. Or her husband. And forgiveness was much further out of reach than Martha might realize. It was something Katie Ann struggled with daily.

"I'll see you tomorrow night."

"Hey, wait." Martha lifted her chin. "You didn't tell me about Eli. How'd it go after I left?"

"Fine." Katie Ann grinned, intentionally fueling Martha's curiosity.

Martha cackled. "Really?" She leaned closer and whispered, "I think that man's got a thing for you."

"Well, you're wrong. We agreed to be friends, though. And that's all. We are at two very different places in life."

A full smile spread across Martha's face. "The fact that you are both trying to clarify the relationship this early on...well, that means something. When are you going to see him again?"

"What makes you think I'll see him again?" Katie Ann fought to hide her expression as she realized that she was looking forward to Tuesday.

Martha tried to snap her gloved fingers. "Aha! You are going to see him again. When?"

Katie Ann lifted one shoulder as she pulled her eyes from Martha's. "Tuesday."

Martha's eyes grew round. "Fabulous!"

"We're going to travel together to see the sand dunes, as *friends*. Eli is hiring a driver."

Martha crossed herself, which she often did, even though she wasn't Catholic. "Thank God. I've been praying for you to find someone." She let out a heavy sigh. "In case I kick the bucket, you'll have someone to take care of you."

Again Katie Ann felt sure Martha was exaggerating, but the comment was disturbing nonetheless. "Don't say things like that, Martha."

Martha hugged Katie Ann. "Don't you worry about a thing." She kissed Katie Ann on the cheek and closed the door behind her.

And for the first time since she'd met Martha and nursed her through a host of ailments, some real, some not so real—Katie Ann felt truly worried about her friend.

Chapter Five

Lucy thanked her hostess at the Mansion Bed-and-Breakfast after a meal that should have been more than satisfying. Eggs Benedict were her favorite, and the fruit bowl and homemade granola also topped the list of her preferred breakfast items. But this morning her stomach roiled with anxiety, and she wondered if coming all this way to see Katie Ann was a mistake. Ivan's wife might be Amish, but she was still human, and Lucy had seen the loathing in Katie Ann's eyes on Saturday. She wished this trip hadn't been necessary, but after much deliberation, she didn't see any way around it.

She carted her red suitcase to her rental car, popped the trunk, and stored the luggage inside. It was only ten miles from the B and B in Monte Vista to Katie Ann's house, and she planned to drive as slowly as possible. She'd hoped to get this dreaded visit over with on Saturday and be back in Lancaster County by now, but she was certainly willing to work around Katie Ann's schedule. That was the least she could do.

As she pulled off the main highway, she touched her hand to her stomach and felt the baby kick. In the darkness of the other night, and with a heavy coat on, her pregnancy hadn't been noticeable to Katie Ann. The last thing she wanted to do was cause the woman more pain. But she didn't have a choice. Ivan was gone, and he'd been the only person who could explain the contents of the box he'd left behind. Lucy's future depended on Katie Ann being able to identify the picture.

She took a deep breath and tried to calm her rapid heartbeat. So many times she'd wanted to defend herself to Katie Ann and the members of her community. She knew that everyone in the Old Order district thought she'd seduced Ivan away from his wife, that surely no good Amish man would pursue an *Englisch* woman. If they only knew.

She thought back on Ivan's many advances and wished more than anything that she could go back in time, wished she had never agreed to have lunch with the handsome Amish man who was clearly unhappy at home. One lunch led to another, until eventually Ivan had kissed her. She ended it after that, but Ivan only tried harder. Every day he would wander into the café where she worked. He'd also call her from a cell phone he was hiding from Katie Ann. And when he said he never loved anyone the way he loved her, she had melted. All she'd ever wanted was to be loved, and she'd managed to go thirty-two years without true love. Until Ivan.

She pulled into the driveway that led up to Katie Ann's house. She glanced to her left at the house she knew to be Samuel and Lillian's. She hoped that neither of them would be at Katie Ann's when she arrived. Or the scary woman who had been there on Saturday night. It would be hard enough to talk to Katie Ann without an audience.

Katie Ann pulled the last of the clothes through the wringer washer, then began to hang the wet items in the mudroom. Temperatures had dropped during the night, and a blanket of frost still covered everything at nine o'clock this morning. She'd tried to stay busy for the past four hours, since she'd gotten up to nurse Jonas. After feeding her little one, he'd drifted back to sleep, and Katie Ann had busied herself cleaning and washing clothes. Anything to keep her mind off Lucy's impending visit.

She didn't know the woman well at all. She had worked at a café back in Lancaster County, and they'd only spoken a handful of times before Katie Ann caught Ivan kissing her one day. After that, her husband had promised her that he'd stopped seeing Lucy, that there'd never been more than a shared kiss and a few phone calls. Katie Ann knew now that Ivan had lied to her, and she couldn't help but wonder if there were other untruths built around his relationship with Lucy. Maybe he had tried to end it with Lucy, but Katie Ann could still remember the way she begged Ivan not to leave their marriage. She and Ivan had relocated to Colorado for a new beginning, but Ivan's heart had remained in Lancaster County. And even though Katie Ann had adjusted nicely to her life in Colorado, Lancaster County was where her own roots were. She wondered if she would ever move back there.

As she clipped a towel to a hanger, she recalled Ivan's funeral a few months ago. Lucy had been racked with grief, and Katie Ann almost felt sorry for the woman. Almost. But there was always enough bitterness in Katie Ann's heart to drown out any sympathy for Lucy. Perhaps she shouldn't have even agreed to this meeting. *An urgent matter?*

She thought about what Martha said. Could Lucy be coming to ask for money? When she heard a car pulling in, she left the rest of the wet clothes in the laundry basket. Her stomach clenched tight as she smoothed the wrinkles from her black apron and moved through the house. Her heart felt like it would beat out of her chest as she stood on the other side of the closed door, waiting for Lucy to knock. She listened to her heels click up the porch steps, then a soft tap against the door.

Katie Ann opened the front door, took one look at Lucy, and almost gasped. A knot formed in her throat, and she couldn't speak.

"Hello, Katie Ann." Lucy tried to pull her long beige coat tighter around her, but it didn't hide her enlarged belly.

Katie Ann managed to open the door and motion for Lucy to enter.

"Come in," she finally said after Lucy was already inside the living room and Katie Ann was shutting the door. She could hear the tremble in her voice, and she wondered if Lucy was half as nervous as she was.

"I guess you must have noticed…" Lucy's voice trailed off as she placed both hands on her stomach. "I'm six months pregnant."

"Ivan's?" Katie Ann asked.

Lucy looked down at her brown boots. "Yes."

Katie Ann moved as if she were a character in someone else's nightmare, unable to believe that this adulteress was in her home. Any earlier thoughts of polite small talk or an offer of coffee slipped from her mind. Still standing, she asked, "What do you want, Lucy?"

Lucy's bottom lip trembled as she avoided eye contact with Katie Ann. "First of all, I want to say how very sorry I am. For everything."

She looked up at Katie Ann as a tear rolled down her cheek, and Katie Ann stared at her, knowing she didn't have one ounce of forgiveness for the woman, despite what she'd said, thought, or prayed about in the past. And she had no plans to make this visit easy on her.

"What do you want?" she asked again.

Katie Ann was surprised at how plain Lucy looked. She didn't have on the heavy makeup she'd seen her wear before, and her clothes were conservative, not as if she'd selected them that morning with the intention of seducing someone's husband. Perhaps being pregnant had humbled the woman.

Still standing, Lucy reached into her oversized brown purse and pulled out a wooden box. "I found this after Ivan died." She held out a small cedar container for Katie Ann to see.

Katie Ann recognized the box right away. It was half the size of a shoe box, and Ivan's father had made it for him when he was a boy. He'd always kept it on their dresser.

"What about it?" Katie Ann couldn't imagine why Ivan's old keepsake would have brought Lucy all the way to Colorado.

Lucy leaned forward slightly and grimaced.

Instinctively, Katie Ann took a step toward her. "Are you all right?"

"Yes, just a hard kick from the little one."

Lucy smiled a bit, and Katie Ann stiffened. But despite her resentment of Lucy, she asked her if she would like to sit down.

"Thank you." Lucy kept her coat on, thankfully, and sat down on the couch.

Katie Ann sat in the rocking chair across from her. "Lucy, I'm sure you didn't come here to show me Ivan's box." She folded her hands in her lap, bit her bottom lip, and waited.

"Actually, it's what I found in the box." Lucy unlatched the tiny clasp and pulled out a photograph. She reached across the coffee table and handed it to Katie Ann, who took it hesitantly. It was a picture of a house, a beautiful white house with black shutters and a white picket fence.

Katie Ann handed the picture back to her. "Why are you showing me this?"

Lucy's voice wavered as she spoke, her eyes watering. "I was hoping you might know where this house is." She reached back into the box and pulled out two keys. "These keys were in the box also. I think Ivan bought us a house somewhere, and—"

Katie Ann blinked her eyes a few times. "What?"

"I'm sorry, Katie Ann. I'm so sorry. But our bank account is wiped out, and I think Ivan used the money that was in there to purchase this house. But I have no idea where it is. I know that sounds crazy, but I can't afford to keep making the mortgage on our current house. They've cut my hours at the café, and I'll need to stop working when the baby comes."

Katie Ann rubbed her forehead and tried to picture Ivan cleaning out their bank account. "That doesn't sound like Ivan."

"The money was his. I mean, I had very little when we moved in together. So it isn't like he stole my money or anything." Lucy stood up. "I think he was planning to surprise me with a new home."

Katie Ann thought about all the ways Ivan used to surprise her in the past, whether just a bouquet of flowers, or even once a new buggy. She thought for a moment. "That doesn't make any sense. Ivan would have put your house on the market to sell before he invested money to build a new one." Katie Ann shook her head. "I can't believe this is what you came here to talk to me about."

She wondered how much money Ivan had put in Lucy's bank account. He'd told her he left with very little, but Katie Ann had never been familiar with their finances...until she'd started to run out of money several months after Ivan left her. Then the mysterious box of money showed up on her doorstep.

"After Ivan was killed, I went to check our bank account," Lucy said. "His landscaping company had been doing very well, and the money he'd been saving was gone. I haven't made a mortgage payment since he died. We bought the house I'm in together, and I can't afford it on my own. I'm going to lose my home, and I'm pregnant. So if I don't find out if this is our house, I'm going to be homeless."

Katie Ann tried to absorb what Lucy was saying, but it still didn't make sense. "If Ivan bought a house, there would be some paperwork or something. How could you not know about it?"

Lucy raised her palms in the air. "Exactly. I was wondering if you knew anything about it."

"Why would I know? Ivan left me a year ago." Katie Ann reached down, picked up the picture from the box on the coffee table again, and stared at it, resentment filling every pore.

Lucy sat down and put her head in her hands. "I don't know. It was a long shot coming here. But I have no paperwork, nothing. Just money missing, a picture of a house, and two keys. It was the only thing I could think of, that Ivan used the money to buy us another house, then died before he had a chance to tell me about it." Lucy started to sob. "I'm going to have a baby, and I'm going to lose my house. I never even wanted…" She stopped and looked up at Katie Ann, and her face reddened.

"You didn't want a baby?" Katie Ann felt like this surreal conversation was choking her.

Lucy sniffled. "I don't see myself as a very good mother. I don't know the first thing about babies."

Katie Ann eased back into the rocking chair, feeling nauseous. All she'd ever wanted was a baby, and for her and Ivan to have a family together. Now his mistress was sitting on the couch crying. "Being a mother will come naturally to you."

Lucy swiped at a tear. "Do you think? Did it come naturally to you?"

Katie Ann didn't like being compared to Lucy, and she didn't want to share such an intimate detail with her. "It came naturally. And it will for you too."

Lucy lowered her head again. "I just don't know what I'm going to do. I took an advance from work to be able to make this trip." She stared up at Katie Ann. "Do you think Ivan bought this house for us? To surprise me?"

Katie Ann studied the woman's expression. "I don't know."

"It's the only thing that makes sense." She put a finger to her lips for a moment, then asked, "You haven't gotten any mail regarding this, have you?"

Katie Ann recalled a letter she received from Ivan's attorney a while back, but there was no mention of any house. "No. I haven't."

Lucy started crying again.

"Can I get you something to drink?"

"Maybe just a glass of water." Lucy pulled a tissue from her coat pocket and blew her nose.

Katie Ann left her in the living room and returned a moment later. She handed the glass of water to her, then folded her arms across her chest. "How much do you need?"

Lucy swallowed a gulp of water. "What?"

"How much money do you need to keep your house from going into foreclosure?"

Lucy stood up and faced Katie Ann. "I didn't come here to ask you for money. I just came here to see if you recognized that house, or knew where it might be located."

Katie Ann gazed into Lucy's eyes, and for some reason…she believed her. She left the room, and a minute later she returned with her checkbook.

"Katie Ann, I will not take any money from you."

Katie Ann scribbled out what she thought would be enough to carry Lucy for several months. She tore the check out and handed it to Lucy. "Take it. You are going to give birth to Jonas's brother or sister."

Lucy stiffened her arms at her sides and shook her head. "I can't." Then she covered her face with her hands. "How could you even make this offer, after what I did to you?"

Tears poured down Lucy's face, and Katie Ann dabbed at her own eyes.

"I'm the most horrible person on the planet, and if I could go back, I would have never, never…" She sobbed harder. "Please forgive me, Katie Ann." She looked up at her. "Please. I need to be forgiven."

Katie Ann swallowed back a lump in her throat.

She knew that she could ease Lucy's pain by telling her that she was forgiven, but the words just wouldn't come. The image of Ivan walking out the door, abandoning their life together, kept flashing before her.

She pushed the check toward Lucy. "Take the money, Lucy. If not for you, for the child."

Lucy slowly reached for the check. "Ivan should have stayed with you. You're a much better person than I am."

Katie Ann wanted to say, "Yes, he should have." Instead she moved toward the door, hoping Lucy would follow.

She did.

Lucy stepped out on the porch and then peered at Katie Ann through the screen, tears still streaming down her cheeks. "I loved him. And I miss him very much."

Katie Ann took a deep breath, rubbed her forehead, and thought about how much she missed Ivan too.

"Ivan and I had a fight the night he was killed." Lucy closed her eyes tightly for a moment before she looked back at Katie Ann. "We said ugly things to each other, then he left." She locked eyes with Katie Ann and tipped her head to one side. "I always wondered if he was going back to you."

A tear rolled down Katie Ann's cheek, and with

Lucy's eyes still locked with hers, she closed the door. Katie Ann knew that she would spend the rest of her life wondering too now.

Martha sat down in her recliner, bumping the small table next to her chair for the thousandth time. Katie Ann asked her why she didn't move the table over, but once she was settled in her chair, the table was close enough to reach her hand lotion, the remote for the television, and the phone without even having to stretch a muscle.

She stared at the empty space a few feet away where Elvis's cage used to be. It had been almost a year, but she sure missed that bird. Sometimes she could still hear him saying her name. She tapped her fingernail on the hard surface of the table next to her. That parrot should have outlived Martha, but the Lord had seen fit to call her beloved Elvis home. She'd thought about getting another parrot, but it just didn't feel right.

Closing her eyes, she thought about Arnold. *Why did you take him, too, Lord?* Her close friend and companion didn't go home to see the Lord, but instead went to Georgia to be with his dying son. How could Martha fault the man for that? But she sure missed him. They exchanged the occasional letter, and Martha had sent flowers when his son passed, but Arnold had decided to stay on in Georgia instead of returning to Canaan. He had kinfolk there, and he'd reestablished those relationships. Martha was glad for Arnold. He deserved to be happy.

She thought back a couple of months to when Arnold had asked if he could come for a visit. As much as she'd missed him, she made up an excuse for him not to come. She just wasn't sure her heart could take another good-bye. Easier to just leave the past in the past without stirring up old feelings. But after her appointment with the doctor today, she had the strongest urge to call Arnold. Part of her wanted to share her news with him, but she feared Arnold would feel obligated to hop a plane to see her. She didn't need his pity.

Laying her head back against the recliner, she thought about Katie Ann. She sure hoped that Eli Detweiler would fall madly in love with Katie Ann. Her friend needed someone to take care of her and Jonas, and clearly Martha wouldn't be around forever. She opened her eyes, placed her hand on the telephone, then tapped her finger on the table again.

She picked up the phone, and this time she managed to dial nine out of the ten numbers before she placed the telephone back in the carrier.

"Oh, why not," she said aloud as she picked up the phone again. She dialed the numbers quickly, knowing that once the phone rang once, there was no turning back. Arnold was a nonprogressive man—as anyone would know by looking at his outdated clothes and truck—but even he had caller ID.

Her heart raced as the phone rang a third time, then a fourth, and she was about to hang up when she heard the soft, gentle voice of a man she still loved.

"Hello, Martha."

"Hi, Arnold. How are you?"

"Still missing you."

Martha put a hand to her chest and closed her eyes as she pictured Arnold's kind face. The man made her want to be a better person, and he'd introduced her to the Lord, something she'd always be grateful for. "How's the weather there?"

"Chilly. But not as cold as in Colorado, I reckon."

There was silence for a moment, and Martha struggled to keep her voice in check as a tear rolled down her cheek. "Temperatures dropped last night. They say it will be mighty cold by Thanksgiving."

"What are your plans for the holiday?"

"Oh, I'll be with Katie Ann and Jonas. Probably at Lillian and Samuel's house. What about you?"

"My son's wife invited me to Thanksgiving at her folks' house, and a cousin of mine invited me, but…" He sighed. "I think I'll probably just stay home."

"Now, Arnold Becker, I've never known a man to love turkey as much as you do. It's not right for you not to have any on Thanksgiving." Martha realized that she was hinting toward an invitation and quickly backtracked. "But I guess it's your choice."

"How's your back?"

Arnold always asked about Martha's back, even though most of the time it was fine.

"Feeling pretty good." She dabbed at her eyes. "I have to go. I was just checking on you."

A long silence ensued, but Martha was choking back tears and afraid to speak. Finally Arnold did.

"I'm fine, Martha. As I said, I'm just missing you."

Well, if you cared about me half as much as I care about you, you wouldn't have stayed in Georgia. She'd wanted to say it a dozen times, but for reasons she wasn't sure of, she never did. "You take care, Arnold."

"You, too, Martha."

She hung up the phone as another tear rolled down her cheek. She clicked on the lamp on the table. Nightfall was settling in, and normally she would have been at Katie Ann's by now. She hated to miss a day with Katie Ann and Jonas, but Katie Ann would know something was wrong, and that girl had enough on her plate. She didn't need to be worrying about Martha.

And curiosity was nipping at her, making her wonder how Katie Ann's visit with that hussy Lucy had gone. Martha was still sure that Lucy had come calling for money.

* * *

Katie Ann watched Jonas sleep, her own eyelids growing heavy. She tucked his small quilt around him and made sure he was warm enough, then forced herself to leave his bedroom. She wondered if there would ever come a time when she wouldn't worry so much about him. God had taken Ivan away, and the thought of losing Jonas, too, was more than she could bear. All this fear and worry went against everything she'd been taught. She knew the only way to bring peace and calm was to believe in God's will, to pray about it. She was sure she couldn't trust another man the way she'd trusted Ivan, but had she stopped trusting the Lord as well?

In the living room, she lifted the lantern until a reflection lit the clock on the wall. Surely if there had been a problem at the doctor, Martha would have been at her house in an instant. Katie Ann would have showered her with sympathy, even though she suspected that Martha simply had a bad cold. Probably best that she didn't come over and expose Jonas. Martha went to bed early, so it was too late to call her, but Katie Ann decided to go out to the barn to see if she had left a message on the answering machine.

A light snow dusted her black coat as she walked across the yard. She pushed the barn door open, waking some of the residents. One of the pigs snorted as a chicken flapped across the space in front of her. But nestled in the corner on the quilt, Dash slept peacefully.

Katie Ann tiptoed to the workbench and shone the light from the lantern onto the answering machine. No messages. She leaned down, hoping to pet the sleek black cat. But as her hand drew near, the animal hissed, and within seconds he resembled a porcupine, every hair on his body standing straight up.

"It's okay, fellow. You can trust me." But the cat hissed again, cowered for a moment, then leaped underneath the workbench and around the corner where he'd retreated before. She reached into her pocket and pulled out some leftover scrapple she'd put in a plastic container, unsure if the cat would be interested in the cornmeal mush.

After giving each of the three horses a quick scratch on the nose, she made her way back to the house. She checked on Jonas, who was sleeping soundly. He was still having bouts with a gassy tummy, but Katie Ann had been practicing Eli's technique, which continued to work well. She carried the lantern back into the living room and placed it on the coffee table in front of her, then sat down on the couch with a book. It was so quiet, except for a coyote howling in the distance. After only a few minutes of reading, she felt fidgety, so she got up and put another log on the fire.

It was bizarre. Ivan always had a good business sense about him, and buying a new house before he sold the old one just didn't make any sense. She knew Martha would scold her for giving Lucy money, but someone had given Katie Ann money when she needed it the most, so it seemed the right thing to do. Or had she done it to ease her own conscience because she couldn't forgive Lucy, or Ivan? Was it her way of trying to get right with God? She wasn't sure, but she hoped that it was enough money to keep Lucy far away from Canaan.

Lucy sat at the airport, waiting for her flight to board. She kept thinking about Katie Ann's generosity, and she wondered whatever had made Ivan choose her over his wife. The woman seemed so unselfish and filled with goodness. Lucy, on the other hand, didn't think life could get any worse. She'd sunk lower than a snake by accepting Katie Ann's money, and the only man she'd ever loved was gone. Along with his money. It hadn't been a ton of money that he'd brought to the relationship, but it was substantially more than Lucy had ever had, and his contribution to their bank account had always given her a sense of security.

But Ivan had always loved to surprise her, like with the new car he'd bought her a few months ago. He had adapted well to his job in the outside world doing landscaping projects, saying it allowed him to keep a small part of his past, his love of the land. And the money had been good, but old habits die hard, and Lucy was always on edge about money.

She recalled the fight they'd had the night Ivan was killed in the accident. Lucy was concerned about their finances, and Ivan said that was all she cared about—money. The last thing he did when he left was to mumble something in Pennsylvania *Deitsch*, and Lucy had no idea what he'd said in his native dialect.

She rubbed her tired eyes for a moment as she wondered once again what Ivan's final words had been. She'd pushed him to get a divorce, but Ivan said he didn't believe in divorce, which Lucy found ironic since the man was sharing her bed.

Sometimes Ivan said one thing but did another. She knew he felt bad about their living arrangements, but he still insisted divorce from Katie Ann wasn't an option. He also said that he knew he'd failed in the eyes of God, that he missed his relationship with the Lord. Most of the time Lucy didn't understand his reasoning. She just knew she loved him.

Lucy stood up when people started to board the plane. She picked up her carry-on bag and edged toward them. A woman in front of her moved to the front of the line, since she was boarding with a small baby. Lucy touched her stomach with her free hand and wondered for the thousandth time what in the world she was going to do with a child.

Chapter Six

Eli asked the driver to wait while he went to get Katie Ann and Jonas. He was worried that Katie Ann would cancel because of the snow, but the driver had the car toasty warm, and Eli had an umbrella opened to protect them from the light flurries. Although he wasn't sure a trip to the sand dunes was the best plan. He'd wait until they were on the road to mention it and suggest an indoor outing instead.

Katie Ann opened the door a few seconds after he knocked, with Jonas bundled in her arms, a car seat at her feet, and a diaper bag over one shoulder. "We're ready," she said.

Eli was thrilled to hear excitement in her voice. And the woman looked absolutely beautiful. A faint alarm rang in his head, reminding him that they could be nothing more than friends, but he ignored it, picked up the car seat, and motioned Katie Ann ahead of him, holding the umbrella over her head.

"Careful down the steps," he said, latching onto her arm.

Once they had Jonas secure in the backseat, Eli offered to sit there with him, but Katie Ann insisted on being close to the baby. So Eli sat in front with their driver, Wayne, an older man whom Vera had recommended. Vera said he was a regular driver for the few Amish in their small community.

The car hadn't even pulled out of the snow-covered driveway when Katie Ann spoke up. "Would you mind if we make a stop around the corner before we go to the sand dunes?"

Eli was surprised that she was still open to seeing the massive dunes with the weather as it was. He twisted his neck to face her. "*Ya*. Wayne can take you wherever you need to go."

"I want to check on my friend Martha." Katie Ann frowned. "She comes to see me and Jonas every day, and she didn't come last night." She hesitated. "And Martha had a doctor appointment yesterday."

Wayne reached the end of the driveway. "Which way to your friend's house?" The gray-haired man looked over his shoulder at Katie Ann.

Eli had liked the *Englisch* man right away. He was soft-spoken with a gentle smile.

"Turn right here," Katie Ann said. "Then it's the

second right, and Martha's house is the third one on the left."

Wayne did as he was instructed, and in five minutes they pulled into Martha's driveway. It was snowing harder.

"If it's all right, I'll just leave Jonas in the car and run in to check on Martha." Katie Ann opened the car door after Eli nodded.

"What a beautiful woman," Wayne said as they watched Katie Ann walk up the sidewalk to Martha's front porch.

Eli cleared his throat. "*Ya*, she is." Stroking his beard, he kept his eyes on her.

Katie Ann knocked hard on the door until Martha finally answered in her pink housecoat and matching slippers. Her hair was atop her head in the butterfly clip.

"I'm just checking on you."

"Come in out of the cold." Martha grabbed her arm and pulled her across the threshold, then peered past her to the car in the driveway. "Who's that, and where's my baby?"

"Eli hired a driver. His name is Wayne, and Jonas is in the car. I only have a minute. I just wanted to hear what the doctor said. Do you just have a bad cold?"

Martha nodded. "Yes. Just a cold. I'm fine. Now you go play with that handsome Eli."

She grinned, but Katie Ann was not fooled. Martha was the first one to complain about the slightest ailment, and it was disturbing that she wasn't offering up much information.

"Did he give you some medicine? Is it the flu?"

Martha tugged Katie Ann toward the door. "Yeah, yeah. I've got medicine."

Katie Ann shook free of Martha's grip and squinted her eyes as she spoke. "Martha, are you not telling me something?"

"Oh, good grief. I'm fine, Katie Ann. Go and have fun today." Martha opened the door and pushed the screen wide as she stepped out on the porch in her robe. She cupped a hand above her brow and peered across the yard. "Although this weather isn't the best."

Katie Ann moved onto the covered porch, pulled her black coat around her, and glanced up. "*Ya*. It's snowing even harder now."

Martha chuckled. "Good snuggling weather, I'd say."

Katie Ann narrowed her eyes at Martha. "What did I tell you? Eli and I agreed to be just friends."

"Whatever." Martha rolled her eyes, then her expression suddenly changed. "Hey, real quick. What did Lucy want? Money, huh?"

"I'll explain later."

"I knew it." Martha shook her head. "The tramp wanted money, and you probably gave her some."

"We'll talk about it later. I have to go." Katie Ann turned her back to Martha and eased down the porch steps. She glanced over her shoulder. "Stay out of the weather and get well."

"Katie Ann Stoltzfus!" Martha yelled, and Katie Ann cringed. "Did you give that woman money?"

Katie Ann raised her hand and waved Martha off as she neared the car.

"I knew it!" Martha yelled as Katie Ann opened the door and crawled back in.

She'd deal with Martha later. Today she was looking forward to seeing some sights in the San Luis Valley, although as it snowed harder she started to worry about having Jonas out in the cold.

"I'm afraid most of our sightseeing may have to be done from the car." Eli twisted in his seat and smiled.

He smiled a lot, and Katie Ann thought again about what Martha had said, that the man was just happy. Katie Ann knew it couldn't hurt her to have a bright light in her world, and as Eli waited for her to answer, she wondered if she should have agreed to this outing. She reminded herself that a person can never have too many friends and that as long as she kept her relationship with Eli in perspective, all would be well.

"It's snowing harder," she said softly, wondering if he was going to cancel their outing.

"There's a diner about fifteen miles north of

here," Wayne said. "If you folks are hungry, they have the best pancakes in the area. Maybe this snow will ease up while you're eating."

Katie Ann could see Wayne struggling to see through the flurries coming harder now. She waited for Eli to respond.

"I could go for some pancakes." Eli patted his stomach in the front seat before twisting around to face her. "Katie Ann, what about you?"

She'd eaten cereal that morning, but a cup of hot coffee sounded nice. "*Ya*. That's fine."

Jonas stretched in his seat, his eyes wide, but Katie Ann was glad that he appeared content. On the way to the diner, Eli questioned Wayne about the area…and about farming. Katie Ann had heard Samuel talk about the challenges of farming in Colorado, since the state only had a few months of frost-free weather. Wayne told Eli that he farmed a few acres just for his family.

"It's not so bad once you get used to the climate," the older man said.

Eli stroked his beard. "Lots of solar panels here, *ya*?"

Katie Ann nodded but quietly listened as Wayne answered.

"Yep. Since we have over three hundred days of sunshine on average per year, the solar panels make sense." He turned slightly to face Katie Ann and smiled. "And they are permissible for you folks."

Katie Ann had considered purchasing some of the solar panels for heating, but hadn't as of yet.

Wayne pulled into the diner. "I've got to go to the post office while we're near town, if that's all right with you. And I need to stop at the pharmacy to pick up something for the wife." He put the car in park. "So, okay if I'm back in about an hour? Maybe the snow will have eased up by then." He leaned his face closer to the windshield and looked up.

"That sounds fine." Eli opened his door, and before Katie Ann could climb out of the car, he already had Jonas's car seat out and was hurrying toward the diner entrance with the umbrella protectively shielding Jonas from the snow. Katie Ann hurried behind them.

Eli pushed the door open, got Jonas safely inside the warmth of the diner, and held the door for Katie Ann. "I'm sorry," he said softly. "I should have waited for you."

Katie Ann smiled. "No. I'm glad you didn't. You made sure my Jonas was warm and protected."

Eli's face reddened a bit as he pulled his eyes away from her. "Habit, I guess. Tending to the *kinner.*"

A young waitress asked them to follow her to an empty booth toward the back of the diner. Eli got Jonas situated on one side of the booth, waited for Katie Ann to sit beside her son, and took a seat across from them.

After they scanned the menu, Eli ordered pancakes, and Katie Ann opted for coffee and a banana nut muffin. Then they slipped into a conversation with surprising ease, and Eli's infectious smile set the tone as he talked about his children and grandchildren.

"Did I tell you that Ida Mae has twin boys?" Eli raised a brow. "Luke and Ben are almost a year old." He chuckled as he reached for his coffee. "Cutest little fellows in the world, but they're a handful, like most *kinner* that age. Luke is already walking, but Ben hasn't quite gotten there yet."

Katie Ann was mesmerized as she listened to him go on about his other grandchildren. It was so unusual for an Amish man to carry on this way, and she found it endearing. She felt so at ease with him, she even shared some of her fears about motherhood. Eli was polite and affirming, assuring her that she was a great mother.

"It's just wonderful the way you've raised your *kinner.*" She paused, unintentionally locking eyes with him. "And very…touching, the way you talk about your grandchildren."

Eli kept his eyes fused with Katie Ann's. "The Lord saw fit to take Sarah, but He sure did bless me in other ways." He looked down for a moment and shook his head. "Believe me, there were many days when I didn't think I would make it. Days when I needed to work the fields, but two or three of the *kinner* would be sick and I couldn't leave them. Or there was the time when Jake toyed with the idea of leaving the community, and…" Eli took a deep breath. "I don't know what I would have done." Then he grinned. "Do you know what Frieda did when she was seven years old?" His hazel eyes grew round as his voice rose an octave.

Katie Ann smiled. "I'd love to hear."

"She cut her hair!"

Katie Ann brought a hand to her mouth in an unsuccessful attempt to stifle a laugh. If she hadn't felt the laughter all the way to the warm pit of her stomach, she might not have recognized it. It had been so long. "What did you do?"

Eli grunted. "What could I do? The damage was done." He chuckled. "She had a bob for a long time until her beautiful blond hair finally grew past her shoulders."

"Did she say why she did it?" Katie Ann leaned back a bit as the waitress arrived with their food.

Eli gave a nod of thanks as the young woman put his pancakes in front of him. "She said that it took too long to dry and that long hair was hot in the summertime."

"But surely she knew that it is not our way to cut our hair."

"*Ya*. She knew." He shook his head. "But that's my Frieda. Always thinking practical."

Katie Ann bit her bottom lip.

"Go ahead and laugh. I know it's a bit funny." Eli took a big bite of his pancakes. "Did I mention that she cut it about fifteen minutes before church service?"

Katie Ann put a hand to her chest, but a giggle escaped just the same. "Oh no."

"*Ach*, I've got about a thousand more stories I could share, but I don't want to bore you."

"I can't imagine getting bored hearing stories about your *kinner*." She glanced down at Jonas, who was sleeping soundly. "I'm sure Jonas will fill me with surprises. I can't wait."

"He will grow to be a fine boy."

Katie Ann circled the rim of her coffee cup with her finger. "I hope I'll be a *gut mudder*."

"You already are." Eli's voice was gentle, his eyes soft. "Jonas is blessed to have you."

As she added a pat of butter to her muffin, Katie Ann struggled to ignore the other thoughts fighting for space in her mind. Was it possible that Ivan had been coming back to her on the day he died, as Lucy thought? Would they have been a family again?

"You look a million miles away," Eli said after a few moments. "And I bet I know why."

Katie Ann picked at her muffin but didn't say

anything. He reached across the table and put his hand on hers. She was too stunned to move.

"I know this isn't how you thought your life would unfold, but I know God has big plans for you. You're going to do just fine." He pulled back his hand, but Katie Ann could still feel his touch long afterward.

"I hope so," she finally whispered. Fearing the conversation was drifting to a place she didn't want to go, she decided to change the subject. "So tell me more about your plans to travel."

"I will still work hard. I won't be traveling all the time."

Katie Ann waited while he finished off his last bite of pancakes.

"I have cousins in Indiana, and I know folks who have traveled to Florida, so I think I'll start with those two places." He shrugged. "I haven't decided where else."

"Lots of folks in Lancaster County travel to Florida to vacation. They love spending time at the beach."

"Did you always live in Lancaster County before you moved here?" Eli laid his fork across his plate.

"*Ya*. But my folks aren't alive anymore. I don't really have family there, but I have Ivan's…" She glanced up at Eli. "…Ivan's family there. His sisters, Rebecca and Mary Ellen, live there with their families. And Ivan's brother Noah and his family live there."

"You don't have any *bruders* or sisters?"

She thought about Annie. "No."

"What made you move to Colorado?"

So many questions. She wasn't sure how much to share. "I guess you could say it was a fresh start for me and Ivan." She paused but avoided eye contact. "A fresh start that didn't work out." She finally looked up at him. "Did Vera or Elam tell you what happened?"

"Ya." For the first time since they'd been at the diner, Eli frowned. "I can't imagine an Amish man shirking his duties."

She knew she should be embarrassed, but something about the warmth in his tone coaxed her to just accept the compliment. "*Danki* for saying that."

They were quiet for a few moments, then Katie Ann said, "The woman you saw at my house, Lucy, she is the one who…" She lowered her chin, surprised at how easily she revealed the information, but caught off guard by it too.

Eli folded his arms across the black coat he was still wearing. "Does she live here in Colorado?"

"No. She traveled from Paradise, Pennsylvania, to see me."

Eli's brows lifted, and Katie Ann surprised herself even more by telling Eli about most of her conversation with Lucy, except for the part about giving Lucy money.

"I see." Eli nodded. "And she's pregnant?"

"With Ivan's child."

"I think the woman had a lot of nerve to seek you out to ask about a *haus*." Eli accepted the bill when the waitress returned, and he quickly pulled cash from his pocket and placed it on the table. "Today it is my goal to make sure that your mind is not on anything to do with Ivan or Lucy. We are going to enjoy this day…" He strained to see out a nearby window. "Snow or no snow."

Katie Ann leaned to her left to see outside too. "Look, the sun is shining."

Eli nodded. "*Ya.* It will be a *gut* day."

Eli watched Katie Ann take Jonas with her to the ladies' room for a quick diaper change before they got back on the road. He couldn't believe how easy she was to talk to, or had he just gone so long without female companionship that he'd forgotten? She seemed like a good Amish woman, too, who deserved a husband and someone to take care of her and the *boppli*. Eli knew he'd need to tread carefully, always making it known that he only had friendship to offer her. It was dangerous territory for him because he was the type to nurture, no matter how uncharacteristic it was for an Amish man. He'd spent much of his life tending to the needs of others, and even at this point in his life it came naturally to him.

He sat a little taller, resolved that he had his life planned out and there was certainly no room for romance with a new mother, no matter how beautiful she was.

When Katie Ann returned, they glanced out the window and saw Wayne waiting in the car outside. The hour-long ride seemed to fly by as the three of them talked. Wayne shared the history of the Great Sand Dunes, and Eli was glad to see Katie Ann involved in the conversation, laughing and appearing to have a good time. He might not be able to take care of her the way she needed, but it gave him satisfaction to bring some joy into her life.

Before they reached the National Park and Preserve, they could see the majestic dunes nestled against the rugged Sangre de Cristo Mountains, and as Eli peeked over his shoulder, he saw the twinkle in Katie Ann's eyes as she peered through the window.

Wayne pulled into the entrance of the park. "Amazing, isn't it? These dunes are a landmark for travelers. Did you know they are the tallest dunes in North America? They cover nearly twenty thousand acres." He chuckled. "Just a little history for you."

Eli glanced at the massive dunes for as far as he could see, but his eyes kept veering back to Katie

Ann. As her smile widened, her eyes glistened like the tiny specks of snow-covered sand that stretched before them, and Eli smiled along with her. She seemed so different from the first couple of times he was around her. She seemed happy, and her fulfillment sparked something inside of Eli that he hadn't felt in a long time.

He forced himself to look away from her and focus on the beauty of the mountains.

Then she leaned forward and touched his shoulder. "Look, Eli!" She pointed to her left, but Eli's eyes were on her hand on his shoulder. "There are two elk."

Eli glanced to where she was pointing. "*Big* elk," he said as his eyes drifted back to her hand. Her touch sent a thrill up his spine, and he was again reminded how long it had been since he'd been in the company of a beautiful woman. As his eyes trailed up to her lips, Eli pictured his mouth pressed tightly against hers, a vision that he suspected he would replay in his mind long after this day ended.

After about thirty minutes, they got back on the road. Wayne explained more about the dunes. "You folks really should see them when the weather is better and they aren't covered in snow. Each time you climb over one of the dunes, there is another one waiting on the other side. They go on forever."

"They're beautiful, even covered in snow," Katie

Ann said, keeping her eyes on the mountains as they pulled out of the park.

She was chatty all the way back to her house, talking about the garden she planned to have in the spring, the black bear she'd seen a couple of weeks ago out her window, and the repairs she needed to do on her house, most importantly a leak in her roof that Samuel had tried to repair twice without success. She mentioned several times how fortunate she was to have her brother-in-law and his wife living next door.

It was almost three o'clock when they pulled into her driveway, and little Jonas was beginning to fuss. Couldn't blame the poor fellow. He'd been cooped up for hours in the car, but he'd fared well, not even a whimper until now.

Eli opened the door, unhooked the car seat, and lifted Jonas out. He met Katie Ann on her front porch and waited for her to open her front door. Once she was inside, he handed the carrier to her, wanting more than anything to step inside. He waited, but she merely thanked him for a wonderful time.

"Why don't I have a look at that leak in your roof? I'm a pretty good carpenter."

Katie Ann peered over Eli's shoulder. "Wayne is waiting for you. Besides, I can't let you do that. I'm sure Samuel will have another look at it."

"Do you have any tools?"

She nodded. "*Ya*, a few, but…"

"If I send Wayne home, I can walk to Vera and Elam's *haus* from here." He pushed back the rim of his hat. "And I'm willing to have a look at your roof in exchange for a hot cup of *kaffi*."

She tapped her finger to her chin, grinning. "Hmm…I do need to get it repaired before the next storm." She nodded. "All right."

Eli shuffled down the porch steps to the car. He quickly paid Wayne, thanked the man, then started back to the house. He stopped and looked up at the roof, causing a burst of adrenaline to shoot through him. In truth, he preferred to keep his feet on solid ground.

Katie Ann had left the door cracked, so he walked in. She wasn't anywhere in sight, so he busied himself by starting a fire. She walked in a few minutes later.

"Jonas went back to sleep. Hasn't he been a *gut boppli* today?" She folded her hands in front of her, eyes glowing.

"*Ya*. He's like Maureen." He added another log to the fireplace. "Maureen was happiest when I had to hire a driver to take us somewhere."

As he built the fire and finally got it lit, he thought about Katie Ann having to do this by herself every day. "Why don't you invest in some solar panels for heat?"

"I've thought about it." She shrugged. "I guess I just haven't gotten around to it."

Eli blew underneath the logs until a small flame caught onto the wood. "What about in Jonas's room? Is he warm enough in there?"

"I have a small battery-operated heater that I keep in there, plus once the fire is going, it heats this small *haus* nicely."

After Eli got the fire going strong, he shed his coat and hat, and Katie Ann quickly took them from him and hung them on the rack by the door. He glanced at the clock and realized he'd better have a look at her leak and see if he could get it repaired before dark, or he'd be walking to his cousins' house in freezing temperatures.

"Where's your leak?"

Katie Ann motioned for him to follow, talking as she walked. "You really don't need to bother with this. I should have declined the offer…"

Eli pretended to be listening by giving her an occasional nod, but his eyes roamed around her bedroom. A queen-sized oak bed topped with a yellow and blue quilt took up most of the space in the small room, and there was a fragrance in the air teasing his senses, lavender perhaps. On the nightstand, several books were piled next to a lantern, along with a pair of gold-rimmed reading glasses and a box of tissues. It felt intimate, being in her bedroom.

He crossed the room to where she was standing, her arm stretched and pointing to the ceiling. Maybe it was the dim natural light coming through the window, the floral scent wafting through the room, or the way her mouth moved when she spoke, but Eli closed the space between them until he was standing a few inches from her. He touched her cheek with the back of his fingers, fully expecting her to step back. But she didn't. And as their eyes locked and held, Eli knew what was coming, and he was helpless to stop himself.

Chapter Seven

Katie Ann was paralyzed by the feel of Eli's touch, and any rational thoughts she had about how inappropriate this was left her when he leaned in and kissed her. As he cupped her cheek, his mouth lingered on hers with more intimacy than she could recall ever having with Ivan, but even as her body reacted to his touch, it was still Ivan's face that flashed before her, and she reminded herself that this man was not her husband. She eased away.

"I know I'm supposed to say I'm sorry, Katie Ann." Eli put his hands on his hips and stared at the floor for a moment, then looked back up at her. "But I'm not."

"I think you'd best leave." Katie Ann walked out of her bedroom, and Eli followed. She pulled his coat and hat from the rack and handed them to him. "*Danki* for a lovely time sightseeing, but I think I'll have Samuel look at the leak on another day."

Eli didn't take the items. "No, Katie Ann. Don't do this. I like you, and I want us to be friends, so let's talk about what just happened."

She could feel her cheeks reddening, embarrassed about her own desires and wondering if he noticed how she trembled when his lips were pressed against hers. "I don't want to talk about it." She pushed the coat and hat forward until they hit his chest and he was forced to take them.

He locked eyes with her. "I guess I *am* sorry. If this is going to keep us from being friends, then I regret my actions."

Katie Ann put a hand to her forehead, not wanting to look at him, but not wanting him to leave either. He gently cupped her chin and raised her face.

"I'm sorry. I really would like to fix your leaky roof." He smiled. "But maybe you'd better stay in the living room."

The way he said it caused Katie Ann to smile.

"Okay, *gut*. A smile. All is not lost." He hung his hat and coat back on the rack, then pointed a finger at her. "Now you stay here. Don't even think about coming into the kissing room…" He let out an exaggerated gasp. "I mean bedroom."

He gave his head a quick shake as he walked across the living room and toward her bedroom, and she put a hand over her mouth to stifle a grin. He wasn't just handsome, caring, and nurturing…

he was funny too. Strangely enough, she began to feel a bit more at ease.

"I'll make us some *kaffi*," she said as she walked toward the kitchen. She filled the percolator, the kiss playing over and over in her mind. But with each recollection, the image seemed to transform itself from Eli to Ivan, then back again. She should never have let it happen.

Eli walked into the kitchen. "I can see where Samuel repaired the area, but I'm going to need to get up on the roof to figure out why it's still leaking. When is a *gut* time for me to come back tomorrow?"

"I appreciate the offer, and if it had been something simple to repair today, I would have been grateful, but I can't let you come back and start on a project like this." She raised an eyebrow. "You have sightseeing to do, remember?"

Eli waved a hand. "Plenty of time for that. What if a storm comes?"

"I'll put a bucket under the leak, as I have done in the past."

Eli pointed to the living room. "*Kaffi* by the fire?"

Katie Ann noticed him shivering. He must be finding the Colorado weather awfully cold. "All right."

She followed him to the living room, thinking how inappropriate this would be if they were not grown adults. Then she found humor in that thought. As a teenager, she never would have kissed a boy in her bedroom, and yet as an adult, she'd let it happen. She sat in the rocking chair, and Eli sat on the couch across from her.

"So how long will you be staying in Colorado?" she asked.

"Until next Tuesday. Another week. I want to be home for Thanksgiving." He stroked his beard for a moment. "Who will you spend Thanksgiving with?"

"Lillian and Samuel are having Thanksgiving, and Vera, Elam, and all their children will be there, and of course the newlyweds, David and Emily. And Martha." She took a sip of coffee. "I'll be making sweet potatoes and bringing the butter bread."

"Sweet potatoes are my favorite food at Thanksgiving."

"Really? So will one of your daughters prepare them?"

"Hannah. My oldest *dochder*. She's made them every year for as long as I can remember." Eli paused, took a deep breath. "And I hope that Hannah will be making our family sweet potatoes for many, many more years to come."

Something about the way he made the comment left Katie Ann unsure what to say, so she waited.

"Hannah had breast cancer last year." Then he

smiled. "But *mei* girl is a fighter, and she beat it. She's doing very *gut* now."

Eli's love for his children shone in everything he said.

"I will pray for Hannah," Katie Ann said. "I'll include her in my daily devotions and pray for continued *gut* health."

Thinking about illness made her think about Martha, and she wondered if her friend would be coming over this evening. Katie Ann hoped so. She didn't believe Martha had been entirely truthful with her about her doctor appointment.

"*Danki*, Katie Ann." Eli stood up, and so did Katie Ann. "I haven't had a lot of time over the years to have any really close friends. I mean, I've always had *mei kinner*, but now that I have some time, I'd like to have some adult relationships." He stepped closer to her but kept a safe distance. "Please don't let one kiss keep us from being friends. I haven't kissed another woman since my wife. I don't know what got into me…" He lowered his gaze and took a deep breath.

Katie Ann was equally as concerned about what had gotten into her. She'd not only allowed it—she'd kissed him back. She started toward the door, and Eli followed. "I think you're going to regret taking on this project. Samuel tried twice, and it still leaks."

Eli stroked his beard. "You're probably right."

Katie Ann's eyes rounded. She hadn't expected him to agree so easily.

"You should probably cook me supper, no?"

She crossed her arms across her chest. "Hmm…I might be able to do that." She grinned. "Martha might be here. She's here most nights."

"*Gut*. A chaperone." He winked, then headed out the door.

Katie Ann watched him walk into a light flurry of snow, glad it wasn't a far walk to Vera and Elam's house. She closed the door, leaned her back against it, and couldn't help but smile. She was mourning her husband, and Eli had big plans for the second half of his life. But her new friend was a big distraction from everything else on her plate. And she was looking forward to cooking for him tomorrow night.

Eli fought the chill in the air on the way back to his cousins' house. He stuffed his hands in the pockets of his long black coat and gazed to the east at the Sangre de Cristo Mountains, then to the west at the San Juan Mountains. He knew from his research about the area that Sangre de Cristo meant "blood of Christ," and as the sun eased below the horizon, he could see how the mountain range got its name, as an orange glow could be seen on the opposite horizon. The phenomenon was known as an alpenglow, he had read, and it was an amazing sight.

He replayed the kiss with Katie Ann over in his mind, leaving him feeling both elated and like a heel. A woman like Katie Ann needed a husband and father for Jonas, and Eli knew he was not that man. Kissing her was wrong on several levels, and he would make sure it never happened again. But there was no mistaking the fact that she had kissed him back…and that thought was going to keep him up at night.

"Whoso findeth a wife findeth a good thing, and obtaineth favour of the Lord."

The scripture had come into Eli's mind many times over the past seventeen years, and he often wondered if he was failing God by not remarrying. But it seemed like betrayal—to Sarah. Perhaps it was God he was betraying.

Once again he questioned the path he'd chosen for himself—one filled with travel and less responsibility.

As he rounded the corner to Elam's house, he knew he was going to face a lot of questions from his cousins about his outing. He could see Vera sweeping snow from the front porch as he grew closer.

"How was your day, Eli?" She sent him an all-knowing grin as she pushed the fluffy powder from the porch with her broom.

"It was a *gut* day. The sand dunes were a sight to see." He walked up the freshly swept steps.

Vera stopped sweeping and put her hand on her hip. "And Katie Ann? Did you enjoy her company?"

Eli thought about the kiss. "*Ya*. Very much."

Vera's face lit with a smile. "Wonderful!"

He could see where this was going, and as much as he'd like to please his cousins, it probably wasn't right not to be honest with them. "I suspect Katie Ann and I will be *gut* friends." He eased closer to his cousin's wife, lowered his gaze, and spoke firmly. "But nothing more."

Vera scowled. "You never know, Eli."

"*Ya*. I do know, Vera. Katie Ann is lovely, but she is a new *mudder*, and I've already done all that. I'm not going back there." He waited for her to absorb what he was saying. "It might sound selfish, but I have a plan for the rest of my life, things I want to see and do. So I don't want you to be thinking there will be a romance with me and Katie Ann."

Guilt pinched at Eli's heart as he wondered again if he was failing God.

Vera smiled. "Well, you just go ahead and make all the plans you want to. Sometimes God has His own plans in the works." Then she winked at him and moved into the house.

Eli shook his head. Katie Ann deserved someone

committed to the idea of marriage, not a man committed to his own pursuits. Then he thought about fixing Katie Ann's leak tomorrow afternoon and having supper with her afterward. There was absolutely no reason why he and Katie Ann couldn't be friends.

Martha parked her car in front of Katie Ann's house, then clopped across the snow, scowling. She was going to have to tell her friend about her surgery that was now scheduled for the week after Thanksgiving—in case she didn't survive. She tucked the envelope closer to her chest as she moved up the steps.

"I was hoping I'd see you tonight." Katie Ann was holding Jonas when she opened the door. Martha fought tears as she thought about not being able to see that little bundle grow into a man.

"I don't like to miss a meal. What are we having?" Martha dropped her coat on the rack, glad to see there was a good fire going.

"Meat loaf."

Martha sighed. It wasn't her favorite, but it was food. "I'm not contagious, so let me have my precious baby."

Katie Ann handed Jonas to her. "I made you some creamed celery. I'll just go finish up in the kitchen."

Creamed celery. Thank goodness. *The meal has*

been saved. She sat on the couch with Jonas and leaned down and kissed him on the cheek. "I love you so much, my little man." She dabbed at one eye, determined not to cry in front of Katie Ann. Her friend was going to take the news hard. "You always take care of your mama, you hear?"

Martha leaned against the back of the couch and pulled Jonas up on her chest. She loved the way the baby smelled, a combination of powder and Katie Ann's homemade lavender soap. She held him close until Katie Ann walked back into the room.

"Supper's ready."

Martha did her best to eat Katie Ann's meal, but her stomach was a mess. She'd wait until a bit later to talk to her friend. "How was your day with Eli?"

"It was nice. We saw the sand dunes, and they were amazing."

Katie Ann's smile told Martha how much she liked this Eli Detweiler. Martha grinned as she swallowed a spoonful of creamed celery.

"Don't give me that look."

"What look?"

"The one on your face. There will be no romance between me and Eli."

"You are the one who is always telling me that God has His own plan, so don't go planning your future just yet." She pointed her fork at Katie Ann. "Now you tell me the truth, Katie Ann… Did you give Lucy Turner money?"

Katie Ann pulled her eyes from Martha's and sighed. "It is none of your concern."

Martha wanted to tell her that it was her business. She'd given Vera a box of money last year and told the woman to find someone who could use it. That was before Martha knew Katie Ann very well. Martha was glad that the money ultimately ended up with Katie Ann, but she sure didn't want that trampy Lucy to have any of it.

"I knew you'd give her money," Martha said before taking another bite of celery. "How much?"

"It doesn't matter. Just enough for her to get by."

Martha shook her head, then listened as Katie Ann told her a bizarre story about a house that Lucy thought Ivan bought. On another day Martha would have voiced her opinion about all of this much louder, but today her thoughts were on something else. She waited until they were having coffee in the living room.

"What's wrong, Martha?" Katie Ann held Jonas on her lap, rubbing his tummy the way Eli had shown her. Martha knew that she'd be praying every day she had left that Eli would step up to the plate and take care of Katie Ann and Jonas.

"I'm sick."

Katie Ann looked up at her with fearful eyes. "What did the doctor say?"

"My cold was just a cold, but when they x-rayed my lungs, they found something else. I've got a tumor the size of a grapefruit in my belly." She rolled her eyes. "And all this time, I just thought I was fat."

Katie Ann put Jonas in his carrier, then edged closer to Martha with tears in her eyes.

Martha latched onto Katie Ann's hand. "Now don't you go falling apart." Martha swiped at a tear that rolled down her own cheek. "Argh! I was determined not to cry."

"Tell me what the doctor said." Katie Ann pinched her trembling lips together.

"Well, apparently, the thing has to come out. I'm a goner for sure if I don't have the operation. So that dumb doctor over in Alamosa referred me to a surgeon. That's who I met with yesterday, and I'm having the surgery the week after Thanksgiving." Now here was the hard part. "I likely won't survive."

Katie Ann pulled her hand from Martha's and slapped it over her mouth.

"It doesn't look good." Martha shook her head. "And I'm so sorry to have to tell you this." She reached for the envelope. "Here's everything you'll need to know about my business. I've left everything to you."

"I don't need that envelope," Katie Ann said as she blinked back tears. "Because you are going to be just fine."

Martha shrugged. "Maybe. But I doubt it." She

dropped the large manila envelope in Katie Ann's lap. "So you just keep this." She patted Katie Ann on the leg. "Now, now…no tears. You and Arnold introduced me to the Lord, and I'm in pretty good standing with Him, so I know where I'm going."

"Don't talk like that." Katie Ann sniffled. "Have you told Arnold?"

Martha pointed a finger at her friend. "No, I haven't. And don't you tell him either. He'd feel obligated to come, and I don't want that. If the man loved me enough, he would have already moved here to be with me."

Katie Ann blew her nose, which was as red as Martha's fingernail polish. "That's not true. Arnold just said he wanted to get to know his relatives again. He's invited you there several times and asked if he could come here. You always say no."

"Because saying good-bye is just too hard." She raised her chin. "I don't want to talk about Arnold." She cut her eyes at Katie Ann. "But you'd better not tell him about my diagnosis or I will be very upset with you."

"I think he needs to know."

"Katie Ann, do you hear me?" Martha raised her voice.

"Ya."

They were quiet for a few moments. Then Katie Ann reached for Martha's hand and squeezed. "I will be there with you for everything."

Martha returned the squeeze. "I wouldn't have it any other way."

They were quiet again, and Katie Ann fought tears. She knew she needed to be strong for Martha. In the past, Martha had been a hypochondriac, but Katie Ann always knew that her friend just sought attention and love. But this was different. If she was having surgery, her condition was serious, and the thought of anything happening to Martha terrified her.

"Eli is coming to fix my roof tomorrow night," she finally said.

Martha smiled as she leaned over and pulled Jonas from his carrier. "Is he now?"

"Don't presume anything, but I am making supper for him for his efforts."

Martha rocked Jonas as she spoke. "Well, I'm not coming for supper tomorrow night, so the two of you can have some time alone together."

Images of the kiss flashed through Katie Ann's mind. "No, Martha. You *must* come."

"No."

"But…I need you here. You're here most nights for supper, and especially tomorrow night—"

"No. I'm not coming. I'm sick, Katie Ann. I can't come over here every single night."

Katie Ann frowned. "Are you sure you're not just saying that so that I'll be forced to be alone with Eli?"

Martha handed Jonas to Katie Ann and shook her head. "It's not all about you right now, Katie Ann. It's about me. I'm sick."

"Of course, I know that." Katie Ann elbowed her gently. "But how do you know you'll feel bad tomorrow night?"

"Because I feel bad now." Martha let out a heavy sigh. "Meat loaf is not my favorite. Gives me gas." She turned to Katie Ann. "You know that, and I don't know why you still make it."

Katie Ann cradled Jonas as she followed Martha to the door. She waited until she pulled her coat on to give her a sideways hug so she didn't squash Jonas. "I love you, Martha. And I know everything is going to be fine."

"I love you too. I guess all we can do is pray."

Katie Ann watched Martha leave, knowing that praying wasn't all she would do. First thing in the morning, there was something else she was going to do. Whether Martha liked it or not.

Chapter Eight

Katie Ann visited Lillian Wednesday morning and told her the news about Martha.

"Can you watch Jonas for a few minutes while I go to the barn and make a phone call?" she asked. She felt inside her apron pocket to make sure she'd brought the number.

"Of course. And you're doing the right thing."

"I'll be right back." She buttoned her long black coat and stepped outside, expecting a burst of cool air, but just in the hour since she'd been at Lillian's, the sun had peeked over the mountains and tricked their part of the world into thinking it was warmer than it really was.

She traipsed across the snow to the barn, knowing Martha would be furious with her.

"Hello, Dash," she said quietly, pleased to see the cat curled atop the quilt. He opened his green eyes and squinted in her direction. She moved slowly, picking up the empty container she'd left on her prior visit. "You must like scrapple after all, no?" She stood up, surprised Dash hadn't held to his name and sprinted around the corner. She squatted down and eased a bit closer. The cat's ears went back, and his tail took the shape of a bottle brush. "It's all right, boy."

She leaned closer, earning a small hiss from her new friend, and noticed Dash's protruding belly. "Oh my. I guess I will have to call you *Mrs*. Dash." Katie Ann reached out her hand. "When are you due, little mama?"

Mrs. Dash made her escape faster than in the past, disappearing around the corner. Katie Ann suddenly wondered if there was a Mr. Dash anywhere.

It's hard to raise kinner *on your own, girl.*

She made her way to the phone on Samuel's workbench and dialed Arnold's number. He answered on the second ring.

"Hello, Arnold. This is Katie Ann Stoltzfus calling."

"Is Martha all right?" he asked at once.

Katie Ann could hear the concern in his voice. "*Ya*, she's fine, Arnold." She paused. "But…she's… well, she's going to be having some surgery soon, and I thought you would want to know."

"I'll come right now. Thank you, Katie Ann."

"Wait…I mean, maybe you should wait until the week after Thanksgiving."

Katie Ann smiled at Arnold's reaction. She'd prayed hard about whether or not to tell him, despite Martha's wishes, but she felt called to let him know. She knew he still loved Martha.

"She's having the surgery the week after Thanksgiving. I can call you when I know the details."

"What's wrong with my Martha, Katie Ann? How serious is it?"

Katie Ann took a deep breath and blinked back tears. "I think it's serious. She has a tumor in her stomach that has to be removed."

"Oh no. Oh no."

Katie Ann could hear the elderly man's voice breaking up.

"But let's don't worry too much just yet. You know Martha. She's as tough as they come, and I'm sure everything will be fine."

"Please call me the minute the surgery is scheduled. Are you sure I shouldn't come now to be with her?"

"No." Katie Ann brought a hand to her chest. "Actually, Martha doesn't even know I'm calling you. She would be very angry with me. I don't think she wants to worry you."

"I've begged her to let me come visit her, or for

her to come here. Surely that woman knows how much I love her."

Katie Ann wasn't sure if it was her place to comment, but she'd been as curious as Martha about why Arnold hadn't moved back here. "I think, Arnold, that since you made a decision to stay in Georgia...well..."

"I had to stay. At least for a while. It's a long story. But I will be there as soon as you tell me to be."

Katie Ann smiled. "I know you will. Have a wonderful Thanksgiving next week, Arnold. And I will call you back as soon as I have the details."

After she hung up the phone, she peeked around the corner. No Mrs. Dash. She reached into her pocket and left some scraps of bacon in the container, then went back to Lillian's. She'd never wanted to tell anyone anything as badly as she wanted to tell Lillian about Eli's kiss, but she knew she couldn't. It was inappropriate, and she was much too embarrassed. But she did tell her that Eli was coming to repair her roof and that she was making supper for him.

Lillian stomped a foot before she went to the sink to wash her hands. "I told Samuel that he needed to go back and fix that roof correctly!" She joined Katie Ann at the kitchen table and grinned. "But I guess it's a *gut* thing he never got around to it."

"No matchmaking, Lillian."

Lillian pouted. "Why not? He's perfect for you."

"No. He's not. And I'm even less perfect for him. Eli has big plans to travel and do all the things he couldn't do while he was raising six *kinner* on his own." She picked up Jonas's carrier. "I'm heading home. I have much cleaning to do. *Danki* for watching Jonas."

"I love watching the *boppli*." Lillian snapped her finger. "*Ach*, I've been meaning to ask you—have you seen a big black cat in the barn lately? That thing scared the daylights out of me the other day when I went to collect eggs."

"You mean Mrs. Dash." Katie Ann grinned.

"Mrs. Dash?" Lillian frowned. "You've named that poor animal after a spice?"

Katie Ann shifted Jonas's carrier from one hand to the other. "A spice? What do you mean?"

Lillian walked to the kitchen cabinet, pulled out a yellow container, and pointed to the name. "Mrs. Dash is a combination of different spices."

Laughing, Katie Ann said, "Why do you buy those store-bought spices when you can get fresh herbs at the market in Alamosa?"

"This is easier."

"No matter. Next year I think we should have our own herb garden."

Ignoring the comment, Lillian cocked her head to one side. "That cat is solid black. Bad luck." She crinkled her nose as she shook her head. "Don't let it run across your path." She pointed to Jonas. "And don't let it near Jonas. I already told the girls not to go near it. It hisses and balls itself up like a porcupine! And he—or *she*—is big!"

Katie Ann knew most of her people were superstitious, a part of their upbringing that had clearly rubbed off on Lillian. "That's rubbish," she said. "Mrs. Dash isn't bad luck. And she's big because she's pregnant."

"Oh." Lillian twisted her mouth from one side to the other. "Hmm…maybe that's why she's so skittish."

"Maybe." Katie Ann walked toward the door as Lillian followed.

"What did Arnold say? How did he take the news about Martha?"

Katie Ann smiled. "He was ready to leave right this very minute to come and be with her. I told him to wait until the week of the surgery, after Thanksgiving." She cringed. "Martha is going to be so mad at me."

Lillian put her hand on Katie Ann's shoulder. "Martha gets mad about a lot of things, but you were right to call Arnold. I'm glad he's coming."

It was two o'clock in the afternoon when Eli loaded up his cousin's buggy with tools and headed to Katie Ann's. When he pulled up the driveway, she was carrying firewood from the barn to the house.

Eli hurried from the buggy and tethered the horse. "Wait! Let me help you with that." He ran toward her and pulled three small logs from her arms. "You should have waited for me to get here."

"Eli Detweiler, I am perfectly capable of carrying a few logs." She turned his way and smiled. "But *danki*."

Once inside, Eli placed the logs in the carrier by the fireplace. Katie Ann already had a small fire going. "It smells *gut* in here," he said.

"I'm slow-cooking a stew."

"Well, I'd better get to work then. Elam sent along just about every tool he had, along with some extra shingles he had left over from when they re-roofed their house last year, so I'm sure I can get your leak fixed. I just need a ladder."

"In the barn. Do you need anything else?"

He took a deep breath and lied. "No, I'm all set."

What he needed was a quick cure for fear of heights. Thankfully, his oldest son didn't suffer from the same affliction, and from the time Jake was ten years old, Eli had given him all the chores that required climbing, especially on the roof. Jake loved being the one to clean the gutters. It practically made Eli break out in hives.

But here he was. And up the ladder he would go. For Katie Ann.

"See you shortly."

Eli propped the ladder against the house and thanked the Lord that it was only a one-story home. He eased up the steps and prayed that he could make any repairs from the ladder, without actually crawling onto the roof. Two rungs from the top, and he could already feel his legs shaking. He scanned the area and saw the loose shingles. Shaking his head, he took one more step up and realized that he was going to have to climb up on top of the roof to be able to get to the problem area. Most of the snow had melted from the afternoon sun. He slung Elam's box full of tools onto the roof, along with a few shingles he had tucked under his arm.

As luck would have it, the shingles slid right off the roof. He started his descent back down the ladder, sighing. *This had better be the best stew I ever had.*

Katie Ann took a bite of stew, closed her eyes, and savored the taste of the seasoned beef, carrots, and potatoes. "I wish you were old enough to try this, Jonas." She took another sampling before putting the lid back on the pot.

She pulled a loaf of bread from the oven and began to set the table with chow-chow, butter, and several jars of jam. She couldn't stop thinking about Martha and wished her friend would join them for supper.

Sunshine poured through her window in the kitchen and bounced off her shiny wood floors that she'd cleaned earlier in the day. She could still smell a hint of ammonia, but mostly she smelled stew and burning cedar in the fireplace. Everything was ready, so she picked up Jonas and laid him in the playpen in the living room so she could keep an eye on him while she and Eli ate. She expected him to fall asleep soon since she'd just nursed him.

She could see the ladder propped up against the house from her window in the living room, and while she'd been cooking, she'd heard activity on the roof. As she walked closer to the window, she looked up and saw Eli working, so she went back to the kitchen. She'd just set the table with her best china and laid out napkins when she heard a thud. Followed by a groan. Gasping, she feared the worst as she ran through the living room and bolted out the door.

Sure enough, Eli was sprawled out on his back in the snow, and he wasn't moving. Katie Ann got to him as fast as she could and leaned down over him as her heart beat out of her chest. He crinkled his forehead and slowly opened his eyes.

"*Ach*, thank goodness you're not dead." Katie Ann cringed as she realized what she'd said.

"*Ya*. Thank goodness." Eli laughed but quickly moaned, closing his eyes again.

"Should I go call for help?" She touched his

shoulder but pulled back when he clamped his eyes closed and groaned again. "How badly are you hurt?"

"I don't know yet. I'm afraid to move. I guess I lost my footing."

"I'm going to go get Samuel." Katie Ann started to stand up, but Eli opened his eyes and grabbed her arm. He eased her back down.

"Please don't. I'm embarrassed enough." He slowly sat up, and Katie Ann was horrified to see blood in the snow where his head had been.

"You're hurt." She reached up and gently twisted his head so she could try to inspect his wound. "I think we'd better get you to a hospital."

"Really? Because I'd rather not." He bent his legs, propped one arm against the ground, and tried to stand up, but lost his balance.

Katie Ann put an arm around him. "Here, let me help you."

"I should fall off the roof more often." Eli leaned into her and smiled.

"You will not be getting back on my roof."

"Don't need to. It's fixed." He glanced upward. "Although Elam's toolbox is still up there."

"We'll get it later. Let's get you into the *haus* so I can have a look at your head."

Katie Ann knew that she shouldn't be thinking about the way Eli's arm was draped around her shoulder, or the way that her arm was around his waist. She got him situated on the couch, checked on Jonas in his playpen, and hurried to the kitchen for a wet rag. When she got back, Eli was standing in the middle of the room.

"I was dripping blood on your couch." He lost his footing, and Katie Ann was afraid he was going to fall over.

"I don't care about that. Sit down." She helped him back to the couch and began dabbing at the back of his head. "You must have hit a small rock or something. There's a jagged little cut, and I really think you need some stitches."

"Can't you just put a butterfly bandage on it?"

Katie Ann smiled at his sad, puppy-dog eyes. "Eli Detweiler, are you afraid of a few stitches?"

"No. I'm *hungry*." He drew in a long deep breath. "I've been dreaming about that stew the whole time I was working."

"Well, all right. I'll be right back with my first aid kit, and I'll bandage you up as best I can."

"Maybe some aspirin too?"

Katie Ann nodded as she headed down the hall to the bathroom. She quickly found some bandages, antibiotic ointment, and aspirin in the medicine cabinet. After getting a glass of water, she gave him the aspirin and got to work doctoring his head. It seemed much too intimate to be running her hands in his hair to clear the area for the bandage.

"I still think you need to have a doctor look at it." Katie Ann stood up.

"*Danki*, Nurse Katie Ann. But I feel *gut* as new." He rose from the couch. Slowly. He grabbed his back as he straightened. "Okay, maybe not exactly *gut* as new." He grinned. "But still hungry."

"Come, come." She motioned with her hand for him to follow her to the kitchen.

After they both prayed silently, they ate with little conversation. Eli helped himself to some butter bread and finished three bowls of stew, commenting several times about how much he liked it. Katie Ann was pleased that he enjoyed her cooking. Ivan had rarely said anything about her meals, especially the last few years. It was nice to have a man enjoying her efforts.

Katie Ann brought coffee into the living room while Eli stoked the fire. As darkness set in, she lit the two lanterns in her living room and one by the front door. Jonas started to fuss in his playpen, but before she could go to him, Eli had picked up the baby and settled back on the couch with Jonas in his lap. Katie Ann sat down beside him.

Eli looked up at her. "How's his tummy been?"

"Much better. If he doesn't have a hearty burp after his feeding, I rub his tummy, and that seems to solve the problem. He's sleeping much better during the night." She smiled. "And so am I."

Eli let out a quiet moan.

"I bet *you* won't sleep well tonight, though. I'm so sorry that happened, Eli."

"Me too." He chuckled. "I'm feeling a little stiff. But…all worth it to have that stew. Katie Ann, that was mighty *gut*. Some of the best I've had."

Katie Ann tucked her chin, feeling her face heat up. "*Danki.* I was happy to cook it for you." She looked back up to see him gazing into her eyes, and a faint alarm went off, but she knew she wasn't going to ask him to leave. As much as she loved Martha's company in the evenings, it was nice to have a man in her home, sharing a meal and conversation.

For the next four hours Katie Ann sat on one end of the couch, facing Eli who was at the other end. Jonas was in between them, sleeping soundly on a blanket. As the fire crackled and lit the room, Katie Ann watched the shadows dance across Eli's face as he talked about his childhood, his teenage years, and how he met Sarah.

"I was with her when she took her last breath, and the last thing she said to me before she died was that I should find a new *mudder* for the *kinner* right away." Eli blinked several times and avoided Katie Ann's eyes. "I failed her." After a few moments, he looked back up at her. "I know it's our way to remarry as soon as a spouse passes, but I just couldn't. Sarah was my everything, and replacing her just seemed so…so wrong." He leaned back against the couch. "I didn't even really try. I mean, everyone in the community was trying to fix me up with someone, but I just wasn't interested. And not only that, I didn't have time for dating. I had six *kinner*."

"It must have been so hard for you." Katie Ann couldn't remember having such a deep conversation with Ivan. Ever. This was nice.

"Looking back, I should have tried harder. I'm sure Sarah was right. It would have been better for the *kinner* to have had a *mudder*, and it was selfish of me not to have tried harder to find them one." He took a sip of his coffee. "There were babysitters and family members who helped, but I was young, and I thought I could do everything myself. Prove to Sarah that I didn't need anyone else." He put his coffee on the coffee table, then reached over and touched her hand. "I'm sorry. I've mostly been talking about me. Tell me about you."

Katie Ann told Eli about her childhood...and even told him about Annie. "*Mei* sister was only four months old when she just went to sleep and didn't wake up."

Eli's eyes never left hers as she spoke, and even though he didn't seem to have any words for her loss, his eyes blinked with sadness and compassion. She also told him how she and Ivan tried for years to have a baby, but she skimmed quickly over the part about Lucy and how Ivan eventually left her.

"That must have been so hard for you."

She wasn't sure if Eli meant when Ivan left or when he died. In some ways, it was as if he died the day he walked out the door.

It had been a surprisingly good evening. They'd taken turns getting coffee refills and even shared a piece of shoofly pie. But it was getting late. She glanced at the clock as she stifled a yawn.

"I saw that." Eli grinned. "I remember how it is to have a little one. You're probably already thinking about how many times you will be getting up with him during the night. I'm going to go. It's almost nine o'clock."

Katie Ann stood up, tired, but not anxious for him to leave. "I've enjoyed tonight."

"Me too."

She followed him to the door and waited as he got bundled up. "I'm sure Elam and Vera have a heavy blanket in the buggy. You'll need it." She handed him his hat. "How is your head? And your back?"

He grimaced a bit as he put his hat on. "I might be a little sore, but I'll think of you fondly." He laughed before he leaned down and hugged her. Then he kissed her on the cheek. "*Danki.* For everything."

"You're welcome. See you at church on Sunday?"

"If not sooner." He winked as he headed out the door.

Katie Ann picked up Jonas and carried him to his bedroom. As she dressed for bed, she realized that this had been the best night she'd had in years. And for the first time since she'd met Eli Detweiler, she regretted that all they would ever be is friends.

As Eli drove home, he thought about the way Katie Ann always seemed to have one eye on Jonas, especially when the baby was in Eli's arms. But hearing her story about Annie explained why she might be unusually jumpy and protective about the child. He was glad that she'd shared some intimate details about her life and wondered when he would see her again. Then he remembered that he had left Elam's toolbox up on her roof and smiled to himself.

If only he'd met Katie Ann sixteen or seventeen years ago, right after Sarah had died. But no sooner had he had the thought than he wondered if he would have felt the same way about her. His grief for Sarah probably would have kept him from seeing Katie Ann. Not only that, but Eli knew that he was not the same person he was seventeen years ago. He tried to speculate what Katie Ann must have been like as a younger woman.

Why, Lord, is she in my path now? Eli was not going to veer from the plans he'd made, but he found himself caring about Katie Ann in a way he never anticipated. But he would be leaving on

Tuesday, and once he was back in his surroundings, he'd work for a few weeks, then schedule one of the many short trips he'd planned to take. Maybe he would send her a postcard from his travels, check on her and Jonas occasionally.

Then that kiss flashed in his mind again and he shivered, only partly from the cold.

Chapter Nine

Katie Ann dressed in a new green dress for worship service, one she'd just finished hemming a few days ago. She bundled Jonas in a thick blue jumpsuit, a handmade gift from Lillian. Sometime over the past three days the toolbox had slid off the roof, and she'd repacked all Elam's tools to take to him today. It was already loaded in her buggy, and she tried to shed the disappointment she felt that she hadn't heard from Eli since he left Wednesday night. She'd thought he would at least come by to pick up the tools. Or to say hello. Something. Maybe he hadn't enjoyed their time together as much as she had.

She'd treasured her time with Martha on Thursday and Friday evening. Thursday, Katie Ann cooked what she and her friends called Lazy Wife's Dinner, a casserole with noodles, cheese, potatoes, carrots, and beef. And she prepared a side dish of

creamed celery for Martha. On Friday night Martha
brought supper—a pizza she'd picked up in Monte
Vista, and that was just fine by Katie Ann. Martha
tried to grill her about Eli, but Katie Ann wiggled
her way out of saying too much, especially since
she hadn't heard from him since he left.

On Saturday, Martha had stopped by early in
the afternoon, saying she wasn't feeling well and
that she wouldn't be at church service the following day. "Everyone will probably think I croaked,"
she'd said.

Katie Ann's stomach churned.

Once Jonas was buckled in beside her, she
clicked her tongue, setting the buggy in motion.
Church service was being held at the home of Vera
and Elam's oldest son, Jacob, and his wife, Beth
Ann. It was their first time to host worship service
since their wedding the year before.

She wondered how much more sightseeing Eli
had done over the past three days. The weather had
been unusually warm for mid-November, sunshine
and mild temperatures. She fought the feeling of
disappointment that he hadn't invited her to tag
along.

It was almost eight o'clock when she pulled into
Jacob and Beth Ann's driveway. In their small community, there were never more than about fifty
people at worship service—a small crowd compared to the hundred and fifty or so back home in

Lancaster County. With only thirty-two families in the Monte Vista area, they were split into two districts with one bishop serving both. Bishop Esh actually held worship service every Sunday, alternating between the two districts.

After she tethered her horse, she carried Jonas in his carrier toward the house. She knew she would be walking in right as the service started, and she quickly found a seat in the back next to Vera. As she got settled, she glanced across the room to where the men were sitting, but she didn't see Eli.

"I don't see Eli this morning." She tried to sound casual as she whispered in Vera's ear.

"Didn't you hear? I assumed that somehow word had gotten to you. We had to get a driver to take him to the hospital on Thursday. I was concerned because he had such a bad headache." Vera leaned closer to whisper since the bishop was entering the room. "He had to have four stitches in his head, and he has a concussion. The doctor told him to rest for a few days."

Katie Ann gasped as she brought her hand to her mouth. "I knew he should have gone to the hospital after he fell off my roof. I tried to get him to go, Vera. Really I did."

"*Ach*, I'm sure you did. It took me forever to convince him to let us call a driver to take us all. None of us can figure out why he offered to fix your roof."

Katie Ann lowered her chin. "I know. I'm so sorry. It wasn't his place, and I shouldn't have let him."

"No, dear." Vera grinned. "That's not what I meant. Eli has been terrified of heights his whole life. Elam said he couldn't believe that he asked for tools to fix your roof." Her grin broadened. "He must have really wanted to make an impression."

"Afraid of heights?" Katie Ann bit her bottom lip and shook her head. "I didn't know."

As much as she tried to focus on worship, her mind kept drifting back to Eli and what she could do to make up for his fall at her house. *Off* her house. She mentally scanned her recipe box at home, trying to think of something she could make to take to him, but she knew Vera was an excellent cook. Most likely Eli had everything he could possibly want to eat already. Then she remembered something she had at home. Something that would be perfect for Eli.

She was glad when church service ended a little early, and as she helped the other women prepare the noon meal, she found Vera and pulled her aside. "I feel terrible about Eli. Would it be all right if I come by this afternoon and bring him a small gift?"

Vera's face lit up. "That would be very nice. I think a visit from you will cheer him up."

"I don't know about that." Katie Ann felt her

cheeks brighten as she lowered her chin. "But I do feel bad." She looked back at Vera. "I'll come by later."

Eli kicked his feet up on the coffee table and looked at the clock. He estimated about another hour before everyone came home from church. Smiling, he flipped through a gardening magazine he'd found in the kitchen, and he shoved another handful of roasted pecans into his mouth.

Peace. Quiet. A magazine. And a snack.

He felt a little guilty that he hadn't gone to worship, especially when he was feeling one hundred percent better. But when Vera insisted he stay home and rest as the doctor said, well…who was he to argue? Although he did miss Katie Ann, and now that his head didn't throb as though it might fall off his shoulders, he couldn't wait to go see her. He still needed to pick up Elam's tools, so that would be his excuse. He couldn't recall having as much fun as he'd had with her Wednesday night. And it seemed like a lot more than four days since he'd seen her.

He closed the magazine when he heard the family buggy pulling up the drive.

Betsy was the first one to bolt through the door. She didn't take off her coat or bonnet before she started to talk, and Eli struggled to understand her as she tried to catch her breath.

"Katie Ann is coming to see you today! *Mamm*

is very happy about that!" She took another big breath. "But *Daed* says you will break Katie Ann's heart if you get too close to her…because you are leaving and all, and Levi said—"

"Betsy!" Vera gently grabbed her young daughter by the arm and helped her out of her coat. "Must you repeat everything you hear?" She glanced at Eli but quickly looked away.

Levi trailed in behind Vera. "I told you to be careful what you say in front of Betsy Big Ears." He grinned as he nodded at Eli and headed up the stairs.

Betsy slammed her hands to her sides as her mother struggled to untie a knot in her bonnet strings. "I don't understand why people say things if they don't want them repeated." She pulled from her mother and leaned her head toward the stairs. "I do not have big ears, Levi!"

"Be still, Betsy, so I can get this knot out." Vera finally pulled the bonnet from the child's head.

Eli had gotten used to the bedlam in his cousins' house. Most of the time. Occasionally, Betsy screamed at the top of her lungs when she was angry, and that had been a bit rough when he'd had his headache. But he'd lived through the chaos of family, and he figured himself to be somewhat immune.

He recalled what Betsy said. Katie Ann was coming to see him?

After Betsy marched upstairs, Vera sat down next to Eli. "I'm sorry about that." She tapped a finger to her cheek and took a deep breath. "How are you feeling?"

"*Gut* as new." He cringed a bit, knowing he'd need to put in some extra devotion time this evening to make up for playing hooky.

"No more headache?"

"No. I really do feel much better."

Vera frowned. "I'm sorry you had to hear all that."

"So…" He lifted one brow. "Katie Ann is coming to see me?"

"*Ya.* She feels bad that you fell off her roof." Vera grinned. "I still can't believe you were up there in the first place. Elam says you're terribly afraid of heights."

Eli chuckled. "I was hoping I was over it."

"I'm sorry you didn't get to do any more sightseeing. And you're leaving day after tomorrow. Maybe you'll come back for another visit? There's lots to see and do around here." She paused. "Maybe in the springtime, when it's warmer."

"I'd like that. Despite the fall, I've enjoyed my time here. I wouldn't have missed David and Emily's wedding, and I enjoyed seeing the sand dunes."

"And spending time with Katie Ann?" Vera bit her bottom lip. "Sorry, I couldn't help myself."

"Vera…" Eli sighed. "We talked about this. And I know you're still trying to play matchmaker."

She batted her lashes playfully. "Whatever do you mean?"

"Uh, if I didn't already know, I think Betsy just confirmed it." He chuckled. "But a reminder… Katie Ann and I are in two different places in our lives. She's just starting out with a new baby. And, Vera…I've done all that. Six times." He waited for a response, but Vera just lowered her head a bit. "But Katie Ann and I are friends, and I expect us to stay that way."

Vera stood up from the couch, put her hands on her hips, and stared down at him. "Well…as a reminder, you just never know what the Lord has planned for your future. 'For I know the thoughts that I think toward you, saith the Lord, thoughts of peace, and not of evil, to give you an expected end.'" She gave him a smug smile and headed toward the kitchen.

Eli knew exactly what the Lord had planned for his future, and it didn't include raising a new family. And he was starting to resent the butterflies that danced in his stomach at the very mention of Katie Ann's name. He sat taller, knowing he needed to keep his priorities intact. He'd be leaving in two days.

* * *

Katie Ann knocked on the Detweilers' door with Jonas cradled in one arm and a plastic bag in the other hand. She was glad she could remember where she stored the travel guide, the one she'd picked up years ago when she thought Ivan might take her to Florida or one of the other beach destinations described in the book. Her people didn't usually fly on a plane unless it was an emergency, but most of the places listed could be reached by bus. She certainly didn't have any use for the book anymore. Maybe Eli would enjoy it, possibly travel to one of the locations pictured within the covers. Perhaps even send her a postcard?

"Hello, Katie Ann." Elam stepped aside so that Katie Ann could enter, and she gave him a nod.

Eli stood up from the couch when he saw her. She walked toward him and held out the bag as Elam left the room.

"It's a gift for you because I feel so bad about what happened."

Eli smiled. "Katie Ann, you didn't have to do that. It was just an accident." He opened the bag and took a peek inside.

"I thought it might be helpful for your travels." She paused while he pulled out the guide and flipped through the pages. "Although it's mostly beach locations, so I don't know if—"

"It's wonderful. *Danki*." His eyes were fixated

on a page for a moment, then he closed the book. "Where did you get this?"

"I've had it for a long time, and I don't see where I'll be needing it anytime soon." She repositioned Jonas in her arms, smiling. "*Ach*, and I sent your tools with Elam. Vera told me at worship that you have a concussion."

Eli grimaced. "Please tell me that you didn't climb up on the roof to get them?"

"No." She chuckled. "They slid off the roof at some point."

He sighed. *"Gut."*

"Because of your fall, you didn't get to do any more sightseeing as you'd planned. I'm so sorry about that."

"I have one day left. Tomorrow." He reached out his arms. "May I?"

Katie Ann handed Jonas to Eli, and Eli sat down on the couch. He laid Jonas faceup in his lap, and once again he talked to her son in baby talk. It was endearing, and she still couldn't recall seeing another Amish man carry on that way about a baby.

"Are you up for another day of sightseeing tomorrow?" Eli raised an eyebrow. "I was thinking about taking a trip to Alamosa, since it's only about twenty minutes from here by car. That would be easy on our boy here." He gently ran the back of his hand along Jonas's cheek, and Katie Ann felt a warm glow flow through her.

"I love Alamosa. I don't get there as often as I'd like since it's quite a haul by buggy, but I keep up with the Amish folks there by reading *The Budget*." Katie Ann sat down next to Eli on the couch.

"Then it's a date."

"Gut." She smiled and pretended not to notice his choice of the word.

Eli lifted the heels of his feet up and down, bouncing Jonas slightly in his lap. She noticed he was without his shoes, and his left sock had a tiny hole near the toe.

Then Eli stood, smiled, and handed Jonas back to Katie Ann. "I'll go to the barn and call Wayne, see if he can take us tomorrow. But either way, I'll make arrangements. Eight o'clock all right?"

"Perfect." Katie Ann bundled Jonas in his blanket and tucked his wool cap tight around his ears. "Then I'll see you tomorrow."

Eli walked her to the door. "Looking forward to it."

She nodded as butterflies played in her stomach. She wished she were looking forward to it a little less.

The next morning Eli watched the sun rise above the mountains as he crossed the snow-covered yard to get in the car with Wayne.

"Glad you were free today," he said as he climbed into the front seat.

Wayne looked up through the windshield. "You've got a great day for travel. No snow predicted, and lots of sunshine…if not a bit chilly." The elderly man smiled. "Are we picking up Katie Ann and the child again?"

"*Ya*. She doesn't have an opportunity to go by car much, so…" Eli shrugged, wondering if Wayne could sense his excitement.

Wayne nodded, but he didn't say anything.

A few minutes later Eli walked up the path to Katie Ann's porch. By the time he climbed the stairs, she had opened the door and was ready and waiting, Jonas in a carrier at her side.

"*Guder mariye.*" He picked up the carrier and put a gentle hand on her arm as he carried Jonas down the steps. "Careful."

"*Guder mariye* to you too."

Eli tried to calm his racing heart as he helped her and Jonas into the backseat. He'd been like a kid the night before, barely able to sleep. Just the thought of spending the day with her sent his adrenaline pumping. And the thought of leaving them tomorrow caused him a bit of grief. But he wasn't going to think about that today. He was going to make sure she had another wonderful outing.

During the short drive to Alamosa, the three of them chatted, and Eli was surprised to learn that Katie Ann's favorite flower was an orchid. Like Maureen's. Katie Ann also shared a little about their move from Lancaster County to Colorado, and how difficult it was. In addition to the repairs that had to be done on the property and houses, she said she had missed Lancaster County for a long time, especially after her husband left to go back.

"Do you think you'll ever move back there?" Eli twisted in his seat to face her.

"I don't know. I have more friends and extended family there." She shrugged. "Sometimes I'd like to go back, but I've made a home here in Canaan, and I'd miss Lillian, Samuel, Emily, David, and of course Vera and Elam and their family." She paused with a sigh. "And then there's Martha. I don't know if I could ever leave Martha. At least not anytime soon. She's having surgery next week. She has a tumor in her stomach." Katie Ann's forehead creased as she bit her bottom lip.

"That sounds serious. I'll pray that she makes a full recovery."

"Danki."

Wayne slowed the car as they stopped at a light. "This is it. Alamosa. What would you like to do first?"

Katie Ann's face lit up as she spotted an Amish furniture store to their right, so Eli suggested they have a look.

"I've been in this store, and it's very nice, run by Amish folks."

Eli couldn't take his eyes from her, and he really

didn't care what they did today. Just being in her presence made him content. More alarms rang in his head, but he was leaving tomorrow.

Today was a day to spend with Katie Ann. And Eli planned to enjoy every minute.

Chapter Ten

Lucy sat down at her kitchen table with all of her bills in front of her. For the first time since Ivan's death, she wasn't afraid to sort through them, and she knew she would have enough money to pay them all. Thanks to Katie Ann.

She didn't recognize the envelope on the top of the pile addressed to Ivan, and she instantly wondered if it might have something to do with the mystery house. She ripped into it, but it was only an advertisement for landscaping supplies. Tossing it aside, she laid her head down on the table and wept. She wondered if the crying would ever stop. It had been months since Ivan's death, but she couldn't wrap her mind around the fact that he was never coming back. He was the only man she'd ever loved, and her life seemed pointless at the moment. She rubbed her belly, then cried even harder.

After a few minutes she forced herself to sit

up and focus on the bills, reminding herself that things could be much worse. If it hadn't been for Katie Ann's generosity, Lucy wasn't sure what she would have done. She still couldn't get over the fact that Ivan's wife had given her money—a substantial amount of money that would enable her to stay afloat until she found the house that she hoped existed. She was sure there had to be a house somewhere. Nothing pleased Ivan more than to surprise her, and that was the only explanation for why his money was gone from their account and there was a picture of a house and two keys in his cedar box.

She'd driven the countryside looking for the white house with black shutters, surrounded by a white picket fence, but she hadn't found anything.

After taking a deep breath, she pulled the mortgage bill from the envelope. A mortgage she couldn't afford on her own. She'd barely signed the check when someone knocked at the door, and she hurriedly swiped at her puffy eyes. It had been almost a week since she'd even put any makeup on.

She looked through the peephole to see a uniformed man, a cop. The last time a police officer showed up at her door, it was to tell her that Ivan was dead.

She eased the door open, no longer concerned about her puffy eyes or the tears now streaming down her cheeks. "Yes?" She sniffled, pushing back a strand of hair.

"Ma'am, are you okay?"

She put her hand across her stomach. "I don't know. I guess it depends on what you're doing here."

"Lucy Turner?"

"That's me."

"I'm sorry, but this is a court summons." He pushed an envelope toward her before he slowly turned and walked away.

She closed the door, sat back down at the table, and stared at the unopened envelope, wondering which credit card was suing her. Katie Ann's gift hadn't come in time, and she wondered how she was ever going to make it. She'd called a Realtor the day before, and even though the woman said she thought she could sell the house quickly, Lucy knew she didn't have enough equity to afford anything else—barely a small apartment to raise her child in.

She lowered her head and did something she rarely did. She prayed. But no sooner had she asked God to help her than a sharp pain seared across her abdomen, and within minutes she felt her water break. Gasping, she rushed to the phone to call her boss at the café, her only real friend. As she dialed the number, another sharp pain almost brought her to her knees.

She knew it was way too early to be in labor. She didn't know if God really existed, but if He did, this must be His punishment for her living with another woman's husband.

* * *

Katie Ann was thrilled to meet some of the Amish women in Alamosa, and as she browsed through the shop owned by an Amish widow, she felt a sense of hope. Maybe someday she could own a shop like this in Canaan, even if on a much smaller scale. She could make all kinds of handmade items—pot holders, lap quilts, soaps, dolls, and even jams and jellies. Maybe her nephew David would put a few pieces of his furniture in her store. He'd recently acquired a furniture store in town, and he was a fine craftsman.

Katie Ann loved being a mother, but she couldn't help but fantasize about providing goods for the few tourists who found their way to Canaan, and perhaps even for the local *Englisch* folks.

"How long have you lived in Alamosa?" Katie Ann picked up a business card holder with an Amish buggy etched on the front. Before the woman could answer, she asked, "Who made this? It's lovely."

"*Danki. Mei sohn* did."

Katie Ann put the card holder back on the shelf, wondering how old the woman's son was. By the time Jonas was old enough to help Katie Ann with a shop, she figured she might be too old to take on such a project. The woman excused herself to tend to another customer, and Katie Ann scanned the shop until she found Eli, who was carrying Jonas, and Wayne.

Her eyes stayed glued on Eli as she watched him tenderly shift Jonas from one shoulder to the other. But the longer she stared at him, the more she saw Ivan, and as the image of Eli returned, she reminded herself that no matter how wonderful Eli might seem, trust would not come easy for her.

And as hard as it was to trust Eli, she was having an equally hard time trusting God's plan for her life. She prayed the same amount of time that she always had, but she knew her communion with God was not the same. To hear Him, to know Him, and to understand the wonder of His love—one must trust Him completely.

"See anything you can't live without?" Wayne asked as he and Eli walked up to her. She cleared her thoughts and shook her head.

"No. But they have some finely crafted goods here." She smiled, focusing again on Eli with her precious Jonas. "Want me to take him?"

"Only if you want to. I think he's happy looking at the manlier items in the back of the store, like the workbench." He winked at Katie Ann before he looked back at the baby. "Aren't you, Jonas?"

Katie Ann couldn't help but smile at the tender tone of voice Eli used with her son. "Are you fellows ready?"

"*Ya*. Jonas is hungry." Eli grinned, and Katie Ann laughed.

"*Jonas* is hungry? Did he tell you this?" She glanced at the clock on the wall and knew it would be time to nurse him soon. And her stomach was growling more than normal for this time of morning.

Eli held his head close to Jonas. "*Ya*, I'll tell your mommy that you'd like some pancakes or maybe an early lunch. I think the *Englisch* call it brunch."

"Give me *mei boppli* before you confuse him with all your silliness." She gently eased Jonas from Eli's arms.

They were almost out of the store when Eli stopped and took a final look around. "I always wanted to own a place like this. Maybe something smaller, but still like this."

He smiled at Katie Ann, but she stood motionless. God's timing had never seemed more off.

Martha jotted down the details of her surgery as the nurse on the phone rattled them off.

"Are you sure I can't eat breakfast? Because I'm not going to be in a very good mood when I show up at your hospital at seven o'clock in the morning hungry. I have cereal and a muffin every morning at six thirty. I really don't like to miss my breakfast."

She rolled her eyes when the woman insisted

that she couldn't have breakfast that morning, nor could she eat anything the night before after midnight. Surgery was scheduled for the Wednesday after Thanksgiving, and even though her appetite had been declining, Martha didn't like to be told when she could eat.

"Fine." She forced herself to thank the woman for calling, since she was working on being nicer. If her time was coming, she wanted God's most recent memories of her behavior to be good ones.

After she hung up the phone, she got comfortable in her chair and thought about Katie Ann. She sure hoped that girl was having fun with Eli, and she wished there was some way to get that man to stay longer. She'd plotted and planned in her mind, but every time a lie for the good of all concerned came to mind, she was reminded that God was watching and her time was drawing to an end.

She arched a brow and glanced up. "I won't pull any tricks to get that man to hang around, but, Lord, I sure hope You can see Your way clear for him to stay. He needs to fall in love with Katie Ann and take care of her and that baby."

She picked up the newspaper and flipped the pages until she came to the obituaries. Using a red pen, she circled the ones that were nicely written and drew an X across the ones that didn't do justice to the deceased. She wanted to write her own obituary, to make sure it was done correctly, but that seemed a little over the top. Instead, she'd give her recommendations to Katie Ann and pray her friend could get it right.

"Lord, I'm going to miss Katie Ann and that precious baby."

She leaned her head back against the chair, resolved she wouldn't cry. If it hadn't been for Emily and David—and Arnold—she might not have found her way to God. She'd grown close to Emily and David last year when they were doing some work at her house, and those kids had such a strong faith, she couldn't help but be curious. Arnold drove it on home. The man's faith in God was amazing, and when Martha opened her heart to the Lord, nothing had been the same. She knew exactly where she was going when she left this world, but she sure was going to miss everyone here.

It was nearing dark when Wayne pulled into Katie Ann's driveway. Jonas was screaming, and had been for most of the drive back from Alamosa. They'd stopped twice during the short drive back— once for Katie Ann to change the baby's diaper, and the other time for her to rub his tummy, thinking maybe he was having stomach problems again. Nothing worked.

"I'll get the carrier. You get Jonas in the *haus*." Eli held the car door open while Katie Ann got Jonas out of his car seat, then stepped out of the car, thanking Wayne for driving. Eli settled with Wayne and followed her inside.

She paced the floor with the baby while Eli offered to get the percolator going. Jonas was soon fast asleep in Katie Ann's arms, and she worried that she shouldn't have had him out all day again. They'd hit several more shops in the area and eaten two meals while they were out. Tiptoeing, she eased down the hall to Jonas's room and laid him in his crib.

When she returned to the living room, Eli met her with a cup of coffee.

"I feel like a terrible mother. I shouldn't have had him out and about so much today."

Eli sat down on the couch, and Katie Ann sat down beside him.

"You're a *gut mudder*, Katie Ann. But I imagine the *boppli* is tuckered out."

She took a sip of her coffee. "It was probably too long a day for him."

"I hauled Maureen everywhere with me from the time she was born." Eli took a sip of his coffee. "Did you have a *gut* time today?"

"Very much." She'd brought back all kinds of knickknacks for Lillian, Vera, Emily, and Beth Ann, and of course something extra special for Martha—a quilt for a single bed, with scripture readings all over it. Katie Ann hoped Martha would take it to the hospital with her when she went to have her surgery.

She put her coffee on the table in front of them. "I need to light some lanterns before we're sitting in the dark."

Eli touched her arm. "You sit and rest. I'll light the lanterns." Then he rubbed her arm in a way that made Katie Ann want to curl up in his arms. It had been so long since she'd felt loved, she wished she could pretend, just for a while.

He knew where the lanterns were, and as she watched him light each one, she allowed herself a few moments to fantasize about what it would be like to have Eli around all the time. But before the vision could come full circle, she imagined him leaving her. They weren't even a couple, but Katie Ann could see him walking out on her.

Tomorrow he would go home, as planned. And Katie Ann was sure this was a good thing, before she got too attached.

A minute later, Eli sat back down on the couch. "Why are you looking at me like that?"

Katie Ann blinked her eyes a couple of times. "Like what?" She hoped her expression didn't reveal her thoughts, how she wanted for him to hold her in his arms, even if it wasn't love. Even if it wasn't real.

Eli gazed into her eyes, and Katie Ann felt like she might cry, for reasons that confused and embarrassed her. As a woman, she found herself desiring Eli in a way that wasn't appropriate. She'd been a married woman for many years, and as such, she knew the comfort of a man's embrace. The kiss they'd shared began to replay in her mind, and she wondered if Eli was thinking about it too.

After a few moments Eli shrugged. "I don't know. You were just looking at me like…" He shrugged again, then smiled. "Never mind."

Katie Ann felt comfortable sitting on the couch with Eli as orange sparks shimmied up the fireplace and shadows from the lanterns danced around the room. It took everything in her power not to move closer to him. If only she could lean her head on his chest, listen to his heart, and have him wrap his arms around her. That was all she needed.

She felt a wave of goose bumps run the length of her body when he grabbed her hand in his.

"Katie Ann…"

His smile was sensuous, and for a moment she wondered if his intentions would exceed her needs. She couldn't allow him to kiss her again, but every part of her wanted him to. She swallowed hard as he finished his sentence.

"Meeting you has been the best part of my trip here." He gently squeezed her hand.

She knew she was in a dangerous place, longing and desiring a man who wasn't available, but it would be hard to say good-bye to him.

"I've enjoyed our time together," she finally said. "*Danki* for taking me and Jonas on your sightseeing trips."

He eased his hand away from hers, stroked his beard, and locked his eyes with hers. Katie Ann braced herself for whatever he was about to say. She took a deep breath.

"Katie Ann…"

"Ya?"

"Are you hungry?"

She grinned, relieved, but slightly disappointed for some unknown reason. "I'm guessing you are, no?"

His smile broadened. "Maybe a sandwich?"

"I think I can do better than that. I have some leftover stew in the freezer that won't take long to heat up."

Eli rubbed his belly. "I can't believe I didn't eat it all when I was here before. Is it too much trouble?"

She stood up, a bit hungry herself. "Not at all. I'll just run it under some warm water and put it on the burner to heat."

"And I'll keep our fire going." Eli walked to the fireplace and glanced at the wood in the carrier. "Only one log left. I'll go carry in some more." He walked toward the door, and Katie Ann nodded as she moved toward the kitchen.

Twenty minutes later they were back on the couch with bowls of stew in their laps, both agreeing it was too cold to eat in the kitchen. Once they were done, the conversation turned to Katie Ann and Ivan, which wouldn't have been her first choice, but she found herself confiding in Eli in a way that surprised her.

"I'm not shocked about Ivan buying a house and not telling Lucy." She grimaced as she spoke. "Ivan was big on surprises, but also big on secrets."

Eli twisted to face her. "Katie Ann, I am so sorry for everything you've been through." He shook his head. "That's just so wrong."

She wasn't seeking his pity, and she was starting to wish she hadn't shared so much, so she shrugged. "All in God's plan, I suppose." She winced, as she could almost picture God staring down on her and shaking His head.

"I know it's hard not to question the Lord's plan for us when something so unforeseeable happens." Eli's brows narrowed as he sighed, and Katie Ann suspected he was referring to his wife's death. Then his face brightened, and he locked eyes with her. "But I'm thankful that it was part of His plan for us to meet. I'm grateful for this new friendship."

His presence gave her joy, even if she didn't understand the Lord's plan, or completely trust it. "Me too."

Eli shifted his weight and crossed one ankle on his knee, his body still turned toward her. "Katie Ann…" He paused. "I'd like to write to you. Would that be all right? I mean, I'd like to know how you and Jonas are doing."

"I'd like that." She playfully tapped him on the shoulder. "I want to hear all about your travels, the places you'll see."

He chuckled. "I know it's strange for an Amish man to take on such excursions, but I still plan to work hard too."

"You don't need to justify your intentions to anyone except God. I think you've earned some time to yourself."

"*Danki* for saying that."

"Where will you go first?"

"Indiana. Jake's wife, Laura Jane, has family there. They've invited me to stay with them, and I've never been to Indiana. Then I'll go back home and ready my land for planting. And after that, I plan to take a short trip to Florida."

Katie Ann knew envy was a sin, but the emotion surfaced just the same, and she fought the memories of all the times Ivan promised to take her on a vacation there. "I think that's wonderful."

"It will seem strange, being away from the *kinner*. Even now, being here, I can't help but worry about all of them." He chuckled. "That was the one thing the Lord couldn't have prepared me for with six children. No matter how old they get, I still worry."

"I can understand that."

Eli sat taller. "Do you have a phone?"

"I share the same phone that Samuel installed in the barn. We know lots of folks have cell phones these days or phone ringers in the *haus*, but I agreed with Lillian and Samuel that it's best to keep the ringers out of the house, especially when Jonas is sleeping. And Lillian wants her *kinner* to grow up without the invasions of the outside world."

"Can I call you sometimes?"

"I'd like that." She twisted away from him toward the table by the couch, found her small pad of paper and a pen. She scribbled down the phone number and address and handed it to him.

"Could you take my phone number and address down, in case you or Jonas need anything? I'm going to get a cell phone soon so I can be in touch with my family when I'm on the road, but for now I have a phone in the barn."

Katie Ann passed him the paper and pen. He handed it back to her with his phone number and address.

He glanced at the clock and grinned. "Time sure does fly when I'm with you. I guess I need to go." He stood up, and Katie Ann did the same. "My bus leaves early in the morning, and I'll have to catch a taxi ride to the bus station."

Katie Ann couldn't think of a single thing to say to get him to stay just a little longer, and she dreaded saying good-bye. She followed him to the door and waited while he pulled on his long black overcoat and put on his black felt hat. When he was done, he just stared at her. She didn't move, but as he inched closer her knees began to shake and her pulse quickened. He cupped her cheek.

"I've been dreading having to say good-bye to you," he said.

His touch was unbearably tender, as was the sound of his voice, sending a warm shiver through her. As his lips slowly descended to her cheek, she felt both relief and disappointment, then he kissed her again, this time closer to her mouth, and when his lips brushed hers there was an intimacy that she knew she would recall for a long time, and she was going to savor every second.

After what seemed like a long while, he eased away, picked up her hand, and pressed a kiss into her palm. "Take care, my friend."

Under any other circumstances, and with anyone else, it would have seemed a strange thing to say.

"You too." She fought the tremble in her voice. "Safe travels."

He smiled as he closed the door behind him.

Katie Ann watched Eli through the window as he walked down the driveway to go back to Vera and Elam's, a light snow falling. She touched her lips and fought the urge to cry.

"Be blessed and safe, my friend," she whispered as he disappeared into the darkness.

Chapter Eleven

Middlefield welcomed Eli back with slightly warmer temperatures than he'd left in Colorado, but with snow just the same. He thanked the cab-driver, noticed all the buggies in front of his house, and wondered what was going on. Hurrying into the living room, he was surprised to see all five of his daughters inside.

"What in the world are all you *maedels* doing here?" He looked at each one of them. "And where are all my grandchildren?"

Hannah waved her hand in the air. "They're with Laura Jane."

"And why does she have all the *kinner* this fine afternoon?"

"Because we want to talk to you, *Daed*." Ida Mae sat down on the couch next to Karen and Frieda. "Sit down and tell us all about your trip."

Eli narrowed his brows. Something was up. His

daughters all led busy lives, and he was going to see all of them here the very next day for Thanksgiving. "I could have told you all about it tomorrow, *mei maedels*."

"We couldn't wait!" Maureen was still standing, and she bounced on her toes as she spoke. "Tell us about..." She grinned. "Her."

"Who?"

"Katie Ann."

He glanced around the room at his five daughters. Why were they gathered here and asking about Katie Ann?

"*Aenti* Vera told us you spent a lot of time with her while you were in Canaan." Frieda pushed back a strand of hair that had fallen from beneath her prayer covering. "So we were just wondering..." She gave a little shrug.

Eli slowly took off his coat, then his hat. He hung them both on a rung by the front door and folded his arms across his chest. You could have heard a pin drop on the wooden floor beneath his feet. "And which one of you called *Aenti* Vera to check on me?" He tried to keep a serious voice.

Hannah laughed as she took a seat in a rocking chair in the corner. "We didn't have to call *Aenti* Vera. She called us. We're so happy for you, *Daed*. We've been praying that you would find someone to share your life with. You deserve that, and Katie Ann sounds wonderful, perfect for—"

"Whoa, whoa, whoa." Eli held his palm toward Hannah, whose expression dropped. "There is no romance between me and Katie Ann."

His kiss with Katie Ann flashed through his mind, and he knew it was the most romantic thing that had happened to him in seventeen years, but he wasn't about to admit that to his daughters. "We are friends. That's all." He looked at all of his daughters, one by one. "Now, why the long faces?"

Maureen was standing across the room, her expression possibly the most forlorn of the group. "We were hoping you'd found someone special."

To insinuate that Katie Ann was not special caused a knot in Eli's stomach. "She *is* special. A special *friend*." Eli unfolded his arms from across his chest and put them on his hips. "Since when did all of *mei dochders* become so interested in *mei* personal life?"

"Maureen is married and out of the house now, *Daed*. We're all out on our own." Hannah walked closer to Eli. "It's time for you to find someone to grow old with."

Eli chuckled. "In case you haven't noticed, I *am* old." He walked to the coffee table and picked up his mail. "And none of you needs to be fretting about me." He flipped through the envelopes. "Besides, I told you girls that I planned to do some traveling."

"First of all, that's just not normal." Frieda

scowled. "What sort of Amish man wanders the countryside?"

Eli put down his mail, rubbed his forehead, and wondered when his daughters all grew into such headstrong women. He looked at Frieda, stroked his beard for a moment, and then shook his head. "I've told all of you that I plan to take some time for myself."

"Well, that was before you met a woman who is perfect for you."

Maureen leaned back against the couch, her pouting expression reminding Eli of when she was a small girl.

"*Ya*. And you're going to blow it, *Daed*." Karen also leaned back against the couch, folding her arms across her chest.

"Perfect for me?" Eli faced off with all his girls, glancing around at each one of them in turn. "She is not perfect for me. Katie Ann has a baby that is almost three months old. She is just now starting her family. I've raised six wonderful *kinner*, and I think I deserve a little time on my own."

Ida Mae huffed. "That sounds mighty selfish, *Daed*."

Hannah spoke up next. "Hush, Ida Mae." She turned to Eli. "It's not selfish, *Daed*. And we do think you should have some time for yourself, but—"

"*Danki* for your permission, Hannah." Eli

smiled, but when Hannah's eyes teared up, he silently reprimanded himself for the comment. Hannah was his most sensitive child, even though she was the oldest daughter. "Girls," he said softly, glancing at each one of them. "If ever there was a time when I needed a *fraa*, it was when you all were young. I regret that you grew up without a mother for so long, and some of you not at all. So I'm going to say this one time, then that's the end of it. Katie Ann is a beautiful, wonderful person. We grew close while I was there, and we plan to stay in touch. As friends." He pointed a finger around the room. "Everyone clear about that?"

The girls all gathered near the door, nodding as they bundled up in coats and bonnets. They each kissed him on the cheek and rattled off what they were bringing for the Thanksgiving meal the next day. As the others scurried across the porch toward their buggies, Ida Mae hung back. She wrapped her arms around her father. "We just want you to be happy, *Daed*. That's all."

Eli eased away and cupped Ida Mae's chin. "I know you do, *mei maedel*. And hard work mixed with travel will make me happy."

She nodded, and Eli watched his very independent, strong-willed daughters hitch up their buggies to head home. Pride was something to be avoided, but Eli was proud of each one of them just the same.

He waved at the departing buggies, then walked

back inside. Again his mind replayed his kiss with Katie Ann, the way it had been since the moment his lips left hers. She was as wrong for him as any woman could be. And it wasn't just Jonas and the new family she was beginning. Eli could tell from their conversations that Katie Ann was struggling to trust again. Maybe she had forgiven her husband and his mistress, but he sensed that trust was still a far cry away.

He didn't ever want to do anything to cause her to distrust him. What about the kiss? Shouldn't she have been able to trust him not to be so forward? Eli supposed he should feel guilty for both times that they had kissed...but he didn't.

Nothing had ever felt so right.

Katie Ann buttoned her coat, tied her bonnet, and gathered up the extra-large batch of creamed celery she'd made to take for the Thanksgiving feast. She'd taken Jonas over earlier and was sure that Anna and Elizabeth were entertaining him. As she closed the door behind her, she stumbled, then grimaced when she saw what almost caused her to trip. *A dead mouse*. As she eased around the poor critter, she noticed he wasn't frozen, but freshly dead. Then something darted from underneath the house and raced toward the barn.

Mrs. Dash turned around once to look at Katie Ann before scurrying through a barn window and out of sight. Katie Ann looked again at the dead animal, then eased down her porch steps. She'd been feeding the cat leftovers most every morning and night. Katie Ann still couldn't get close to her, but perhaps this was Mrs. Dash's way of returning the favor—ridding the barn of mice.

She was almost to Lillian's front door when she heard a car. Spinning around, she saw that it was Martha. It was too cold to wait for her, so she headed into Lillian's large kitchen through a second door on the porch.

"It's toasty warm in here," she said as she put the creamed celery on the table. She scanned the room and saw everyone but the newlyweds. "Where're Emily and David?"

"They're here." Lillian pointed to the living room. "With Elizabeth, Anna, and Jonas."

Katie Ann peeked her head into the room and watched Emily and David fussing over Jonas. She smiled, sure that the couple was probably planning to start their own family soon. "Hello, everyone. Happy Thanksgiving."

After she'd hugged those in the room, she walked back into the kitchen just as Martha came through the door from the porch into the kitchen. Lillian disliked the fact that everyone used that door, but it was just so convenient. Martha elbowed her way through the crowd in the kitchen.

"I made a cheese ball." She handed it to Lillian.

"Because that's just all the energy I could muster up this year."

Lillian took the ball wrapped in plastic wrap. "Martha, you didn't have to bring anything. I told you that." She tenderly rubbed Martha's arm. "How are you feeling?"

Martha shrugged. "As good as anyone who has a big tumor in their stomach could feel, I guess."

Katie Ann rubbed her forehead. Despite Martha's nonchalance, she knew her friend was scared.

"I want to know every little detail of your visit with Eli yesterday," Martha whispered in her ear. "You and I are going to your house directly this afternoon, and don't hold back any details."

"Martha, there isn't much to tell. We went to Alamosa, and—"

"Whatever. I want to hear it all anyway."

Katie Ann could feel her cheeks reddening just thinking about last night.

An hour later, a meal that took many hours to prepare was consumed in less than fifteen minutes, and the men retired to the barn while the women cleaned up.

"Oh, I need to tell you all, I got the details for my surgery next week." Martha handed Vera a plate to be washed. "They're cutting me open on Wednesday. I have to be there early in the morning, and…" She paused with a huff. "Can you believe I can't eat breakfast that morning? Not that I would have been thrilled to have cereal and a muffin as my last meal, but…"

Vera was running soapy water in Lillian's sink, and Emily handed her another plate as she turned to Martha. "Martha, first of all, it's not your last meal. Don't say things like that."

Emily's eyes were starting to tear up. Katie Ann knew how much the girl—and David—loved Martha. They all did. But Martha needed to be careful how she spoke about her upcoming surgery, especially around the younger folks.

Katie Ann patted Emily on the shoulder and whispered, "Everything will be fine. You know how Martha gets."

Emily nodded, but Katie Ann was as worried as the rest of them.

"Katie Ann?" David poked his head into the kitchen, grinning from ear to ear. "You have a phone call."

"A call? Who could be calling me?"

Everyone in the room turned to David, and Lillian spoke up. "David, who is it?"

His smile broadened. "It's Eli."

Katie Ann couldn't even look at the women around her, and the heat in her face was evidence of how red her cheeks must be. She tucked her chin as she moved toward the door.

"You go, girl!" Martha's voice boomed above

the whispers in the kitchen, and Katie Ann kept her eyes down.

As she walked into the barn, the men began to scatter. Elam, Samuel, David, Jacob, and Levi all moved toward the door.

"I'm sorry. You don't have to leave."

"Sure we do," Levi said as he winked at her.

Katie Ann took a deep breath and watched as Samuel closed the barn door behind them. She wished she had thought to bundle up before she ran out the door. With chattering teeth, she said, "Hello."

"Happy Thanksgiving."

Her heart came alive at the sound of his voice. "And happy Thanksgiving to you." She put a hand to her chest, hoping to calm her rapid pulse, but it was no use. It hadn't even been forty-eight hours since he left her house, since the kiss, but her lips still tingled at the memory of his touch.

"I had to get away from the crowd for a few minutes. My girls have taken over my kitchen, which is fine. My son and sons-in-law have taken over my living room, which is fine. And my grandchildren are in my bedroom playing board games. That, too…is fine. But…" He chuckled. "I needed a few minutes of quiet. And I thought about you. Are you having a good day with everyone?"

"*Ya, ya*. We all ate too much, as expected." She held her breath for a moment, wondering if their conversation would be filled with small talk, in light of all the deep conversations they'd had over the past couple of weeks.

"I'm not going to keep you from family, but I didn't want the day to go by without wishing you a happy Thanksgiving. And you hug Jonas from me."

Katie Ann was glowing from the inside out, and she didn't even notice the cold anymore. "I will. And you give my blessings to your family as well."

It was quiet for a moment.

"Katie Ann, I'm feeling a little bad about…"

She heard him take a deep breath.

"…about the way I kissed you Monday night."

"It wasn't like it was the first time." Katie Ann slapped a hand across her mouth, not believing what she'd said. She squeezed her eyes closed in horror and waited for Eli's response.

He laughed. "Uh, true. I was just thinking that maybe I somehow took advantage, and—"

"Eli, I'm a grown woman. You didn't take advantage of me."

"Well then, if it's okay with you, I'm not going to feel bad anymore. I'm highly attracted to my new best friend, and I had a weak moment."

"You had *two* weak moments." She squeezed her eyes shut again, but she couldn't stop smiling at how playful they were being with each other and how natural it felt.

Eli's familiar laughter warmed her heart. "*Ya*, I did. And trust me, I think about both. Often."

Katie Ann wanted to tell Eli that she thought about him, too, but there was no way she was going to put her heart out there to a man she couldn't have. She thought about the way he always referred to her as his best friend. She liked that title. It was safe, but she wasn't sure what to say.

"Katie Ann, I'll let you go. Don't forget to hug Jonas for me."

"I won't. And *danki* for calling."

She waited for him to hang up, but she could hear him breathing. "Eli?"

"Ya."

"Is there something else?"

"No. Not really."

Katie Ann waited.

"Okay, I'm hanging up now." Eli laughed. "Talk to you soon."

I hope so. "All right. Bye, Eli." And this time she hung up. She glanced around the barn for Mrs. Dash, but decided there was too much activity today for her to make an appearance.

Her cheeks warmed when she exited the barn and saw the men standing right outside, all shivering. She knew they had to have heard at least part of her conversation. But when she looked toward the house and saw all the women peering out the window at her, she knew what she was walking into.

* * *

It was nearing dark when the last of Eli's kin left. What a grand day it had been, and he felt like sharing the details with someone. Not just anyone. Katie Ann. As he kicked back in his recliner, he adjusted the lantern on the table beside him so he could see better. He searched his pile of papers and mail on the table until he came across a tablet of paper and a pen.

Dear Katie Ann,

He stopped and wondered if the details of his day would be of interest to her. After only a few moments of deliberation, he decided that they just might.

It's Thanksgiving evening, and everyone has gone home. It's quiet in the house. Just the way I like it (I'm chuckling here), but I wish you were here for me to tell you about our day. My oldest grandchild, Leah, sang to everyone in the living room after the meal, and I don't think I've ever heard anything so beautiful. She sang "Jesus Loves Me" and "For God So Loved Us." Do you remember me telling you about Leah? She's Jake and Laura Jane's oldest, my first grandchild. And also today, little Luke fell and bumped his head. It was a touching moment when his twin brother, Ben, touched his head and started to cry, as if he'd felt the pain. Seems like twins are always extra close. Luke and Ben are identical. Did I tell you that?

Sometimes, when it's quiet like this, I'll put out a small radio I have hidden in my bedroom and listen to country gospel music. Sometimes I turn it on really softly in the background when I pray. Mei kinner all know I have it, and I suspect that one or two of them might have a radio as well, but our bishop has a habit of showing up unexpectedly, so I keep it hidden in a drawer in my nightstand. I'm such a rule-breaker, no?

Eli stretched his socked feet out on the recliner and leaned his head back for a moment. He closed his eyes and let his last visit with Katie Ann play out in his mind for the hundredth time. When he'd relived the moment several times, he resumed his writing.

I hope that when you receive this, it will put a smile on your face. You need to smile more. It's healthy. Or so I'm told (chuckling again). Either way, I love it when you smile.

Eli reminded himself not to come on too strong. He knew he should pray for Katie Ann to find a wonderful man to take care of her and Jonas, but he just wasn't sure he liked that idea. Actually, he was sure he didn't like that idea. *I'm a selfish man.* He scratched his forehead.

> *What are your plans for Christmas? Will you celebrate First Christmas at Lillian and Samuel's haus, or will you go somewhere else? Mei dochders will take over mei haus again for First Christmas, then on Second Christmas we usually spend the day visiting friends and shut-ins. We always visit Annie Hostetler and her husband, John. Annie has Alzheimer's, and they don't get out much. That disease scares me. And we always end the day by having pie at Miller's Pantry. Best pie in the world, I think.*
>
> *I'll close for now. I hope to hear back from you. Sending blessings to you and Jonas.*
> *Best friends, in His name,*
> *Eli*

He put the letter on the table, planning to mail it first thing in the morning. His fire was dwindling, and as he got up and threw another log on it, he thought about the fires he'd tended at Katie Ann's house and the time they'd spent talking while sitting on her couch. He shook his head and knew that he was going to have to clear his mind. It was fine to think about her. Just not all the time.

When he got cozy in his chair again, he thought about the next trip he'd be taking after Christmas. But he clearly needed to focus on something else besides Katie Ann.

On Tuesday morning Katie Ann helped Martha pack her suitcase to take to the hospital the next day. She worried her friend wouldn't bring what she needed, plus she was hoping Martha would take the quilt she'd brought back for her from Alamosa. She recalled her trip with Eli to the neighboring town, and she wondered what he was doing today. She hadn't talked to him since he called on Thanksgiving Day. Not that she expected to.

"Martha, I don't think you're going to need all those hair accessories at the hospital." Katie Ann watched as Martha loaded up a huge blow dryer, large pink curlers, several kinds of hair product, and of course…the butterfly clip.

"That's easy for you to say. It doesn't matter how your hair looks because it's always covered up by that prayer *kapp*." Martha grabbed Katie Ann's arm and pulled her to the bed. She eased her down on the pink and white comforter that Katie Ann had gotten her for her birthday last year. "Now, honey. Listen to me. I know you're scared about my trip to the hospital, but you've shown me the way to the Lord." She sat taller and raised her chin. "I'm not afraid to go."

As Martha dabbed at her eyes, Katie Ann knew that wasn't true, so she took a deep breath and tried to be strong for her friend. "You're not going anywhere yet. Everything is going to go fine, and you'll be home recovering in no time."

"I don't think so."

Martha lowered her head, but Katie Ann saw a tear trickle down her cheek. She looked up and swiped at the tear.

"I've never been knocked out. I know that's hard to believe at my age, but I just know I'm not going to wake up."

"Of course you'll wake up." Katie Ann was surprised to learn that this was Martha's biggest fear. Katie Ann was much more concerned about the surgery itself, and she planned to talk to the doctors as soon as she and Martha arrived at the hospital, something she should have already done. Had she not been so preoccupied with Eli...

"Where's that quilt you gave me, that lovely spread with the Lord's Word all over it?"

Katie Ann pointed to a chair across the room. "There it is."

Martha walked to the chair and picked up the

small quilt. "We'll just carry it in, since it won't fit in my suitcase."

Katie Ann was thinking it might fit if there weren't so many hair supplies, but she didn't say anything. She glanced at the clock on the wall. Arnold would be arriving later in the afternoon.

Martha pushed the quilt toward Katie Ann. "You make sure I'm covered in this when they wheel me into surgery."

Katie Ann remembered when David had his kidney transplant. She was pretty sure they wouldn't allow the quilt to go into surgery with Martha, but she didn't say anything. At least Martha could sleep beneath it before and after.

"Let's pray for a while." Martha slowly eased down onto her knees and propped her elbows on the bed, folding her hands in front of her. Katie Ann slid down beside her. "And let's don't do it silently like you people usually do. Can you please pray aloud?"

Katie Ann blinked back tears. "Of course."

"Don't cry." Martha reached over and grabbed onto Katie Ann's hand. "Have I told you how much I love you?" Martha smiled. "Like you are my own daughter."

And no matter how hard she tried, Katie Ann couldn't keep the tears from spilling down her cheeks as she answered. "And I couldn't love you any more if you were my own mother."

* * *

Katie Ann grabbed her mail from the box at the end of her driveway on her way home from Martha's. She tucked it into her apron and went to Lillian's to pick up Jonas, who was sleeping soundly in a playpen in the living room. It wasn't until after she was home and had Jonas in his own bed that she saw the letter from Eli.

She wanted to enjoy every word, so she bathed, made coffee, got a fire going, and curled up on the couch. She was surprised that she hadn't heard from Arnold, but hopefully he had a safe trip and they would see him at the hospital tomorrow. She peeled the envelope open and read. Smiling, she could almost hear him chuckling as he wrote, and she felt a part of his life as he detailed memorable moments from his day. She couldn't wait to write him back.

Dear Eli,

I so enjoyed your letter and hearing about Leah and the twins. It sounds like you have such a wonderful family, and I loved hearing about them. Tonight, worry fills my heart, as tomorrow morning I will be taking Martha to the hospital to have the tumor removed. Lillian will keep Jonas for me. I've prayed hard about tomorrow, and I know that worry is a sin, but on this night I'm afraid I'm filled with concern. You probably only saw one side of Martha (now I'm chuckling), but I promise you, she has a huge heart, and she is very dear to me, as if she were my own mother.

Katie Ann tapped the pen to her chin as more visions of Eli's kiss raced through her head.

*It has gotten much colder since you left, dropping into the single digits the last few days. I will be glad when spring is here. Last year, Lillian and I didn't have a garden. We weren't sure what to plant. The growing season is so different here, with only three months of frost-free weather. But after talking with some other folks, we have a plan. We will grow peas, tomatoes, sweet corn, potatoes, and onions. And we're told that cauliflower, cabbage, and broccoli will do **gut** in this climate. I'm looking forward to that, but our last day of frost will not come until mid-June.*

Jonas continues to amaze me on a daily

basis, and he smiles every time I say his name. What a blessing he is to me so late in life.

I've been quilting pot holders in the evenings, and I'm working on a cookbook. Someday I would like to have a small shop to sell things like that, something very small.

She recalled how Eli mentioned that he'd always wanted a shop, but she decided not to bring that up.

I will close for now, as I want to spend extra time in prayer tonight. May this letter find you well in all the ways of the Lord.

She paused, thought for a minute, and decided to sign her letter the same way he had.

Best friends, in His name,
Katie Ann

She folded the letter, put it in an envelope, and found Eli's address on her end table. She'd drop the letter in the mailbox on the way to the hospital in the morning. She'd tried to get Martha to spend the night with her, but Martha was insistent that she wanted to spend her last night on Earth in her own bed.

Katie Ann closed her eyes in prayer.

Please, Lord, don't let Martha die. Please.

Chapter Twelve

"It stinks in here." Martha was dressed in a purple pants outfit, and Katie Ann could tell that her friend had spent extra time on her hair this morning. Not one strand was out of place, and it was tightly secured under the butterfly clip. And her makeup was perfectly applied, right down to her bright red lipstick. "And I don't even want to talk about how hungry I am."

"I'm sure they'll let you eat not long after the surgery."

They wound their way down the hall to admissions. Martha said she'd already preregistered at the hospital, so it wasn't long before she was shown to her room and settled into her bed. Much to her chagrin, it was not a private room.

"Katie Ann…" Martha motioned from her bed for Katie Ann to come closer, then she whispered, "Go find out why that person is in my room. I specifically asked for a private room, and I am paying good money to have one."

In the next bed, a woman was lying on her side facing the window, only her long blond hair visible atop the covers.

"All right." Katie Ann patted her on the arm, although she wasn't as concerned about Martha's roommate as she was about finding the doctor and getting some details about Martha's surgery. "I'll be back in a few minutes."

She turned when she got to the door. Martha was wearing a white hospital gown and was tucked beneath the quilt Katie Ann had given her. "Do you need anything?"

Martha pointed to the bed next to her and mouthed, "I don't need a roommate."

"Okay," Katie Ann whispered as she left the room.

Martha tried to calm her breathing. They'd be coming for her soon. She closed her eyes and prayed silently. *Please, Lord, if You could see fit to have me wake up and live a few more years, I'd sure be grateful to get to see my little Jonas grow into a small person. If I leave now, he won't remember me.* She sighed. *But if it's Your will to take me home, please take care of Katie Ann and Jonas. And, Lord...can You make this as painless as possible? You know how much I hate pain.*

Her prayer was interrupted when she heard whimpering to her left. She turned to face the back of the person in the bed a few feet from hers. Twisting her mouth back and forth, she watched the woman's body shaking.

"You all right over there?" When there was no answer, Martha asked, "Do you need me to get a nurse for you?"

The woman didn't turn around, but just shook her head.

Martha glanced around the room at all the equipment, wishing she could yank the IV out of her arm, but she figured that would hurt just as much as when they put it in. The woman in the next bed kept crying, and Martha hoped Katie Ann would hurry back and get this person out of here. Last thing she needed was more sadness.

Martha sat up in bed, dropped her feet to the floor, then pulled the IV pole the few feet to where the woman lay. She tapped her on the arm. "Honey?"

"I'm fine, really."

Martha could tell by her voice that she was young, but she wasn't sure how young. Her body stretched the full length of the bed beneath the covers. Martha leaned closer, not sure what to do. "You don't sound fine," she finally said.

"Well, I am." The woman shifted a bit, but she didn't turn around.

Martha wanted to see the face of the person she was talking to. She gently tapped her on the shoulder again. "I'm going to call a nurse if you don't turn around and let me see that you're all right."

As the covers shifted, the woman slowly turned to face Martha, and Martha gasped.

"Do I look all right to you?" The woman could barely move her mouth due to the stitches across her lip, and Martha wasn't sure she'd ever seen a shiner like the one this young woman had. Her left eye was swollen shut, and another gash ran along the side of her cheek with more stitches. "Happy now?" She turned back to face the window.

Martha didn't move or speak for a few moments, then she took in a swift breath. "Whoever did that to you should be shot in the…" She bit her lip and remembered that the good Lord was listening. "Did a boyfriend or husband do that to you?"

No answer.

"Maybe a car wreck?"

The woman eased back around to face Martha. "I really don't want to talk right now. Can you please just leave me alone?" She rolled over again, just about the time Katie Ann walked back into the room.

"What are you doing out of bed?" Katie Ann moved toward her, and Martha reluctantly climbed back into bed. Once she was settled beneath her quilt, which, unbeknownst to Katie Ann, she'd had blessed by both a priest and Bishop Esh, she folded her arms across her chest.

Katie Ann leaned closer and whispered, "They'll be moving that woman out of here shortly, and you'll have the room to yourself."

Martha scowled. "What?"

Still whispering, Katie Ann leaned even closer to Martha's ear. "You told me that you didn't want to share a room, so they are coming to get her soon."

"Well, that's ridiculous." She waved her hand toward the door. "Go back and tell them never mind."

Katie Ann's mouth fell open as she cupped her hands to her hips.

"Oh, don't look so bothered. I'm the one about to get cut wide open. Just go now…" She waved her hand again, and Katie Ann shook her head all the way out the door.

Martha wanted to talk to the woman next to her. Actually, she was more like a girl, maybe sixteen or seventeen. But she wasn't sure how to start up a conversation without irritating her more.

Just then the door eased open. Martha glanced up, and she was sure her heart was going to beat out of her chest. "Arnold? What in the world are you doing here? Now I'm *sure* I'm going to die, or you wouldn't be here."

The love of her life took off a black felt hat, similar to what the Amish folks wore, although Arnold was as Catholic as could be, and he shuffled toward the bed. "Hello, Martha. You should have told me you were ill." He leaned down, and to her surprise, he kissed her on the cheek. "I've missed you."

She swallowed back a lump in her throat. "How are things in Georgia?"

"I had my reasons why I needed to stay there after my son passed, but I am wrapping things up." He smiled. "I'm thinking about moving back here, to Canaan."

"Well, that's just peachy, Arnold. You decide to move back here *now*? When I'm about to kick the bucket?" She rolled her eyes, glanced up, and prayed aloud. "Lord, there is something unfair about this."

Arnold sat down in the chair by her bed, reached for her hand, and squeezed. "You are going to be just fine, Martha. I know it."

"Nope. I'm fairly certain that I'm not going to wake up once they knock me out." She squinted her eyes. "So, Arnold Becker, if there is anything you want to tell me, I suggest you do it right now." She raised her chin.

Arnold chuckled. "Still my same Martha."

His eyes twinkled, and Martha wished she could marry him on the spot.

"My, how I've missed you." Then he frowned. "Why wouldn't you let me come visit you?"

She turned to face the poor girl next to her, who

was still facing the window. "I didn't want to have to say good-bye again." She turned back to him. "But here you are, and I guess I'll have to say it anyway."

"I needed to be with my daughter-in-law and her family. We were all grieving, and I hated to leave them…and…" He pulled his eyes away from hers as he took a deep breath. "I didn't come back to stay because I couldn't provide for you in a proper manner. But I made some investments, and now—"

"Did the good Lord strip you of your senses?" Martha stiffened as she thought about all the months she'd missed this man. "I have more money than I'll ever spend in a lifetime. I thought you knew that."

Arnold stood taller. "But I wanted to be able to take care of you."

She stared into his kind eyes, never more touched—or frustrated. She pressed her lips firmly together for a moment. "On the off chance I pull through this, am I gonna have to tell you good-bye again?"

"Yes, we'll have to part ways once you are better. But I'll be back in a few weeks. To stay, if that's all right with you."

Martha shrugged, elated, but not about to let Arnold know just how much. "It's a free country."

Arnold chuckled again. "Yes, it is."

Martha narrowed her brows. "Who told you I

was getting cut on today?" She waved her hand in the air. "Oh, never mind. I know who it was."

Right then, Katie Ann walked back into the room.

"My goodness, Katie Ann, look who showed up out of the blue!" She lifted one brow at Katie Ann, never more grateful to her friend.

"How about that, Martha. What a coincidence." Katie Ann smiled. She walked closer to Martha and whispered again. "The girl is staying, but I don't know why you can't make up your mind."

"Because I'm old."

Katie Ann grinned. "You visit with Arnold. I'm going to go find out when they are coming for you."

Katie Ann walked to the nurses' station and asked to speak to Martha's doctor. She waited in a chair for almost fifteen minutes before a doctor walked up to her.

"Hi. I'm Dr. Lieberson. Were you asking about Martha Dobbs?"

Katie Ann stood and shook the doctor's hand. "*Ya*. I was." She took a deep breath, unsure how to ask the questions on her mind. "I was just—just wondering about…"

She recalled David's kidney transplant and how everything was always presented to them in percentages. Chance the kidney would fail, 33 percent, or chance of infection, 50 percent. Things like that.

"Can you tell me what Martha's percentage is?"

"Percentage?" The young doctor folded his arms across his chest. "Percentage about…"

Katie Ann bit her bottom lip and avoided his eyes. "What is the percentage that Martha will survive the surgery?" She glanced up at him as her heart thumped in her chest.

He paused. "Well, there are always risks when anyone has surgery, but I don't foresee any problems. Martha should be able to go home tomorrow afternoon."

Katie Ann gasped. "So soon? But won't she have a large cut on her stomach that must be tended?"

"No. It won't be a very big incision at all."

"But if her tumor is the size of a grapefruit, that seems like—"

"What?" Dr. Lieberson pulled off a pair of dark-rimmed glasses and squinted. "Martha doesn't have a tumor the size of a grapefruit. It's no larger than a pea."

"The kind you eat?" Katie Ann felt ridiculous the moment she said it, but she was more than confused already.

The doctor smiled. "Yes, like the kind you eat. We did a biopsy, and the cyst is benign, but it's causing her some irritation, so we're removing it. It's a very simple procedure that should take less than an hour, plus her time in recovery."

Katie Ann laughed out loud. "I'm sorry, doctor."

She put a hand over her mouth to stifle further laughter as relief washed over her. "This is very *gut* news. Martha must have misunderstood her diagnosis."

She wasn't sure if that was the case, or if Martha did what she usually did when it came to medical issues…embellished a bit. Either way, Katie Ann was glad to hear this.

Dr. Lieberson narrowed his brows. "I'm sorry if Martha didn't understand. I spoke to her briefly after she met with her regular physician."

Katie Ann smiled. "It's all right. Martha must have been confused. I'll go make sure she understands."

"Do you want me to talk to her?"

"No." Katie Ann was anxious to get back to the room. "When will they be coming to get her?"

The doctor scratched his cheek. "They should have already been to get her. I can check and see—"

"Katie Ann!"

Katie Ann swung around to see Martha approaching on a gurney with her arm stretched out and Arnold by her side. An orderly was pushing her along.

"They won't let me take my quilt."

"It'll be in your room when you get back."

Martha shook her head. "*If* I get back."

"Martha, your cyst is very small. The doctor said

this will be a very easy and quick surgery. You even get to go home tomorrow afternoon. Isn't that wonderful?"

"Big. Small. Whatever. I have a foreign growth inside of me." She scowled at Katie Ann, then turned to Arnold and batted her eyes. "I'm so glad you're with me during this difficult time."

Once again, Katie Ann put a hand over her mouth. She knew any surgery was risky, but she wasn't sure she'd seen Martha quite this dramatic before. She leaned down and kissed her on the cheek. "I love you. I'll pray that all goes well. And I'll see you shortly."

"Bye, Katie Ann."

Something about the way Martha spoke her name made Katie Ann terribly uneasy, and she didn't feel like smiling anymore. Instead, she stepped aside as Martha's gurney rolled past her, then she slowly followed. Once Martha was settled, she wanted to find the chapel.

Two hours later, Katie Ann was growing antsy, and she could tell Arnold was too. He kept getting up, pacing in the waiting room, then sitting back down.

"Didn't they say it would only take an hour?" he asked Katie Ann for the third time.

She nodded. She'd found the chapel earlier and prayed for the Lord to place His healing hand on Martha, and now, as they waited, she prayed even more.

A few minutes later, Dr. Lieberson came out from behind the double doors that led to the operating rooms. Katie Ann stood up. When she saw him smile, she put a hand on her chest.

"Everything went just fine. She'll be in recovery for about an hour, then she'll be back in her room." He chuckled. "She mumbled something about food when she was first waking up." He stroked his chin. "I thought she said creamed celery, but I'm not sure." He reached out and shook both Katie Ann's and Arnold's hands. "Anyway, she's doing just fine."

"Thank you." Katie Ann turned to Arnold and gave him a hug.

After a prayer of thanks, she and Arnold grabbed a bite to eat before heading back to Martha's room. Martha's roommate was still facing the window, so they were as quiet as they could be in case she was sleeping.

They'd barely sat down when the same orderly as before rolled Martha in.

Martha pointed a wobbly finger at the man. "Creamed celery is what I said."

"Yes, ma'am," he replied with a smile.

A nurse entered the room then, and together she and the orderly got Martha situated in her bed.

Katie Ann quickly found the quilt and spread it on top of her.

"She's still pretty groggy." The orderly lifted the railing on the side of Martha's bed. "And I'm pretty sure she's hungry." He grinned. "You folks have a good day." He waved as he left the room.

Katie Ann and Arnold each went to opposite sides of Martha's bed.

"Hello, sunshine." Arnold leaned down and kissed Martha on the cheek, but Martha turned to Katie Ann.

"I'm alive."

Katie Ann reached for Martha's hand and smiled. "*Ya*, you are."

"In that case, I'm hungry."

"I saw carts of food being wheeled around earlier, so I bet you will have some food very soon." Katie Ann brushed back some of Martha's gray strands that had fallen across her forehead.

"Creamed celery." Martha's eyes were closed as she spoke, and Katie Ann wondered if she would even be able to stay awake long enough to eat.

"I don't think the hospital has creamed celery, Martha."

Katie Ann heard movement to her left, and she turned to catch a glimpse of the battered young woman staring at all of them. The girl quickly turned back the other way. Katie Ann was wondering what happened to the girl when Martha squeezed her hand.

"Katie Ann, I think I need a nap…" Martha closed her eyes.

Katie Ann turned to Arnold. "The doctor said she would sleep most of today."

Arnold nodded, and even though Martha did indeed sleep most of the day, Katie Ann and Arnold both stayed with her until late in the afternoon and finally told her good-bye around four o'clock.

During their time at the hospital, Katie Ann prayed. And she laughed on the inside, wondering if Martha knew how loudly she snored. But Arnold never acknowledged it. Instead, he just mentioned every little while how much he loved his Martha. Katie Ann found herself longing for that kind of love.

Martha pushed the nurse's call button for the third time in the past fifteen minutes. "What if I was dying in here?" she mumbled, glancing at the clock on the wall. Ten o'clock. She could vaguely remember Katie Ann and Arnold telling her good-bye earlier in the day, but foremost on her mind at the moment was the fact that she had apparently missed dinner, and she was sure she'd never been this hungry in her life.

"What can I do for you?" A young woman in

blue scrubs walked into the room and spoke to Martha in a whisper.

"Food. I need food. I must have slept through dinner."

"The cafeteria is closed, but I can probably find some pudding, or maybe some chips. Something like that."

Martha hung her head for a moment. "I was thinking more like a burger and some fries." She looked up at the woman. "But I'd be grateful for anything you can round up."

"Sure." She picked up Martha's chart at the end of the bed and studied it for a moment. "No food restrictions. Let me go see what I can find."

After the woman left, Martha heard rock music coming from the bed next to her, then the girl answered a cell phone with a strained hello.

Martha lowered the volume on her television a bit.

"I don't know when I can go home. They haven't said. I think I'll be in here for a few more days." After a long silence, she said, "I know. That's what you always say." A moment later she clicked the phone closed and stared at the ceiling.

Martha studied the girl for a moment and wondered again what had happened to her.

"Why don't you just take a picture?" The girl turned to face Martha.

Her voice sounded like a reflection of the girl herself. Broken.

Martha took a deep breath as she gazed into the girl's one good eye. "What's your name?"

"Danielle." She dabbed at her lip with her finger and grimaced.

"I'm Martha."

Silence. Martha could tell Danielle wasn't in the mood to be friendly—and who would blame her?—but blatant curiosity drove Martha on. "Who did that to you?"

Danielle slowly twisted her head toward Martha. "Look, lady…*Martha*…I don't mean to be rude, but my situation is really none of your business." She closed her one good eye and winced, clearly in pain.

"Are they giving you something for the pain?" Martha shifted her weight slightly, thankful that she didn't seem to be experiencing near the discomfort as this poor child.

"I guess." Danielle opened her eye and stared at Martha for a few moments. "Is Arnold your boyfriend?"

"He used to be." She lifted one shoulder. "I don't know. I guess maybe he will be again."

"You're not very nice to him."

Martha pressed her lips together, raised one brow, and prepared to lambaste this child. But when the girl grimaced in pain again, Martha said simply, "I'm a lot nicer than whoever beat the snot out of you."

Danielle stared up at the ceiling, and they were both quiet for a while. Martha hoped the nurse would return with some food soon.

"So…" Danielle turned to face Martha again. She could barely move her swollen lips as she spoke, and Martha strained to hear her. "That woman who was here…she's Amish, huh?"

"Yes. Her name's Katie Ann."

Come on with some chow, nurse. Martha glanced toward the door and sighed.

"Those people are weird."

Martha turned to face her, semi-glad that a conversation was ensuing. "The Amish are the gentlest and kindest folks I know." She turned her attention to the door when it swung open.

The same young nurse smiled and entered. "The McDonald's downstairs was still open, so here you go." She placed a bag on the nightstand by Martha's bed.

Martha breathed in the aroma of French fries and wanted to hug the woman's neck. "Honey, my purse is right there inside that drawer…" She started to reach for the drawer of the nightstand, but gasped when she pulled against her incision.

"Now, now. You lie back," the kind woman said. "No need to pay me."

"Yes, I need to pay you. I insist." Martha opened

the bag with the burger and fries. "You are my hero."

The woman chuckled. "I don't know about that, but just pay it forward. Do something nice for someone else." Before Martha could respond, the nurse walked toward Danielle. "Can I get you anything, Danielle?"

Danielle just shook her head.

"Okay." She turned to leave. "I'm here until six in the morning, so let me know if either of you needs anything."

Martha dived into her burger and moaned with delight. Then she glanced at Danielle. "French fry?"

Danielle shook her head. "Those people are holy, aren't they?"

"What people?" Martha asked around a mouthful.

"The Amish. They're like all into God and everything, right?"

Martha swallowed. "They have a very strong faith." She popped a fry into her mouth. "Good folks, the Amish."

It was quiet for a while, only the low buzz of the television, some late-night talk show, and the beeps and sounds from the other side of the door. Normal hospital sounds. Martha was glad she was going home tomorrow, back to her own bed. And surely Katie Ann was at home making her some creamed celery. She smiled.

"I don't believe in God."

Martha snapped her head to the left. "What?"

"You heard me, Martha. There is no God, and people who waste their time praying to Him are doing just that…wasting their time."

Martha thought her heart might break. If this girl needed anyone, it was surely the Lord. "How old are you, child?"

"Seventeen."

"Not very smart for your age, are ya?"

Danielle squinted her eye at Martha and spoke slowly through half-opened lips. "Just because I don't believe in God, that makes me stupid?"

"Correct." Martha shoved the last bit of burger in her mouth.

"You don't know anything about me. I used to make straight As in school, and I even graduated early."

"Micky D's wouldn't normally be my first choice for a meal, but this is the best burger I've ever had." Martha stuffed her trash into the bag and carefully eased it onto the nightstand, careful not to twist too quickly.

"Did you hear me? I'm very smart."

Martha didn't look at Danielle. "Yeah. I heard you."

"People just wrote all that stuff in the Bible to keep us from killing each other."

Martha turned to Danielle and lowered her chin. "Really? Wow, hasn't that worked well."

"You know what I mean. It's all made up, something to keep the masses in order."

"If that's what you choose to believe."

"It's the truth."

"If you say so."

They were quiet for a while, and Martha was starting to feel like she could sleep, but when Danielle spoke again, Martha heard the Lord calling her loud and clear.

"Why do you believe in God? What proof do you have that He exists?"

Martha took a deep breath, clicked the television off, and faced Danielle. "How much time you got?"

Chapter Thirteen

Lucy stared at tiny Benjamin in his incubator in the preemie nursery at Lancaster General Hospital. He was small but healthy, and Lucy missed Ivan now more than ever before.

Ivan, we have a beautiful baby boy.

Leaving him to go home would be the hardest thing she'd ever done, but the doctors had told her that he would have to stay in the hospital for at least two more months until he was closer to full term. He looked like Ivan with his big eyes, and like Lucy with his small pug nose. He was the most beautiful thing she'd ever seen, and she wanted more than anything to be a good mother, even though she and Ivan had never really discussed having a family. Ivan always said that if it was God's will, it would happen.

Lucy wondered what she could do to get on good terms with God. She'd never really had much to do with Him prior to her affair with Ivan, but she was sure God disliked her even more than she disliked herself. She'd been praying every day, asking for forgiveness and begging that God would show her how to be a good mother. She thought about Katie Ann a lot, sure that Ivan's wife was a wonderful mother. Lucy wondered if she and Katie Ann might have been friends in another life, but she knew the answer. Katie Ann was a good person. Lucy wasn't. But as she gazed down at the tiny miracle before her, she had this feeling that maybe there was hope.

Martha cleaned up in the small bathroom in her hospital room, moving slowly, but not in too much pain. Just glad to be alive.

Thank You, Lord.

She was brushing her teeth when she heard a nurse talking to Danielle. She turned off the water and pressed an ear to the door.

"Danielle, we have to discharge you today. We've let you stay an extra two days. Is there someone I can call to come pick you up?"

Martha held her breath and waited. No answer. The nurse started speaking again.

"Honey, are you sure you don't want to visit with that policeman who was here a few days ago? Are you sure you don't know who did this to you?"

Silence again. Martha scowled. That girl had to know who had done this to her. She listened as footsteps exited the room. She needed her butterfly clip from her small suitcase. Shuffling across the floor to her bag, she glanced up at Danielle. She was sitting up in bed, but staring at the floor. Martha had talked to her about God for almost three hours, and even told her some incredibly personal tales about her own faith journey, stories that would have made the average gal shed a tear or two. Not Danielle.

And when Martha had finished baring her heart in an effort for this lost soul to see the Lord for the hero He could be for her, Danielle had merely said, "Is that all you've got?"

Martha had fallen asleep in prayer, telling the Lord that she'd tried her best.

She located her clip and headed back to the bathroom. It took her longer than usual to secure her hair, since it hurt to lift her arms very high. She needed some help and wondered where Katie Ann and Arnold were. She thought they would have been here by now.

As she hadn't completely shut the bathroom door, she went to push it closed when she saw movement in the room. Peering through the tiny crack, she watched as Danielle tiptoed around Martha's bed. She kept watching as Danielle eased the drawer to the nightstand open. It didn't take her long to find Martha's wallet. Instinctively she opened her mouth to tell the little thief to step back, but she didn't.

Danielle had closed the drawer and was back in her bed in less than a minute, and Martha figured it wasn't the girl's first rodeo. She also figured Danielle probably needed the sixty dollars in Martha's wallet more than she did, but lies and thievery irritated Martha more than anything else. She wasn't sure how to handle this.

Once she finally had her hair semi-secure with the butterfly clip, she smoothed the wrinkles from her pink blouse. If she'd known Arnold was coming, she would have brought her matching pink earrings and necklace, but at the time Katie Ann was already scolding her for taking too much to the hospital.

She eased out of the bathroom and slowly lowered herself onto her bed. Now she just had to wait for Arnold and Katie Ann to get here. She gave Danielle an all-knowing smile, but the girl just sat on the edge of the bed, looking down at the floor.

"I heard you tell someone on the phone that you wouldn't be released for a few more days." Martha spoke firmly, tempted to tell Danielle that she was a thief *and* a liar. "But based on what I just heard the nurse say, that was a lie." She pointed her finger at Danielle and leaned forward. "You want to stay here in the hospital because it's *safe*. Right?"

Martha couldn't hold back. "Who did this to you, Danielle?"

Danielle put her head in her hands for a moment, but when she looked back up at Martha, her one functional eye was wild with anger. "Are you always this much in everybody's business?"

Martha sat taller, as tall as she could without putting pressure on her incision. "If I need to be."

"Well, you don't even know me, so stay out of my business."

"Suit yourself." Martha felt sick to her stomach. *Pay it forward. Do something nice for someone.* The nurse's words echoed in her head, but Martha figured she had done something nice. She was letting Danielle keep the sixty dollars she'd stolen from Martha's purse.

As the door swung wide, Martha turned to see Arnold and Katie Ann. "Katie Ann, please tell me that I'm going to a place where there will be creamed celery?"

Katie Ann kissed her on the cheek. "I have a fresh batch at home. I thought you might want to stay with me for a day or two until you're feeling better."

Martha didn't feel all that bad, but being catered to was not something she was going to turn down either. "I guess I'd better." She turned to Arnold. "So what are your plans?"

"I'm going to see that you get settled at Katie

Ann's, then I'll head home." He smiled. "To take care of some things. And pack."

Martha smiled.

"Yesterday I rented a small house." Arnold grinned. "Not too far from yours."

"My house is plenty big. You should have just picked you out a bedroom upstairs. I haven't even been up there in months. It'd be like having your own apartment." Martha braced herself for Katie Ann's rebuttal that was sure to come.

"Martha! That would have been totally inappropriate." Katie Ann raised her chin and glared at Martha, which only made Martha cackle.

"What? You worried about my reputation? At this age, Katie Ann?" She turned to Arnold. "Will we be having lasagna on Wednesdays, like we used to?"

Arnold moved toward Martha's suitcase and picked it up. "I sure hope so."

Martha pointed a finger at him. "Although something has changed since you've been gone, Arnold Becker."

His expression dropped. "What's that?"

"We used to go to your church in Alamosa, but since you've been gone, I've been worshipping with Katie Ann and her people." She glanced at Katie Ann. "I bet they'd let you come too."

Arnold smiled but didn't say anything.

Martha had enjoyed attending Mass with Arnold

before he left, but his lack of response about the matter made her wonder if he'd consider a change to the Amish way of worshipping, which she tended to prefer these days. Martha had disliked the backless benches at first, but mysteriously several highbacked chairs showed up on the worship wagon shortly after she'd complained. She didn't understand most of the service, but after the noon meal, Katie Ann would translate whatever Martha didn't understand, which usually led to a lengthy discussion that Martha always enjoyed. Plus, the meal after worship was always a good one. And if there was another bonus to attending Amish worship, it was the fact that you only had to go to church every other Sunday. Probably because it was three hours long, but Martha was glad to have every other Sunday "off," as she called it.

"We checked at the front desk," Arnold said. "And you are cleared to go."

Martha pulled her purse from the drawer in the nightstand.

Katie Ann picked up the quilt and asked, "Are you sure you have everything?"

Martha shot a slow and coy smile at Danielle. "Probably not, but oh well."

"Guess we're ready then." Katie Ann moved toward the door with Arnold as he carried Martha's suitcase.

Danielle had lain back down on her bed and was staring at the ceiling.

Martha looked at her long and hard and chose her words carefully. "Danielle, I wish you well."

Danielle turned to face Martha and blinked her one eye several times. "You too."

Martha turned to leave before the girl could see the tears welling in her eyes.

Please, Lord...help her to see the wonder of Your love.

Arnold closed the door behind them.

Arnold left on Thursday afternoon after having lunch with Katie Ann and Martha at Katie Ann's house, and by Friday afternoon, Katie Ann could tell that Martha was ready to go back to her own home. She said she was feeling better and had gotten what she called her "Jonas fix." And while Katie Ann loved having Martha stay with them, she was exhausted from tending to both her friend and her baby. She wasn't sure which one was more demanding.

Arnold had driven Martha's car to Katie Ann's, then taken a cab to the airport, promising that he would be back soon and for good.

"Are you sure you can drive?" Katie Ann helped Martha get into her coat, hat, and gloves. It was snowing and cold outside. "I think it might be too soon, and the weather—"

"Katie Ann, you know how I feel about that extra bed of yours. I can only take it for so long. Besides, I'm only going around the corner." She kissed Katie Ann on the cheek. "Tell my baby I will see him on Sunday. I'm going to stay home out of this weather and rest tomorrow."

"I think that's a *gut* idea." Katie Ann waited until Martha's car rounded the corner before she closed the door.

Lillian came over later that afternoon with Anna and Elizabeth, and Emily stopped by also, thinking that Martha was still there. After all her company left, Katie Ann settled in front of the fireplace with Jonas in her lap and reread Eli's letter. She missed his smile, his laughter. As the fire crackled in the fireplace and the wind gently howled outside, Katie Ann wondered what he was doing. If he missed her at all.

The next morning, she heard a truck coming up the driveway. She finished feeding Jonas, laid him in the playpen near the fireplace, and went to the window. A Federal Express man was making his way through the snow and up to her porch.

"Danki," she said as she accepted the small box.

"You're welcome." The young man with a black stocking cap and heavy coat chuckled. "It's a cell phone, in case you didn't know." He paused, rubbing his gloved hands together. "It's been ringing in the truck on and off for the past two hours."

Katie Ann didn't know what to say, and the nice young fellow didn't wait for a response before heading back to his truck. Katie Ann hadn't even closed the door when she heard the faint ring from inside the box. Smiling, she walked to the couch and hurriedly worked to open the package. Only one person she knew would send her a cell phone.

Saturday morning Martha eased into her recliner with a cup of coffee, her thoughts on Katie Ann. She was starting to lose hope for Eli Detweiler. Hard to have a romance when the fellow was in another state. But at least the two were writing to each other, so just maybe…

She noticed a pile of bills on her end table. There wasn't a task she hated more than paying bills. She had plenty of money, more than the average person by far, but it was just a tedious chore. The piles seemed to be screaming at her as she sipped her coffee, so she eventually pulled her purse into her lap and took out her wallet, which also held her checkbook. She thought about Danielle. She'd been praying for the girl every night. That she'd be safe from whoever did harm to her, and that she'd put her trust in the Lord.

Martha hoped Danielle wouldn't steal from anyone else. Some folks might not be as understanding about it as she'd been. She opened her wallet, pulled her pen from its spot, and wrote out a check to the gas company. Then she curiously unzipped the money compartment, wondering if Danielle had taken all sixty dollars.

Martha pulled three twenties from inside and sat holding them for a moment. *Why didn't she take it?* She began to inspect the contents of her wallet, confused. Something had to be missing. What was it?

There were no checks missing. The cash was there. A book of stamps, several business cards she'd collected from local vendors. She drummed her fingers on the end table, holding the wallet with her other hand. She flipped through her credit cards, found her driver's license, her AARP card, and even two extra bobby pins clipped next to her credit cards.

She took a deep breath. Maybe her mind was going. Everything seemed to be just as it should be.

By the time Katie Ann ripped open the box, the portable phone wasn't ringing anymore. She picked it up and searched through the packing for a note, but the only thing besides the phone was what appeared to be an extra battery. She jumped when the phone rang again. She'd used a cell phone on rare occasions before, so she knew how they worked. This one flipped open.

"Hello."

"Katie Ann! *Gut, gut.* You got the phone."

"Eli?" She knew exactly who it was, but she was at a loss for words, so she waited for him to explain.

"I got your letter about Martha yesterday. I went right out and had this phone shipped overnight to you. I charged the batteries at the store before I shipped it." He took a breath. "I realized that by the time you got my letters, then I got yours, well…too much time was passing. How is Martha?"

"*Ach*, she's *gut*. It turned out to be a very small cyst." She still couldn't believe he had sent her a phone.

Katie Ann gave Eli the details of the past few days, even explaining about Arnold.

"Katie Ann, it's so *gut* to hear your voice. And I couldn't have you running out to the barn in bad weather to talk on the phone." He paused. "Is this okay? I mean, the phone?"

"Lots of people have cell phones. Our bishop isn't keen on the idea, but he doesn't make much of a fuss. But the money, Eli…"

He laughed. "They have this thing called the family plan. Only ten dollars! So now we're family."

Something about his statement warmed Katie Ann from head to toe. "I see." She brought her hand to her chest, closed her eyes, and pictured his face.

"Katie Ann, I'm going to Jake and Laura Jane's for supper. I just wanted to make sure you got the phone."

"*Danki* for the phone, Eli. You didn't need to do that." Katie Ann wondered how often he would call her, and if she would ever call him. She knew it would be easy enough to charge the phone at Martha's house.

"Can I call you when I get home later?"

She smiled. "I'd like that."

After they hung up, Katie Ann warmed up some soup. As she sat on the couch eating it, she eyed the box in the corner of her living room. It was an indoor swing for Jonas that Lillian had given her as a gift recently. Lillian had told her that she used a swing when both Anna and Elizabeth were babies, and that it was a lifesaver. Samuel had offered to put it together, but her brother-in-law was so busy that Katie Ann assured him she could do the job.

It was later in the evening, once Jonas was settled, when she started to put the swing together. She searched for the right nuts and bolts to attach the legs of the swing. Even though she'd sorted the parts into piles, she was confused about the directions and frustrated. She jumped when the cell phone rang on the kitchen counter.

"*Wie bischt?*"

Katie Ann smiled when she heard Eli's voice. "I'm *gut*, but I'm having trouble putting a swing together for Jonas. How was your supper with Jake and Laura Jane?"

"Laura Jane invites me to supper when she

makes chicken and wafers, my favorite. What's the problem with the swing?"

"Too many nuts and bolts." She waited awhile for a response, but nothing. "Eli?"

Silence.

She pulled the phone away from her ear and realized the battery was dead. She picked up the extra battery Eli had sent but couldn't figure out where to install it. She tinkered with the phone, then opened the instruction book that had come in the box with the phone. After about fifteen frustrating minutes, she had the other battery installed.

Ten minutes later Eli called again. "Dead battery, no?"

His voice was light and cheerful, but Katie Ann was annoyed by her own inability to handle such simple functions in a timely manner. First the swing, now the phone.

"*Ya*. Sorry it took me so long. I had to get out the instruction book."

"I wish I was there to put that swing together for you. What about Samuel?"

"*Ach*, he offered, but I was sure it would be no problem." She sighed as she eased onto the couch and curled her feet beneath her. She pulled a small afghan onto her lap. "I'll finish it tomorrow."

From there, she and Eli settled into a comfortable conversation. He told her that he was not going to Indiana because of the weather, and had decided to go to Florida instead, but not until after Christmas. Katie Ann told him more about the pot holders she'd been quilting and a cookbook she was putting together.

"It keeps me busy late at night if I can't sleep." She leaned her head back against the couch, tired but knowing sleep wouldn't come anytime soon, and she would rather talk with Eli than sleep anyway. She smiled as she thought about what Lillian and Martha would think if they knew she was casually chatting on the phone with Eli.

"I have a hard time sleeping too." He paused. "I never used to have trouble sleeping. Do you think it's because we're getting old?" He chuckled.

"*Ya.* I guess so." Katie Ann pulled the phone from her ear for a moment, making sure it was still lit up. "How long will this battery last?"

"It should last a couple of days."

Katie Ann smiled.

And she spent the next several hours on the phone with Eli, discussing everything from his Florida plans to her desire to someday sell her handmade goods. Eli encouraged her and told her that she could do anything she wanted to do. Ivan had said that her efforts would produce little income and she'd be wasting her time. But finishing a handmade pot holder or throw quilt gave her a sense of satisfaction, like she was being fruitful.

And she was building up quite a collection. It might not ever amount to much, but it made her happy, and Eli's encouragement warmed her heart.

She didn't think she'd ever enjoyed a conversation more than this one, and during the weeks to follow, their phone calls became a nightly thing. Every couple of days she would charge the phone at Martha's house, even if it meant taking a few minutes of ribbing from her friend. Katie Ann found herself sharing even the smallest details about her day. And when Jake and Laura Jane's baby was born—Eli's seventh grandchild—Eli called her from the hospital, more excited than ever about the new blessing.

He truly was her best friend, and while she knew friends had the capacity to hurt one another, there was something safe about her relationship with Eli. And every time she fantasized about something more than friendship with him, she forced the idea away because she realized that God was answering her prayers—in His way.

"Ask, and it shall be given you; seek, and ye shall find; knock, and it shall be opened unto you."

Katie Ann asked God to forgive her for doubting Him and for the distance she'd put between them. She sought to trust again, and the Lord had opened a new door. It might not have been what she expected, but her friendship with Eli was proving to be a gift from God.

* * *

When Eli showed up on her doorstep two days before Christmas, Katie Ann jumped into his arms without hesitation.

"What are you doing here?" She pulled from the embrace and coaxed him inside and out of the icy weather. "Why didn't you tell me you were coming?"

Eli's smile stretched across his handsome face. "Because I just decided to come this morning—I flew! Besides, it was worth it to see you so surprised."

Katie Ann laughed aloud. "I can't believe you did this."

She'd already mailed him a hand-stitched black vest for Christmas, which he had received and told her fit perfectly. He'd sent her a parenting book that focused on the toddler years, later laughing and telling her to be prepared—that it was a wonderful time but could be challenging. And he'd sent a Bible storybook for Jonas.

Eli moved across the living room to where Jonas was tucked into his swing and sleeping soundly. "I had one of those swings for Maureen. She loved it." He gazed down at Jonas, then back at Katie Ann. "I have to go back tomorrow. *Mei kinner* would be mighty upset if I wasn't there for Christmas. But I just had to see you." He pulled her into a hug and kissed her on the cheek. Katie Ann made no effort to leave the safety of his strong arms.

Finally he eased away and gazed into her eyes. "You look beautiful."

She covered her eyes with her hands. "I do not."

Eli gently pulled her hands away. "Trust me, you do."

Trust. Not so long ago, the word would have stung, been a reminder of all she'd lost.

As their eyes stayed locked together, Katie Ann wished she knew what was going on in Eli's mind and in his heart. They'd gotten so close that under normal circumstances, it would have seemed normal for them to take the next step past friendship. But they both knew that they were not going to make that leap.

"Do Vera and Elam know you're here?" Katie Ann walked to Jonas's swing and cranked the handle so that the swing would keep going.

"They do now. I asked the cabdriver to stop by there on my way here." He laughed. "I had to make sure I had a place to stay tonight."

By now everyone knew that the two of them talked on a regular basis. But Katie Ann wondered what Vera must be thinking about Eli's spontaneous trip to Canaan—by plane, no less.

Eli gently eased Jonas out of the swing. Katie Ann would have reprimanded anyone else for waking him up like that, but as Eli held Jonas up and gazed into his eyes, it was a precious sight that she knew she would cherish.

"How is *mei* little man?" Eli talked in the familiar baby talk to Jonas, and Katie Ann knew that Eli's arrival was by far the best Christmas gift she'd ever received.

They sat on the couch talking and drinking hot tea until the early morning hours, then Eli kissed her tenderly on the mouth and went to Vera's, telling her that he would be leaving early in the morning to catch a plane back to Middlefield. Katie Ann still couldn't believe he'd made the trip. Just to see her. He'd even sought permission from his bishop to do so, since air travel was normally frowned upon unless it was an emergency.

"It was an emergency," Eli had told her earlier in the evening. Although he admitted that the bishop in his district didn't have a stiff rule against flying.

She held her tears until the door closed behind him. And for the first time, she admitted to herself—she was in love with Eli Detweiler. In love with a man who wasn't available.

Eli had plenty of time to think on the plane. He thought back to yesterday morning when he realized he had to see Katie Ann. It was an unfamiliar sensation that he knew wouldn't go away until he laid eyes on her. He admitted to himself at that moment that he had fallen in love with Katie Ann

Stoltzfus. And now that he'd spent more time with her, his feelings were confirmed.

He closed his eyes, the vision of her clouding his senses, blocking the roar of the engine and the light chatter around him. His heart ached, and for a few minutes he allowed himself to visualize a life with Katie Ann and Jonas. He was happiest when he was with her. But he'd made plans. And he'd had those plans a lot longer than he'd known her.

Fearing he'd taken too much of a risk with his heart—and possibly hers—he wondered if it might not be best to pull back some. She had to know they were in a dangerous place, to be as close as they were and not be able to move forward. Or maybe she was happy like this. Eli had thought it was the perfect arrangement. Best friends with a beautiful woman whom he was not responsible for.

Funny thing was—he felt as responsible for her and Jonas as he did any other member of his family.

He unzipped the backpack he'd carried onto the plane and pulled out a brochure about Florida, resolved that he would go there right after Christmas. He was going to need something to distract his heart, and what better way than to pursue the life he'd planned out. Flipping through the pages, he forced Katie Ann out of his mind.

Chapter Fourteen

Christmas came and went, and amid the festivities Katie Ann missed Eli more than ever. It was a blessing to be able to share her first Christmas with Jonas, but she found herself quietly weeping at times. Sometimes because she missed Eli, and other times…because she still missed Ivan. Not so much the man as the memories from their early years. But every time her thoughts drifted to Ivan, they quickly shifted back to Eli, and it was Eli she wished were there to witness all Jonas's firsts. At four months Jonas was making a new sound, a gurgle when he smiled, and Katie Ann thought it was the cutest thing she'd ever seen. Eli would love it.

Lucy had written to say that she'd given birth to a boy and named him Benjamin. He was born very tiny, but healthy. Katie Ann found it strange that Lucy would write to her at all, until she got to the end of the letter—the part where Lucy asked if she'd heard anything about the house she thought Ivan had built or bought. Katie Ann didn't write her back.

Eli still called her, but Katie Ann could feel him pulling back on the friendship. Perhaps he had sensed that Katie Ann cared about him more than just as a friend. Or maybe she just shouldn't have trusted her heart to any man. But each time that notion reared, she'd remember how she and Eli had defined the terms of their relationship early on. So was it really rational to blame him because she allowed herself to get too close?

Either way, Eli was in Florida. He'd left a week after Christmas, with plans to stay until he felt like going home. In the past two weeks, she'd only heard from him twice. In fairness, Katie Ann had his cell phone number, and she could have called him. During his first call, he'd described the beach to her and said that he wished he would have come during the summer, but how the temperatures were still much milder than in Ohio this time of year. He'd read three books, done some sightseeing, and eaten at some fine restaurants.

Katie Ann told him how her inventory of homemade items was growing and how she'd talked to several shops in Monte Vista about taking her things on consignment.

And Eli always asked about Jonas. And if Katie Ann needed anything.

She needed *him*. But she always said that she and Jonas were fine.

Tonight she was waiting for Martha to arrive for their Saturday night meal together. Arnold wouldn't be moving back to Canaan for another week. Martha promised Katie Ann that nothing would change, but Katie Ann knew some things would change, as they should. She hoped that Martha and Arnold would get married. But every time she mentioned it to Martha, her friend changed the subject.

"I'm so tired of this cold weather." Martha walked into the living room, handed a pan of chicken lasagna to Katie Ann, and peeled off her coat, hat, and gloves. After taking a deep breath, she hung her purse on the rack by the door and said, "Now, where's my baby?"

Katie Ann nodded toward Jonas's room. "He's already asleep, but go peek in on him if you'd like."

Martha rounded the corner, and Katie Ann could hear her talking softly. A few minutes later she came into the kitchen where Katie Ann was setting the table. She plopped down in a kitchen chair. "You know, I think I might be losing my mind."

Katie Ann grinned. "Why is that?"

"I'm forgetful." She scratched her head. "I mean, I'm forgetting where I put things."

Katie Ann put two glasses on the table and filled

them with tea. "That doesn't mean you're losing your mind."

Martha grunted. "Well, it sure feels like it." She leaned back in her chair and pointed to the chicken lasagna. "I was sure I bought a loaf of garlic bread to go with that lasagna, but I can't find it anywhere."

"No worries." Katie Ann put a loaf of her own homemade bread on the table. "I always have plenty of bread."

"That's not the point." She looked down at her hands. "I've also misplaced my jasmine vanilla lotion that I like so much."

Katie Ann took a seat across from Martha, and they both bowed their heads in silent prayer. Afterward, Martha scooped a large portion of lasagna onto her plate while Katie Ann helped herself to a piece of butter bread.

"I forget where I put things too." Katie Ann spread some rhubarb jam on her bread. "Especially my reading glasses."

Martha just shook her head as she chewed her food.

"Are you excited about Arnold moving into a house so close to yours?"

"Well, I'd be more excited if I could remember which day he was coming." She lifted her hands in the air. "See what I mean? He told me, but I can't remember. Something as important as that, and I can't remember if it's next Thursday or Friday." She took another bite and shook her head again.

"Just ask him again."

Martha twisted her mouth into a frown. "You haven't mentioned much about Eli lately. The two of you still writing letters?"

Katie Ann shrugged. They'd quit writing letters after Eli gave her the phone. "We talk on the phone, but he's in Florida right now."

Martha tapped her fork to the plate. "I just don't know what to think about the two of you."

"There's nothing to think about. I've told you over and over again…we're just friends."

"That man ever kissed you?" Martha glared at Katie Ann.

"Martha! That is not an appropriate question to ask." She avoided Martha's cool stare and focused on her plate.

"Well, you didn't deny it, so I'm assuming he has."

Katie Ann looked up to see Martha grinning. Katie Ann couldn't help grinning back.

"See, you're smiling. You've done some smooching, huh?"

Katie Ann stood up from the table and carried her plate to the sink. "I'm not discussing this with you."

Not only was it inappropriate to discuss such a thing with Martha, but Katie Ann had been training her mind not to think about those kisses with Eli. It was easier that way. Just then her cell phone rang on the kitchen counter. Katie Ann ignored it.

"Aren't you going to get that?"

Katie Ann started to run hot water in the kitchen sink, and although adrenaline shot through her body, she just shrugged. "No. I'm spending time with you."

Martha cackled. "Don't you dare let me interfere with your love life."

Katie Ann began to clear the dishes from the table. "I don't have a love life." She bit her bottom lip as she walked back to the sink. The phone rang again.

"Well, that's your fault."

Katie Ann spun around in time to see Martha raise her chin, so Katie Ann shot her a twisted smile. "Really? My fault?"

"Yep. That Eli would be a great catch, but you're afraid to let yourself be happy."

Martha huffed, and Katie Ann wanted to tell Martha she didn't know what she was talking about, but she was pretty sure she couldn't do that without crying. She kept her head down as she washed the dishes, hoping Martha would be quiet about it. Out of the corner of her eye, she saw her friend get up and put the jams in the refrigerator.

"Don't you think our little Jonas needs a father?

And what about you? You can't tell me you wouldn't like to have a man to help you out around here."

Katie Ann stayed quiet as Martha shuffled around the kitchen, clearing other items from the table.

"And if you're still mourning that husband of yours—"

"I'm not," Katie Ann interrupted as she slammed a rinsed dish into the drain rack.

"I'm just sayin' that you should give Eli a chance. That's all." Martha walked up beside her and started to dry the dishes.

Katie Ann kept her head down as she chewed on her bottom lip. *Please let it go, Martha.*

"And one more thing…" Martha placed a dried dish in the cabinet as Katie Ann braced herself. "Don't you let what that husband of yours did keep you from loving again, because—"

"Martha, stop it! I love Eli. I love him so much it hurts." Katie Ann covered her face with her hands as she cried.

A moment later Martha was rubbing her back, and they were both quiet for a while. Then Martha spoke softly. "Honey, why didn't you tell me this?"

Katie Ann turned to Martha, then fell into her arms and sobbed, letting go of all the emotion she had built up where Eli was concerned. "Because I can't have him…"

* * *

Eli hit End on the cell phone as he walked to the balcony of his fancy hotel, feeling a bit guilty about the luxury he'd allowed himself for this trip. As much as he'd looked forward to some time alone, the sightseeing, and a new place—it just wasn't all he'd imagined. He'd spent his life working the land, raising *kinner*, and always having someone to take care of. Had he thought of those things as burdens at the time?

He stared out at the ocean as the cool wind threatened to pull his hat off, and he thought about his life. When had he been the happiest? Not a full second passed before he knew. When he was working the land, raising *kinner*, and having someone to take care of. As he contemplated why he'd looked forward to this time in his life, he supposed it was because these things seemed appealing at a time when they were not within reach. Now he could do anything he wanted. And all he wanted to do was go home.

Three hours later he was on a plane back to Middlefield, with more time to think. The bishop had agreed to Eli's request to fly to Florida and back, just as he had agreed to let him go see Katie Ann. But now Eli wondered if he was abusing the bishop's leniency.

As the plane prepared to take off, his thoughts drifted to Katie Ann. He'd tried again to call her from the airport, but she hadn't answered. Maybe she wasn't home or near the phone. Or maybe she didn't want to talk to him. He hadn't called her much the past couple of weeks, and their conversations were shorter these days.

Eli had wondered if—even hoped that—distance and time would help him stop thinking about her so much. Maybe once he got home and things returned to normal, he would. He couldn't help but wonder if his children were right—that it just wasn't normal for an Amish man to travel and shirk responsibility. But even when he considered a new path, one that possibly included Katie Ann, he knew he could never leave his family in Middlefield. He had never been more than a few miles from his children until recently.

He leaned his head back against the seat, closed his eyes, and tried to sleep, but Katie Ann's face was all he could see. She was her most beautiful when she was tending to Jonas, but she was a nurturing person by nature. The tender way she handled Eli, both in conversation and in touch, calmed his mind and soothed his soul. As was his duty, he'd provided for his family, but he'd also been caregiver for the children for many years after Sarah died. A man should be strong and capable at all times, but with Katie Ann, he felt like he could let his guard down a little. And in return, he wanted to take care of her in every way.

Eli knew he couldn't leave his family. And it wasn't right to ask Katie Ann to leave the life she'd built in Canaan. And what about his plans to travel? What about loyalty to Sarah? His thoughts spiraled as they so often did recently. He just didn't see how it could work with Katie Ann.

But he wasn't sure he would ever stop thinking about her.

Katie Ann held Jonas in her arms until long after he was asleep, enjoying the comfort of the one constant in her life. Her baby boy, who filled her with a love more profound than anything she'd ever known. Even when she'd heard the cell phone ringing for the second time today, she'd just sat holding Jonas, hoping the noise wouldn't wake him. Of course it was Eli. But her heart was hurting, and she wanted to blame him for that. Rationally, it wasn't fair, but over the past couple of months, she'd grown to love him in a way that was confusing.

It was late when she finally put Jonas in his bed, and after a hot bath she crawled into her bed, snuffing out the lantern before she tucked herself in. Loneliness settled in, the way it always did this time of night. She regretted that she'd let her emotions get the best of her in front of Martha, but it had felt good to just cry in her arms. Now she didn't feel like she had any tears left, nor did she feel like she could sleep. It was probably fifteen minutes later when she heard the phone ringing on the kitchen counter. Twice she'd ignored Eli's calls, and for him to be calling this late at night now made her wonder if there was an emergency. She leaped from bed and stumbled in the dark to the kitchen. A haze of moonlight lit the kitchen enough for her to locate the phone, but it wasn't ringing anymore. She carried the phone back to the bedroom with her, crawled into bed, and kept it in her hand as she wondered whether or not she should call him back. After a few minutes, she dialed his number.

"I miss you," Eli said before even saying hello. "I miss you so much I can't stand it."

She'd been wrong to think she had no more tears left. Instantly her cheeks were wet as she responded. "I miss you too."

"I've been calling, and I…"

She could hear him take a deep breath.

"I'm back in Middlefield."

"What?" She tried to control the shakiness of her voice. "I thought you were going to stay in Florida longer."

"I was. But I just wanted to go home."

Katie Ann bit her bottom lip. "Oh."

There was an awkward silence for a few moments. "Katie Ann?"

The way he said her name caused her to hold her breath for a moment. *"Ya?"*

"What am I doing?"

"What do you mean?"

He waited a moment before he spoke. "I'm a middle-aged Amish man who dreamed for years about an independent life. And now…"

Katie Ann sat up in bed. "What is it, Eli?"

"Those dreams just don't seem important anymore."

One of the things that Katie Ann loved about Eli was his joyful spirit. She'd never heard him sound so sad. "What do you want?" She closed her eyes, fearful of his answer.

"I don't know."

Another tear spilled down her cheek. What had she been hoping for? That he would say he loved her and wanted a life with her? It was too much to wish for, and anger quickly started to replace the hurt she felt. "I'm sorry your trip didn't go as you'd planned."

She knew her words were clipped, and as she raised her chin in the darkness, she knew that she was going to have to distance herself from Eli. She'd thought she could be happy with her best friend, but she needed more, and Eli sounded like a lost puppy. He didn't know what he wanted, and in truth, Katie Ann wasn't sure what she wanted either. She'd opened her heart to him, trusted again, and now…

"My life is here in Ohio, not out running around like I'm *ab im kopp*."

She pulled the phone away for a moment, took a deep breath, and tried not to sound like a woman on the edge. "I don't think you're crazy, Eli."

"I feel like it."

Katie Ann knew what she'd signed on for, and she knew that a friend should offer a sympathetic ear, but just hearing Eli's voice made her long to be with him. "It's late, Eli. I'm sure you'll feel better tomorrow." She closed her eyes, knowing her own emotions were putting limitations on her ability to soothe Eli's troubled heart.

Silence, until Katie Ann finally asked, "Eli, are you still there?"

"Ya."

More silence followed.

"Katie Ann…" He paused. "Can I come visit you?"

She put her hand over her mouth for a moment to keep from gushing in an inappropriate way. After composing herself, she said, "That would be nice."

"I have to take care of some things here, but what about next week?"

"I'd like that."

After they hung up, her heart fluttered like that of a young girl. Any decision she'd previously made to distance herself from Eli seemed as far away as he was. She couldn't wait to see him.

* * *

Martha eased into her recliner late that evening, her heart heavy for Katie Ann. She should have known the girl's heart couldn't hold up to the boundaries she and Eli had set, and she wondered how Eli truly felt about her friend. She was tempted to find out, but Katie Ann would have her hide if she interfered in her business. Of course, Katie Ann had certainly interfered in Martha's business by calling Arnold. But Arnold would be coming home, and Martha was giddy as a schoolgirl about that. She sure wished Katie Ann's future looked brighter in the romance department.

She remembered the coffee cake she'd brought home from the bakery in Monte Vista yesterday. A slice of cake and some hot tea sounded like heaven right now. As she shuffled to the kitchen, she wondered if Arnold was going to ask her to marry him. Seemed the logical next step. She twisted her mouth back and forth, knowing she was mighty set in her ways. But she sure did love Arnold.

Scanning the countertop, she put her hands on her hips. *Where is that cake?* Finally she spotted it at the far end of the counter. She peeled back the foil and frowned. There was a large chunk missing that hadn't been missing before. She was sure of it. Or was she?

She scratched her head. *Is this what old age is like, Lord?*

She sliced herself a small piece and put it on a plate, then brewed a cup of tea. Once she was back in her recliner, she was wishing she had a nice fire in the fireplace, but that just seemed like too much work. She clicked on the television, put her feet on her ottoman, and savored the delicious coffee cake.

"Reruns. All reruns." She flipped between channels on the television, finally settling on an old John Wayne movie that was nearing the end. She had twenty good minutes of television before the movie ended, and after another round of channel changing, she turned the TV off. Too early to go to bed, but her eyes were heavy. Leaning her head back against the chair, she knew she needed to get to her bedroom before she fell asleep in the recliner. Suddenly, a noise upstairs caused her eyes to bolt open and sent a chill up her spine. She held her breath, trying to identify what she'd heard. Had something fallen over?

Her heart thumped, and she stared at the ceiling as her eyes followed the sound above her head. She recalled the time a squirrel had tried to take possession of her upstairs. She'd had to call David to come get the furry creature outside again. But this sounded larger. Maybe a raccoon. And she knew raccoons could be mean little fellows.

She eased out of her chair, quiet as a mouse, then tiptoed to the kitchen. Once she'd located the broom, she headed toward the stairs, armed and ready to meet her intruder. But when she flung the door open to her extra bedroom and flipped the light switch, she screamed at the top of her lungs.

And so did Danielle.

Chapter Fifteen

Martha edged forward with the bristly end of the broom, poised and ready to pounce. As she made a hissing noise, she pushed the broom within a few inches of the girl.

Danielle stepped backward until she was standing up against the dresser. "Stop it! Are you crazy?"

Martha didn't lower the broom. "With all due respect, missy...you are the one who has broken into my house, and..." She saw her favorite jasmine vanilla lotion on the top of the dresser...next to a half-eaten loaf of garlic bread. She narrowed her brows and scowled. "What are you doing up here?"

Danielle shifted her weight, and Martha noticed that both eyes were wide open and the stitches on her cheek were gone, leaving a red mark down the side of her face. Her bottom lip was still swollen on one side.

"If you'll just move that broom, I'll leave."

Martha raised her chin. "No. You answer the question. What are you doing up here?" Now Martha noticed a bag of Fritos, two of her colas, and three dirty dishes on the floor by the bed. "And exactly how long have you been here?"

"I—I don't know. Maybe a few days. Maybe longer."

Martha thought she might fall over. "So I've been sleeping in my bed downstairs while a thief has been living above me." She shook her head. "Unbelievable."

"I'm not a thief!" Danielle clenched her fists.

Martha nodded to the pile by the bed. "Oh, really. Then what do you call that? Were you gonna leave an IOU?"

"I'll pay you for it."

Martha lowered the broom and held it like a pitchfork by her side. "Fine." She held out her free hand, palm up. "Pay up."

"I—I'll have to go get the money and bring it back to you."

Martha laughed. "Sure you will." She walked to the bed and sat down atop the pine green bedspread she'd had since the sixties. She rubbed her forehead for a minute. "How'd you know where to find me?" She sat taller and frowned. "And *why* did you come here?"

Danielle shrugged. She was a petite little thing,

and leaning up against the dresser, her wounds still not completely healed, she didn't seem very threatening. But surely Martha deserved to know why the child had taken refuge in *her* upstairs.

"If you don't want me to call the cops, I suggest you start talking."

"I'll leave. I'm sorry." She edged toward the door.

"Danielle, wait." Martha stood up, and slowly Danielle turned around. "Are you hiding from someone? From whoever did that to you?"

"I gotta go."

Danielle rounded the corner, and without giving it much thought, Martha yelled the first thing that came to mind.

"You can stay if you want!"

Martha waited, and she heard the footsteps on the stairs stop. A moment later Danielle crept back over the threshold. "Why would you let me stay?"

"Why did you come here in the first place?" Martha had suddenly realized what was missing out of her wallet. An ID card that she carried, which listed her address.

Danielle shrugged, eyes to the floor. "I dunno."

"Sure you do. Something sent you my way."

She kicked at the corner of the doorway with her scuffed-up white tennis shoe. "I heard you say no one lived up here."

Martha fought the urge to make a smart remark. Instead she took a deep breath. "I'm going to bed.

It's late. I suggest you do the same." She pointed to the pile of dishes on the floor. "This is not how we do things around here. First thing in the morning, I expect to see this room cleaned up." She glared at her lotion on the dresser. "And my lotion back downstairs on the table by my recliner, where I've kept it for years."

She walked past Danielle, and was almost to the stairs when Danielle called her name. She turned around. "What?"

"Are you going downstairs to call the police?"

Martha pushed back a strand of hair that had fallen forward and sighed. "No, Danielle. I'm not. Now get some rest."

Good grief. Lord, what have You got in store for me now?

Wednesday afternoon the air was a bit chilly, but the sun was shining. Katie Ann bundled up Jonas and took him out to the barn with her, thinking he could use some fresh air. She had some leftover ham for Mrs. Dash, who'd left two more mice on the porch.

She eased into the barn and saw the cat curled up in a big ball in the corner on the quilt. She squatted down with Jonas. "She's going to have a *boppli*, Jonas. Probably several."

She reached into her pocket and pulled out a baggie half-filled with pieces of ham she'd torn into bite-sized pieces. Expecting the cat to bolt, she was surprised when Mrs. Dash just stared at her. And this time her ears weren't flattened to her head.

"Here you go, girl." She tossed some of the ham closer, then waited. "Mrs. Dash is learning to trust us, Jonas."

She nuzzled Jonas's nose with hers, and he made a strange cooing noise. Katie Ann waited for the cat to sprint around the corner. But instead, Mrs. Dash rose from her spot, arched her back in a stretch, and moved closer to the ham. Katie Ann didn't move. After a few moments, Mrs. Dash was within a foot of her, the closest the cat had ever come.

Katie Ann thought about all the prayers she'd said, asking God to help her trust His plan for her, whatever that might be. Figuring cats didn't pray, she silently prayed that God would take care of this big black cat and that she would deliver healthy little kittens.

And maybe you could send a Mr. Dash to help her.

It was a strange ending, and probably even odder to be praying for the cat, but her father had always said there was a place in heaven for animals.

She rose slowly, so as not to spook the cat. Once she was standing, Mrs. Dash looked up, but quickly lowered her face and finished off the ham. She hadn't even finished chewing her last bite when she went around the corner, but it was progress.

When she got back inside, Katie Ann put Jonas in his swing, which he enjoyed more all the time. She cranked the handle, then went to the kitchen to make sure she had everything she needed to cook supper for Eli that evening, and she tried to keep worry from her heart. She wanted to enjoy her time with him, and she was going to do everything she could to keep things in perspective and to see their relationship for what it was.

Her excitement about his coming overrode everything else. Even Martha's situation with her new houseguest. Martha still came by daily, and twice she'd brought Danielle. The teenager didn't say two words either time, and mostly sat on the couch fidgeting.

Katie Ann had asked Martha privately if she should be housing a child without the parents' permission, but Martha said they weren't very good parents if they had let something like this happen to their daughter. Katie Ann didn't know what to think. Arnold was due back tomorrow, and Katie Ann knew he'd keep an eye on the situation.

She heard a knock and looked at the clock, knowing it was much too early for Eli to arrive. When she opened the door, she saw Lillian.

"Come in out of the cold."

Her sister-in-law didn't take off her coat or bonnet, but instead handed Katie Ann a letter. "The postman brought this to our *haus* instead of here, so I signed for it. It's from Robert Dronberger. Isn't he a lawyer back in Lancaster County?"

Katie Ann took a deep breath. "*Ya.* I believe so. Do you want some tea?" She walked toward the living room.

Lillian followed, still in her winter gear. "Why is he sending you a certified letter?"

Katie Ann turned to face her. She knew exactly why Robert was sending her a certified letter. Most likely because she hadn't responded to his other three letters.

"I—I think he is handling some things." She took a deep breath. "Things for Ivan. I mean, things of Ivan's. I don't know." She shrugged. "I think I am the owner of anything that was Ivan's, since we were still married."

"Oh." Lillian bit her bottom lip and stared at Katie Ann for a moment. "Do you have to go to Lancaster County?"

Katie Ann thought about the past three letters since Ivan's death, all requesting her presence in Lancaster County. "I think so."

"When?"

"I don't know."

"Hmm…I wonder if you will have to go get anything of Ivan's from Lucy's house?"

Katie Ann folded her arms across her chest. "I

don't want anything of Ivan's. Besides, if you'll recall, Ivan left here with almost no money. Any money that he made while he was with Lucy, well, I suppose it should go to Lucy."

Just then Katie Ann had a horrible thought. What if there was money or a house or something that was tied up legally, something that should go to Lucy and her baby? She didn't want anything to do with Lucy, but if there was money that was rightfully Lucy's, Katie Ann didn't want to be the one holding things up. "I'll go soon."

"Well, uh…Ivan's been dead for, uh…"

"*Ya*, I know. Seven months." Katie Ann recalled the first letter, which had arrived about a month after Ivan's death. At the time she had scanned it, but knew she couldn't face a trip to Lancaster County. The second letter arrived a month after that, and the third had come last month. Each time she read the letters, she'd put them away…to deal with another time. Now time must have caught up with her.

"Eli is coming for a visit." She was anxious to change the subject, even though she knew her comment would spark questions from Lillian.

Her sister-in-law smiled. "*Gut* news. How long is he staying?"

"He told Vera he would be staying for a few days."

Lillian shook her head. "I don't know why he doesn't just pack up and move here." She grinned.

Katie Ann frowned. "Lillian, that's impossible. His family is there. And as you know, we are just—"

"*Ya, ya*...I know. Just friends. That's what you keep saying." Lillian sighed. "I have to run. Enjoy your supper." She winked at Katie Ann before she closed the door behind her.

Eli chatted with Vera, Elam, and Levi until he thought he might explode from politeness. All he wanted to do was get to Katie Ann's house. Betsy bounced in and out of the living room, usually with a book in her hand. She'd read for a while, then share something about what she'd read, then mosey back upstairs. January was generally slow for all Amish folks, so it wasn't surprising that Elam and Levi were inside with Vera and Betsy on this cold Wednesday afternoon.

"*Gut* to have you back for another visit." Vera handed him his second cup of coffee.

"*Danki*, Vera." He smiled.

"Stay as long as you like." Vera folded her hands in her lap from where she was sitting across the room from Eli. Then she asked about all of Eli's children, how he enjoyed Florida, and what he planned to plant this spring. But she must have caught him looking at the clock.

"I imagine Katie Ann has supper almost ready. You don't want to be late."

Eli looked at the clock again. It was only three thirty, too early for supper, but he was going to take his cue and go. He stood up, and Elam walked him to the door.

"I'll help you get the buggy hitched up." Elam pulled on a heavy coat and gloves.

Eli pulled his hat and coat from the rack by the door.

"*Danki*, Elam," Eli said once the buggy was ready. His cousin stroked his beard, clearly with something on his mind. "What is it, cousin?"

"I'm not sure there is anything more fragile than a widow's heart, Eli."

"Except maybe a widower's heart," Eli quickly responded. But he knew what Elam was saying. "Are you afraid I'm not doing right by Katie Ann?"

"I didn't say that. I'm just reminding you that she is fragile." He backed up a few steps, waved a gloved hand, and said, "Have a *gut* time."

Eli thought about what Elam had said as he drove through a flurry of snow to Katie Ann's house, and he wondered if being so close to Katie Ann was a good idea. But it wasn't like it was something he could control. He loved her, and he felt led to be here. Despite his own plans for his life, God seemed to have something else in mind. But even if he did trade in one dream for another, how could God expect him to leave his family to be with Katie Ann? It wasn't fair to ask her to leave the home she'd built in Canaan either. He'd have to go home at some point, and how would they both feel?

He shook his head, deciding not to worry about leaving her before he saw her. He parked the buggy, then made his way up the porch steps. She was opening the door just as he held up a hand to knock. He pulled the screen open and stepped across the threshold into the warmth of Katie Ann's home.

"It's *gut* to be here." His teeth were chattering as he pulled off his coat and hat.

Once they were hung on the rack, he pulled her into a hug, wishing he could stay in her arms for the rest of his life. He cupped her face in his hands and kissed her, the way a man kisses his wife, and as the passion built between them, Eli felt her trembling. He eased away and gazed into her beautiful brown eyes. "I—I…"

Eli wanted to say it so bad, tell her how he felt. But Elam's words rang in his ears. Katie Ann's husband hadn't been gone a year, and unless Eli was ready to leave his home in Ohio and be a husband to Katie Ann and father to Jonas, he knew that he would have to keep his feelings to himself. Anything else would be selfish and unfair.

"I know friends aren't supposed to kiss like that," he said after a moment. "But I missed you."

"I missed you too. Very much."

Her eyes twinkled as she spoke, and Eli felt torn between taking her in his arms again or running out the door. There was a struggle going on inside of him—between what he thought he wanted and what seemed to be playing out in his heart. And all the while a passion burned inside of him for Katie Ann that made it almost too much of a temptation for him to even be there.

Katie Ann smoothed the wrinkles in her black apron as she took a slow deep breath and wondered if her heart would ever stop pounding against her chest. She released the air in her lungs only after Eli had turned away and walked toward Jonas's play-pen in the living room. He eased his hand down and touched her sleeping baby on the head with a tenderness that Katie Ann could hardly bear.

A few minutes later Eli was stoking the fire and Katie Ann was brewing coffee. By the time they settled onto the couch and began talking, it was as though no time had passed. Once again, they ate supper on the couch in front of the fireplace, and Eli raved about Katie Ann's chicken and rice casserole. Eli told her all about his trip to Florida, but not with the excitement that she expected.

"I don't know. It was nice, I guess." He set his empty plate on the coffee table and took a sip of coffee. "I felt…" He sighed. "I felt guilty. So much luxury and things that just aren't necessary. You should have seen how many different kinds of soaps, shampoos, and lotions were in the bathroom at the hotel." He chuckled. "I did enjoy the television."

Katie Ann smiled, glad to hear the laughter back in his voice. "I don't think you should feel guilty, Eli." She wasn't completely sure how he should feel, since she'd never known an Amish man to travel.

He looked down, rubbed his forehead, then locked eyes with her. "It just wasn't as much fun as I'd always pictured it."

"I'll be taking a trip soon."

His ears perked up. "Really? Where?"

"Lancaster County. I have to handle some things for Ivan. A lawyer has sent me several letters."

"What about Jonas?" Eli narrowed his brows as he glanced toward the playpen. "Will you take him?"

Katie Ann shook her head. "*Ya*. He's not even five months old yet. I couldn't bear to leave him."

Eli squeezed her hand. "Do you want me to go with you, so you and Jonas don't have to travel alone?"

While she was touched, she also knew that she needed to do this on her own, find some closure with Ivan. She shook her head. "No. I've traveled by plane before. But *danki*."

"When will you go?"

"I'm waiting until after Arnold gets here. I'll feel better leaving Martha." She raised her brows. "You'll never believe what is going on at Martha's house." Katie Ann told Eli about Danielle and how Martha found her living upstairs.

"And she's still there?" Eli sounded as shocked as Katie Ann had been when she found out Martha was letting the teenager stay with her.

She laughed. "*Ya*, she is. And I'm not sure who is having a harder time of it. Martha is a bit"— she paused—"set in her ways. And Danielle is… how should I say this, since I don't know the girl well?" She sighed. "She's a bit…messy. Martha said she leaves plates in her room upstairs, throws her clothes down on the bathroom floor, and never offers to help clean anything up. And…" Katie Ann grinned. "Martha threatened to wash her mouth out with soap if she didn't clean up her language."

"Where are the girl's parents?"

"Danielle says her parents are dead, that she graduated school early while living in foster care, and that her boyfriend is the one who beat her up."

Eli shook his head. "That's terrible. How long will Martha let her stay there?"

"I don't know. Martha has a huge heart, so I suspect it could be awhile."

* * *

Martha put her hands on her hips and eyed Danielle as she stepped out of the dressing room. They were in a store Martha had never heard of. "You are out of your mind if you think I'm going to buy you that."

"Why? What's wrong with it?" Danielle faced off with her, mirroring Martha's stance.

Martha started to tell her that she looked like someone who should be standing on a street corner, but she decided a more tactful approach would be better. "You look like a tramp."

"What?" Danielle shifted her weight, which Martha was impressed with given the skintight pink leggings. "This is what everyone wears."

Martha pointed at the two inches of skin showing between Danielle's sprayed-on pants and matching pink crop top. "And that is not going to fly." She glanced around at the sales staff, most of whom were dressed similarly to Danielle, and shook her head.

"But I like this."

"I told you that if you were going to live with me, you have to get a job. What kind of reputable company would hire you dressed like that?"

"Well, I wouldn't be caught dead in what you're wearing."

Martha gasped, looking down at her red-and-white-checked pants outfit. One thing Martha knew for sure—she was a snappy dresser. She was at a loss for words.

"And why do you always wear that dumb butterfly clip in your hair?"

Martha's eyes rounded with rage as she reached up and touched the precious clip that she'd had since she was married to Herbert many moons ago. "This *clip*, my dear, will never go out of style."

"Whatever."

If that girl said *whatever* one more time, Martha thought she might snap. "I think we'd better try another store."

"Whatever."

Danielle marched back into the dressing room and slammed the door. Martha leaned her head back and looked up. *I have no idea what You want me to do with this girl, Lord, but help me keep my cool.*

Martha raised her chin, then glared at the clerk to her left. She shook her head, amazed that her mother would let her out of the house dressed like that. A few minutes later Danielle popped out of the dressing room. But instead of returning to the jeans and T-shirt that she'd had on, she tried on another outfit.

"What about this one?" Danielle raised her brows and stood taller, which only caused the tiny blue blouse to show even more of her tummy.

Martha shook her head, and Danielle stomped back into the dressing room. She couldn't wait until Arnold arrived tomorrow morning. Maybe he knew more about teenagers than she did.

Chapter Sixteen

Katie Ann was thankful for the four days she had
with Eli, even though her feelings were more unre-
solved than ever before. They had spent each day
together and into the evening. At night, Eli would
kiss her tenderly and go to Vera and Elam's house
to sleep. It had been magical.

But right now, Lillian was watching Jonas, and
Katie Ann's furry friend needed her help. Katie
Ann had witnessed enough calf births to know that
things were not going well for Mrs. Dash. As she
knelt down on the hay in the corner of the barn, she
stroked the cat's head and spoke softly. It was the
first time Mrs. Dash had let Katie Ann touch her,
and the animal's eyes were glassy, barely open.

"It's okay, girl. You can do this."

When the first kitten was born, Katie Ann
watched Mrs. Dash clean the animal, but Katie
Ann's stomach lurched when she realized that the

tiny creature wasn't breathing. Mrs. Dash worked to free the new baby of afterbirth, but when it was time to deliver the next one, she simply pushed it aside. Katie Ann tried massaging the small kitten's stomach, unsure what to do. Nothing. The second kitten and the third kitten, also lifeless. *No, no.*

When the fourth kitten, the smallest one of all, solid black like its mother, was born, Katie Ann watched Mrs. Dash work to clear the mucus from the animal's face. Katie Ann started to cry when this animal also lay lifeless before her. "I'm so sorry, girl. I'm so very sorry."

She stared into the cat's eyes, wondering if the pain of death was as horrible for an animal as it was for a human. If the tale were told through the eyes of Mrs. Dash, Katie Ann would have to say yes. The new mother nudged each of her babies over and over again. She cleaned them as their little bodies tumbled at her touch, as if she could bring them to life with love. Katie Ann prayed silently for all of them.

Even knowing she had to pick up Jonas from Lillian and catch a plane, she couldn't bring herself to leave. She didn't want to leave the cat—with all of this. She rubbed Mrs. Dash's head, and the cat leaned in toward Katie Ann, then looked up at her. Katie Ann rubbed her head as flashes of her sister lying still and lifeless in the crib shook her.

Then there was a movement. The tiny black

kitten moved. Or did it? Katie Ann picked up the little body and moved it closer to its mother. Mrs. Dash worked her tongue across the new baby, and seconds later the little one breathed in life. She watched for as long as she could without missing her plane. "Take care of your little one," she said as she gently touched the new mother on the head.

Mrs. Dash leaned her head back and found the top of Katie Ann's hand. Katie Ann stayed perfectly still as the cat's tongue, like sandpaper, swept across her hand in loving strokes of thanks.

Katie Ann sat on the plane headed toward Lancaster County with Jonas in her lap, her mind reeling with what-ifs.

Eli had told her that he would see her again soon, and he'd also invited her to visit him in Ohio. She'd declined, for the moment at least, knowing she had this trip to Lancaster County to make and unsure how she was going to feel when she returned. She was hoping to get her business taken care of in a couple of days, although she was looking forward to seeing Ivan's brother and two sisters, along with their families.

Arnold had arrived in Canaan before Katie Ann left, and Martha was busy helping him get settled in his new home. And Martha and Danielle were getting to know each other, and although Katie Ann couldn't imagine the two living together, Martha said she felt called to watch over the girl, at least for a while.

She'd tried to ignore the curious stares at the airport, and even now on the plane. Once she got back in Lancaster County, heavily populated with Amish folks, there wouldn't be as many curious sets of eyes. Katie Ann had flown twice before, both times for funerals. The bishop in Canaan frowned upon air travel, unless it was necessary. She found it curious how lenient Eli's bishop was about his travels.

As she laid her head back against the seat, she realized that Eli hadn't mentioned taking any more trips. She wondered what his home in Middlefield looked like and if she'd ever see it.

And she wondered when she would see him again.

Eli spent the days following his return from Canaan staying busy around his house. He'd made repairs to the fence in the far pasture, put a fresh coat of paint on the woodshed, cleaned the barn, and repaired the passenger door on his buggy.

Busy. He had to stay occupied to keep his mind off Katie Ann. He'd come mighty close to telling her how much he loved her more than once, especially when they parted ways this last time. But Katie Ann had much on her mind, and he knew it would be difficult for her to travel back to Lancaster County to settle her husband's affairs. So many times he'd wondered what kind of man would leave a woman like Katie Ann. He would spend the rest of his life loving her, given the chance. But he knew his children and grandchildren wouldn't hear of him leaving, and she had created a new life for herself in Canaan. He wondered if she would consider moving to Ohio.

Even though these thoughts filled Eli's mind, the plans he'd made for years kept bumping around in his head.

He carried a bucket of feed across the snow toward the barn. It was a dreary day, filled with gray clouds and the threat of more snow. He thought about Canaan and how the sun was always shining there, even after a hard snow, lighting the white peaks as if by rays from heaven. And something about the way the Sangre de Cristo and San Juan Mountains hugged the San Luis Valley in a protective embrace made him see why folks would want to live there. The Amish community in Canaan was small, but Katie Ann had told him that the population had more than doubled in the past year, with more and more folks migrating to the area for cheaper land and more room to spread out.

Eli was walking back to the house when he heard hooves padding up the driveway. He turned to see three buggies pulling in, the first of which he recognized as his oldest daughter's. Hannah's horse, Midnight, was a fine animal and easily recognizable with his tall steady gait and coat so black it looked almost midnight blue. Eli pushed back his black jacket and looped his thumbs beneath his suspenders.

Ida Mae was in the buggy with Hannah, and Karen and Frieda were in the next one. Bringing up the rear was his baby girl, Maureen. Whenever all his girls convened like this, something was afoot.

"Wie bischt," he said, greeting them as they made their way across the yard to the front porch, each one toting a casserole dish or bag. It wasn't unusual for his daughters to keep him supplied with casseroles and freshly baked goods, but they didn't make a habit of all arriving at the same time. "Dare I ask what brings all my lovely *dochders* here today?"

Hannah glanced at Ida Mae and shrugged as they brushed past him and toward the porch steps. "Just wanted to visit our *daed.*"

Sure you did.

He walked alongside his other daughters toward the house. Was Jake ever invited to these sessions, he wondered, or did his son just have enough *gut* sense to decline?

"I brought you a chicken and rice casserole," Maureen said as she placed a dish on Eli's kitchen table.

Flashbacks of eating the same casserole with Katie Ann on her couch played in his mind.

"And I made you some fresh granola, *Daed*." Karen put a Tupperware container next to the casserole.

His other three daughters all unloaded more food—chicken noodle soup that Frieda said could be frozen, two loaves of bread from Ida Mae, and a chocolate shoofly pie from Hannah.

"*Danki, danki*. I won't go hungry, no?" He smiled at all his girls, knowing something was coming.

Hannah must have been awarded the job of speaker. "*Daed*, *Aenti* Vera called, and…"

Eli shook his head. He loved his cousin's wife, but that woman could stir things up more than any female he'd ever known, except maybe for his own daughters. "And what did *Aenti* Vera have to share?" He eased into a kitchen chair, sighing as he waited.

Hannah sat down across from him. "*Daed*, she said you've become very close with Katie Ann." She glanced around the room at her sisters. "And we were just wondering if you are going to end up moving to Canaan."

Eli was smiling on the inside, even though he tried to stifle his joy in front of his girls. They *did* need him. He should have known they would be afraid that he would leave them to move to Colorado.

"No worries, *mei dochders*. I'm not going anywhere." Although the moment he said it, his heart sank. Confusing. He glanced at each of his girls. Also confusing. Each one of them was frowning. "What is wrong with all of you?"

Frieda and Karen sat down, too, and Karen spoke up. "We were just hoping you'd found true love." She batted her eyes a few times, and Eli wasn't sure what to say. "We want you to be happy, *Daed*. We thought maybe Katie Ann was the one."

"You want me to move?" Eli recalled how he'd raised each and every one of them. Now they didn't need him anymore?

"Of course we don't *want* you to move, but we don't want you staying, either…because of us." Karen reached over and touched his hand. "We all have husbands to take care of us now."

The statement hurt, but he forced a smile.

Maureen, the newest bride and still filled with romance, spoke next. "Do you love her, *Daed*?"

It was a conversation no Amish man should be having with his grown daughters, but he answered truthfully. "I love her very much."

"Yay!" Maureen jumped up and down, and all his girls laughed and clapped.

"We're so happy for you, *Daed*," Ida Mae said. "We didn't think you would really travel the world like you planned."

"I did," Eli mumbled, even though traveling didn't hold the allure it once did.

"Do you think Katie Ann and her son would consider moving here to Middlefield?" Maureen brought her hands to her chest.

Katie Ann had been through so much, and she seemed settled and happy in her new world. Eli envisioned a life with Katie Ann, surrounded by the mountains, sunshine most days, and—the baby. He would be Jonas's father if Katie Ann would have him. With his children's blessings all around him, he couldn't help but get excited about the possibility of being with Katie Ann and Jonas in Colorado. "I think we would be best to live in Canaan."

"We would miss you so much, *Daed*," Karen said. "But you've given to each and every one of us, over and over again. We will support any decision you make."

"*Danki*, girls." Eli narrowed his brows. "And what does your *bruder* think about this?"

"Jake agrees with us," Hannah said.

Eli rubbed his chin and wondered how hard it would be to be away from his children—and his grandchildren. Could he really do that?

But could he really live without Katie Ann?

Martha knocked on Arnold's front door.

"Why don't you use the key I gave you?" Arnold lifted one eyebrow as he stepped back so Martha could enter.

"Easier to knock." Truth was, it felt odd to walk

into Arnold's home unannounced. Rumors were flying that Arnold was going to propose. He'd been caught browsing among the rings at a jewelry store in Monte Vista. Vera told Martha she'd seen him when she was on her way to the post office, and from that point, everyone in the Amish community seemed to know. And that was okay. Martha didn't mind being the center of attention. But she wondered how Danielle fit into this scenario. Poor girl didn't have any parents, and her ex-boyfriend was certainly a thug. She couldn't turn her out on the street. While she couldn't say she was bonding with the girl, she did feel protective of her.

"How is it going with Danielle?" Arnold sat down on the couch while Martha sat down in Arnold's recliner. She loved the way he always insisted she sit in his favorite chair.

"Funny you should mention that." Martha squared her jaw and leaned her head forward a bit. "Do you know I think that girl could sleep fourteen hours a day if I didn't get her up? And, Arnold, you know I like my junk food, but she survives on it. She ate all my Fritos before I even had a one. And sodas… she'll drink them back-to-back all day long." Martha took a breath. "And she's a slob. Throws her clothes everywhere, leaves plates and food in her room, and her clothing…" Martha rolled her eyes. "And did I mention that she's lazy?"

Arnold chuckled. "Sounds exactly like most of the teenagers I've known."

"None of my Amish family has teenagers that act like that."

Arnold nodded. Martha knew that Arnold and his son had fallen on bad terms until shortly before Greg died. Arnold said he would be forever thankful that they mended their ways.

"Were you a part of Greg's life when he was a teenager?"

"Yes. I was. They are difficult years."

He shook his head, which made Martha wonder if he'd take on Danielle in the marriage proposal too. She wasn't about to ask.

"Where is Danielle at now—home?"

Martha sighed as she rolled her eyes. "Yes, I suppose her home is my home. And that's where she's at. I'm hoping she'll look for a job. Not that money is an issue. But I need her out of the house sometimes. She interrupts my schedule." She crossed her legs. "I have my certain shows that I like to watch on TV. I like to eat supper at exactly seven o'clock. And I don't like anyone else running bathwater at the same time I am. I lose water pressure."

"How long are you planning to let her stay?"

Ah. There was the question. Maybe Arnold was waiting to propose until he found out exactly how long she'd be housing the teenager.

Martha shrugged. "I have no idea."

* * *

Danielle kicked her feet up on Martha's ottoman while she stretched out in Martha's comfy chair. She was sure the woman would have a heart attack if she saw her sitting so smug in the worn-out recliner. After rubbing some jasmine vanilla lotion on her hands, she clicked the television on. For such a big house, this was the only TV, and Martha always controlled the remote. She flipped through the channels, but after a few minutes she hit the Off button. There wasn't anything good on this time of the afternoon, and besides…she couldn't concentrate.

It was only a matter of time before Martha found out she was lying, and then she'd throw her out for sure. And there was no way she was going back to her old life. She reached up and touched the scar on her cheek. The doctor said it would fade over time, but Danielle wasn't sure she'd ever really heal.

She replayed the scene in her mind, wondering what she'd done to provoke it. Closing her eyes, she could almost feel the blows to her face, particularly the curled fist with the chunky gold ring that caught her upper cheek and eye. She'd known when she smelled the whiskey and saw the staggering, she should have run. As she'd done more than once before.

She glanced around Martha's house. The woman annoyed her to no end with her rules about house-cleaning and eating at a certain time, and she had zero sense of fashion—evidenced not only by her own bizarre clothing, but also by her house décor. Danielle looked at the picture of the owls hanging above an outdated red and gold couch and shook her head.

But Danielle liked being here better than any other place on Earth. It was the only place she'd ever felt safe. So even if she wanted to yank that ridiculous butterfly clip from Martha's scraggly hair sometimes…or just for once have the remote control, eat in her bed upstairs, or not be restricted about when she could bathe—some things were worth forgoing. And one thing Danielle knew for sure. Martha would never hit her. She could just tell.

The woman was crabby and a nuisance, but Danielle hoped she wouldn't send her away.

She jumped when someone knocked at the door, then panic set in. She figured she would spend the rest of her days here worrying that she'd been found. It was bound to happen sooner or later, but when she peeked around the curtain in the living room, she saw a buggy and a horse, so she knew it was one of those Amish people coming to visit Martha. They were as strange as Martha, dressed in their funky clothes and living in houses with no electricity. She'd never seen an Amish person until some of them visited Martha in the hospital.

She'd also gone with Martha to Katie Ann's house a couple of times. Danielle couldn't believe they lived like that.

"Martha's not here," she said when she opened the front door. Then she studied the figure before her. If ever there was a hot Amish guy, he was standing in front of her in his black pants, black coat, and one of those funky black hats.

"That's okay. Can you give her this?" He held up a brown paper bag, but Danielle was still summing him up. He reminded her of some of the hockey players back home—tall and athletic, although he wasn't missing any teeth.

"Sure," she finally said as she accepted the bag.

"I'm Levi Detweiler." Mr. Handsome extended his hand, and Danielle slowly latched on. "My mom is a friend of Martha's, and she asked me to bring her this rhubarb jam. I think Martha goes into withdrawal or something if she runs out." He almost smiled. One side of his mouth curved up, but it was brief.

"You wanna come in?" Danielle paused. "I mean, Martha will probably be back soon, if you want to wait."

He grimaced a little. "Is anyone else here?"

Danielle felt her heart skip a beat. Why would he ask that? Would he hurt her in some way if she said no one was home? "Uh, no. But I just remembered Martha will be back *any* minute."

"I gotta go. Nice to meet you."

Danielle watched him leave. He was intriguing, almost in a creepy sort of way. He had those weird clothes that soft voice, and his mouth was crooked in a way that made it hard to tell if he was smiling or angry. But she didn't think she'd ever seen a hotter-looking guy.

"Levi's the quiet one," Martha said as she plopped a bag of groceries on the table. "A fine fellow. His brother, Jacob, got married about a year ago, and his sister Emily just got married this past November. I guess Levi's still looking for his someone special." She pulled a frozen pizza out of the bag, along with some Fritos and a six-pack of soda, and put them all on the table. "We're splurging on junk food tonight, but don't get used to it, missy. I just don't feel like cooking."

"I'll be his someone special," Danielle said as she pulled the bag of Fritos open. "He's hot."

Martha put her hands on her hips. "That is no way for a nice girl to talk, Danielle."

Danielle chuckled. "You're kidding me, right? Just yesterday I heard you say the mailman had nice buns."

"Are you familiar with the expression 'Do as I say and not as I do'?" She reached up and tightened her butterfly clip.

"Well, the Amish guy sure was cute. Levi. I

asked him to come in, but he got kinda weird about it. Then I thought maybe he might be dangerous or something."

Martha cackled. "Dangerous? Levi? Uh, no. He didn't come in the house while you were here alone because it wouldn't be proper."

"I think Amish people are weird."

Martha pointed a crooked finger at her. "There will be no talk like that in this house. There's no finer group of folks."

Danielle shrugged. "Whatever."

Martha stared at her for a moment, then shook her head. "I'm going to heat this pizza. Now would be a good time to shower if you want."

Danielle started to argue that she'd prefer to take a shower closer to bedtime, but the woman had bought pizza, Fritos, and soda for dinner, so she'd go along with her on this. "Okay." She crossed through the living room toward the stairs, then turned around. "Martha?"

"What?"

Danielle waited until she turned around. "Thanks for letting me stay."

Martha rolled her eyes. "Whatever."

Danielle grinned as she headed up the stairs.

Martha waited until the oven heated up before she popped in the frozen supreme pizza. Arnold was going to the gym in town this evening, something he'd started doing twice a week. He said it helped his arthritis. She'd made it pretty clear that she had no plans to join him in that particular activity. Exercise made her nauseous. Besides, she was hoping maybe she and Danielle could chat a little. It bothered Martha that Danielle had no interest in God. Only once since their stay in the hospital had Martha broached the subject, and the girl turned red and marched upstairs. Danielle seemed angry with God. A few years ago Martha would have let it go. But when Arnold, Emily, and David opened her heart to the Lord, her life had changed. She wanted that for Danielle too.

But one thing she was learning about teenagers—if they think you want them to do something, they will do the exact opposite. So Martha knew she needed to approach the subject carefully. She smiled, recalling how she had to find the Lord in her own time, knowing that everything ultimately happens on God's timetable.

She'd just shoved a handful of Fritos into her mouth when she heard a car pull up. No one she recognized, and from the looks of it…no one she knew. A woman dressed in tan slacks and a dark brown coat held her hand in front of her face to block the light snow flurries. Martha had the door open by the time she was about to knock.

She was an attractive woman, midthirties, Martha guessed. She wasn't smiling.

"Are you Martha Dobbs?"

Martha gave her a critical squint. "Who wants to know?"

"I'm—I'm looking for someone. I think she might be here. My name's Vivian Kent."

Martha raised her chin and eyeballed the woman for a moment. "Who ya looking for?"

Vivian pulled a photograph from her purse. "Have you seen this girl?"

Martha stared at the picture of Danielle. "Who are you to her?"

"I'm her mother."

Chapter Seventeen

Martha pulled the door wide. "Come in. Yes, Danielle is here." She wasn't sure what she was most upset about, the fact that the woman might have her arrested for harboring a runaway, or that Danielle had lied to her. "Danielle said her parents were dead."

Vivian folded her hands in front of her and sighed. "I'm not surprised. We've had a lot of trouble with Danielle."

Martha could believe that. The girl was willful.

"She's upstairs taking a shower. She should be down in a minute."

Martha felt a wave of relief. Apparently she hadn't been called by the Lord to straighten out young Danielle. And she wouldn't have to worry about her and Arnold taking on parental roles at their ages. What a mess that would have been.

"Can I get you a soda? Some tea?"

Vivian sat down. In Martha's recliner. Martha fought the urge to ask her to move.

"No, I'm fine. How long has Danielle been here?"

"Oh, a week or two." Martha scowled. "How long has she been missing?"

"Since the hospital. We traveled here from Wisconsin to visit a friend, and then Danielle ended up in the hospital." Vivian hung her head and sighed. "When I couldn't find her, I eventually had to go home."

"Did you call the police, report her missing?" Martha was sitting on the edge of the couch, hands folded in her lap, wondering how Vivian could have left the state not knowing where her daughter was.

"I—I couldn't really call the police. Danielle's been in trouble with the police before."

"Why does that matter? Someone beat the life out of her." Martha leaned forward. "Who did that to her?"

Vivian swiped at her eye. "I don't know. I went out with friends, and when I got back to our hotel room, she—she…" The woman folded an arm across her stomach as she looked at the floor.

Martha wasn't sure what to say, but trouble or no trouble, someone should have called the law.

Vivian straightened. "I'm sorry. I'm so sorry that Danielle showed up here and bothered you."

"She's no bother," Martha said. "How did you

find me, anyway? I mean, I know how Danielle found me. She took an identification card out of my wallet. I was her roommate in the hospital. Hey—I don't remember seeing you at the hospital."

"I was there." Vivian smiled.

Really? "I never saw you."

Vivian fumbled with a button on her coat. "You—you were sleeping."

"Oh." Martha was thinking that if it had been Katie Ann in that predicament, she'd have never left her side. But she sighed, knowing that everyone wasn't so thoughtful.

"And Danielle eventually called a friend of hers back home and told her where she was. The friend's mother knew how frantic I was, so she phoned me right away." Vivian dabbed at her eyes. "All I knew was that Danielle was here in Canaan. I've been asking around and showing her picture for two days, and finally someone recognized her—an Amish girl named Beth Ann said she was staying here."

Martha nodded, then pointed to Vivian's ring, a big gold thing on her right ring finger. There was a time when Martha used to adore big, clunky jewelry. "Nice ring."

"Thanks. It was a gift."

Martha stood up when she heard footsteps heading down the stairs. So did Vivian.

"You've got company, Danielle," Martha said,

ready for her lying houseguest to go. *What kind of kid says her parents are dead?* She shook her head.

"Hi, Dani."

Vivian didn't run up to Danielle as Martha expected, and Danielle turned pale as a ghost, her feet rooted to the floor at the bottom of the staircase.

"Hi, Mom."

"Get whatever things you have here and let's go. You've inconvenienced Martha enough." Vivian readjusted her purse on her shoulder. "Be quick."

Danielle turned around and ran upstairs.

"She really wasn't any trouble." Martha edged toward Vivian. "I sure hope you can find out who did that to her, and prosecute that"—she took a deep breath—"…person."

Danielle was back, carrying a plastic bag, which Martha assumed contained the two changes of clothes Danielle had brought with her, plus the four outfits that Martha had purchased for her, ones they'd finally agreed on, plus some undergarments.

"Good luck to you, Danielle." Martha lifted her chin, feeling unappreciated, but still relieved. *The unruly teenager lies and breaks into people's homes.*

"Thanks for the clothes." Danielle's eyes were locked with Martha's as she blinked back tears. The girl had to be worried about the trouble she was in for running away, but surely Vivian would let it all go, after everything the child had been through.

"I forgot to ask. Where's your dad, Danielle?"

"He died. About six years ago." Vivian bit her bottom lip, then smiled. "So it's just been Danielle and me since then."

"Oh." Martha walked them to the door.

Vivian reached into her purse and pulled out her wallet. "I'd like to pay you for any expense or trouble you went to."

Martha waved a hand in the air. "No, no. Just get Danielle home where she can finish recovering. I still hope you find whoever did this."

Vivian tucked her wallet back in her purse and smiled. "I just want to get Danielle home."

"Bye, Danielle." Martha held the door open for them, but Danielle didn't look at her. As Martha closed the door, she sighed, then watched them through the window, until a chill ran up and down her spine. There was something about the way Vivian was manhandling Danielle to the car. Martha's stomach seized up, a pang in her gut that something wasn't right.

As she watched Vivian dragging Danielle by her arm, the girl stumbled, but Vivian just kept pulling her toward the car.

Martha flung the door wide and stepped onto the porch. "Vivian, you wait just a minute! Do you hear me?" Martha marched down the snowy porch steps, certain that she could take on Vivian if it came to that.

* * *

It was after ten o'clock when Katie Ann heard the cell phone ringing. She'd talked to Eli earlier in the evening, but it was a short conversation, and once again…she felt like Eli was pulling back. She knew he had feelings for her, and maybe it was just getting too hard for him to keep saying good-bye. Katie Ann felt the same way.

But it was Martha's name flashing across the display screen. She quickly flipped open the phone, hoping Jonas wouldn't wake up. She'd just gotten him settled in a playpen next to the bed.

"Is everything okay?" She sat up in the extra bedroom at her sister-in-law's house. Mary Ellen, Abe, and their children were already asleep.

"Everything is fine. I guess."

Martha told Katie Ann a bizarre story about her day. In the darkness Katie Ann listened quietly, her heart breaking for poor Danielle. "You think her mother did that to her?"

"She won't say, but I think so. She wouldn't eat any supper, and she's been up in the extra bedroom for most of the night. I keep checking on her, though. She's not her smarty-pants self, which kinda worries me."

"She's still there? For how long?" Katie Ann wasn't sure she understood all this.

"I have no idea. When I walked outside and told

them to wait, I looked at Danielle and asked her if she wanted to stay. Vivian tried to argue, but I told her to shut her mouth. Danielle ran to me."

"*Ach*, Martha. That's horrible. Poor Danielle. But what are you going to do now? Call the police? Report Vivian?"

"I don't know. I'm going to give her some time. If her own mother did this to her, don't you think she might be kinda messed up?"

"I'm sure of it."

"How are things going there?"

"I meet with the lawyer tomorrow morning at ten o'clock. It's been nice visiting with friends and family, and they love spending time with Jonas."

"Well, I miss my baby."

"I know. And he misses you too."

"I hear Danielle coming downstairs," Martha said in a whisper. "I'll call you tomorrow and see how the lawyer went. I love you, sweetie."

"I love you too."

Katie Ann lay back down and closed her eyes. Being back in Lancaster County had felt so familiar. Now that Ivan was gone, everyone kept asking her if she would move back to Paradise, and she was considering it. She'd left Lancaster County for a fresh start with Ivan, which didn't work out the way she'd planned. Maybe another fresh start was in order.

* * *

The next morning she had breakfast with Mary Ellen's family, and Mary Ellen convinced her to leave Jonas while Katie Ann went to meet the lawyer. She didn't want to be away from her baby, but she knew he would be better off with Mary Ellen, as opposed to going into the city. Mary Ellen had arranged for a driver to pick her up and take her to Robert Dronberger's office.

It was almost ten o'clock when she arrived, and within a few minutes a woman ushered her down a hallway to an office at the end of the hall.

The lawyer rose from behind a large oak desk and extended his hand. "So nice to see you, Katie Ann. It's been a long time." He pointed to two tan chairs in front of his desk. "Have a seat, please."

Katie Ann sat down, her heart thudding against her chest. She'd been dreading this visit, a summary of recent events that she didn't care to revisit.

"I'm so sorry about Ivan." Robert put on a pair of reading glasses and thumbed through a thick file folder on his desk, keeping his eyes down. "As you'll recall, you and Ivan came in here before you moved to Colorado and had a will prepared." He looked up at Katie Ann. "Everything that Ivan owned belongs to you."

"How can that be? He was living with—with another woman." She hung her head. No matter how much time had passed, humiliation still soared through her.

"That's just the way the law works." He sat back in his chair, pulled off his reading glasses, and rubbed his chin. "You are still legally his wife."

Katie Ann knew that prior to his death she hadn't really been his wife for a long time. "There are papers for me to sign, no?" She folded her hands in her lap and hoped this wouldn't take long. She'd asked the driver to wait for her.

"Yes, I have paperwork for you to sign, but I need to explain a few things to you." He sighed. "Whatever money Ivan had, Lucy has now. They had a joint account, which Lucy has closed, so I'm afraid there aren't any liquid assets. But Ivan's personal belongings technically belong to you."

Katie Ann shook her head. "No. I don't want any of it. Lucy can have it all, whatever there is."

Robert stared at her for a few moments. "Katie Ann, there is a house involved. Ivan invested all of his money to build a house about ten miles outside of Bird-in-Hand. He'd hired a builder, and they'd just finished the home a week before he died."

Katie Ann fought the tremble in her voice. "I do not want any house that Ivan was building for him and Lucy to live in."

"I understand. But you can sell the home."

She shook her head, knowing she should have

settled all this way before now. "No. Give the house to Lucy."

Robert shifted his weight in the high-back chair, rubbed his forehead, and locked eyes with Katie Ann. "I went to the house, Katie Ann. I think you should go look at it before you make that decision."

Again she shook her head. "I am not in a position of financial need. Ivan was living with Lucy, so she should have the house."

Katie Ann had realized right away that this would solve Lucy's money problems. It wasn't at the top of her priority list to help Lucy, but there was a child involved. Ivan's child.

"Katie Ann, there's something else." Robert sighed. "There's a mortgage owed on the house. In addition to the cash Ivan put into the house, he also took out a mortgage. Lucy will need to keep up with the payments, which are already behind since we had these legal issues to work out."

"But Lucy can't afford to…" She stopped, knowing it was not her place to air Lucy's business.

"Ivan was optimistic about his business expansion, and he built a fine home." Robert paused. "I think you should go and see the house before you make any decisions. Legally, it's yours."

In a self-destructive way, she couldn't help but be curious about the kind of house that Ivan would build for him and Lucy to spend the rest of their lives in. Were there rooms for children? Did it have an extra-large fireplace, the kind Ivan had always wanted? Was there room for a garden? How big was the kitchen?

One thing she knew for sure. She was not going to make mortgage payments on a house that Lucy would live in. "All right," she finally said.

Robert gave her the address after offering to drive her to the house, but Katie Ann declined. She'd rather be alone when she saw it. If she sold the house, she would give the profits to Lucy. It might not be much, but Lucy deserved whatever money Ivan had earned while they were together.

It was a forty-minute drive from Lancaster to Bird-in-Hand. As they drove down Lincoln Highway through Paradise, Katie Ann glanced at the bakery on her left, the location of her first coffee date with Ivan. To her right was the street that led to Noah's clinic. They passed Black Horse Road, the street she and Ivan had lived on. So many memories. And most of them good. She wondered if moving back to Paradise would be a good move for her. As much as she loved Colorado, the rolling hills of Lancaster County beckoned to her.

She'd been guilty of picturing a life with Eli in Colorado, a fantasy that often made her regret ever meeting him. And he'd seemed distant since his last visit. It was hard having to keep saying good-bye to him. But could she really say good-bye to Martha,

Lillian, Samuel, David, Emily, and all her friends in Colorado?

A few minutes later they passed the sign that read Bird-in-Hand.

When the driver pulled to a stop in the driveway, she recognized the white clapboard house with black shutters surrounded by a white picket fence, and instantly bitterness stabbed at her heart. She'd always wanted a house like this, high on a hill overlooking the valley.

She asked the driver to wait, and she slowly walked up the cobblestone path, then unlocked the door with the key Robert had given her. As she eased into the living room, the smell of fresh white paint hit her, and shiny new wooden floors met with the sun's rays as she slowly walked to the middle of the room.

There wasn't any furniture in the room except for a small desk and wooden chair next to a very large fireplace. Ivan's desk. He'd had the piece of furniture since Katie Ann had known him, a gift from his father when he was just a boy.

She could see a large and welcoming kitchen through a doorway to the right, and again she fought the bitterness in her soul. She'd always wanted a kitchen like this. She ran her hand gingerly along the white countertop. Peering out the window, she saw a nice spot for a garden, then forced herself to see how many bedrooms were in the one-story house.

The master bedroom was roomy and filled with windows. Farther down the hall were three more bedrooms. She grabbed her chest when she walked into the last bedroom on the right and struggled to stay on her feet. There, in that room, was everything she'd ever envisioned for a nursery. A beautiful crib up against the wall, filled with blankets and two stuffed bunnies. And a changing table, dresser, and baby carrier were also in the room. She couldn't stop the tears from coming. Ivan died before he knew that Lucy was pregnant, but they were clearly planning on a family.

She thought about how Jonas would never know his father. Lucy's baby would never know Ivan either. Her heart ached as she eyed the room, feeling a level of pain for Lucy she didn't expect. Lucy didn't even know about the house. It was a surprise for her, and as much as it hurt Katie Ann to witness Ivan's plans for his future with Lucy, she wondered if Lucy's loss was as great as hers had been. Maybe greater.

Swiping at her eyes, she walked into all the rooms several more times, knowing that she would have to tell Lucy about the house, about the nursery. Or maybe she'd ask Robert to do it. Lucy could make arrangements to pick up the baby furniture for Benjamin. And Ivan's desk.

She walked to the wooden chair and sat down, leaning on her elbows and supporting her head with her hands. After a few moments she lifted her head. And that's when she saw the envelope addressed to her in Ivan's handwriting. Picking it up, she feared Ivan's last words to her and the level of hurt she'd endure reading anything he'd written to her. But she slid her finger beneath the seam and pulled out a piece of white paper.

> *Dear Katie Ann,*
> *I hope that this letter finds you well. I wanted to talk to you in person and hope to do so soon, but the distance between us, both physically and emotionally, has made me choose to write you this letter instead.*
> *I know you're pregnant, and my heart jumps with joy about this.*

She gasped as she slapped a hand to her chest, clamping her eyes shut. She took a deep breath and went on.

> *In a community our size, I was bound to find out that you are with child, but I can understand why you would be fearful about telling me, scared I would return out of obligation. I know you so well. But before I found out this news, I was already praying that we could find our way*

*back to each other. I think of you, dream of you,
and my regrets are many.*

*My heart longs to be with you...and our child.
I want us to be a family again.*

Katie Ann sobbed so hard, she was having trouble reading. She dabbed at her eyes and went on.

*I hired help to build a house outside of Bird-in-
Hand, and it is my dream for you and our child
to live there with me, if you can ever find a
way to forgive me. I have shamed you, shamed
myself, and shamed God.*

*Please, Katie Ann. I want to make things
right for you...and the baby. I have always loved
you and continue to love you.*
In His name,
Your husband, Ivan

She put her head down on the desk and cried until she was sure there were no more tears. Lucy's words hung in the air like a thick fog that was choking her. *"I always wondered if he was going back to you."*

"How could you do this to me, Ivan!" she cried when she finally raised her head. Dangling the letter by her side, she got up and walked to what might have been Jonas's room. She leaned against the wall, but the gravity of this news caused her to slide down until she was sitting on the cold wooden floors. She looked around the room and realized what she hadn't noticed until now—no electrical outlets or lighting fixtures.

She stayed on the floor for the next hour, her legs extended in front of her, the letter in her lap. In a daze, she tried to sort out feelings that had nothing to do with Eli, yet it was his face that kept flashing into her mind.

What would she have done if Ivan hadn't died? Would she have received this letter months ago and reunited with him? Would she be living in this house now? A house he'd built for her—behind Lucy's back.

She thought about Lucy and Benjamin. Would Ivan still have left Lucy once he found out that Lucy was carrying his child? Did Ivan suddenly long for a family and either woman would do?

Then it hit her. Ivan was doing to Lucy the same thing that he'd done to her. He might be a man full of surprises, but this house wasn't just a surprise for Katie Ann—it represented betrayal. Again. This time he would slither away from Lucy, just as he'd done to Katie Ann, leaving her without any money or future to look forward to. He might not have taken money for himself, but he'd certainly left her in a bad financial way. Just as he had planned to do to Lucy. He was a selfish man, but Katie Ann still wondered whether or not her love for him would have been enough to open her heart to him again.

After only a short while, she decided not. She stood up, took a final look around, and knew exactly what she was going to do.

She asked the driver to take her back to Robert's office. He was busy with someone else when she arrived, but after about thirty minutes, she was escorted back to his office. She didn't sit down.

"I would like to pay off the mortgage on the house." She raised her chin, determined not to cry.

"Really?" Robert scratched his chin. "So you're planning to move back to Lancaster County?"

She fumbled with Ivan's letter in the pocket of her apron. "No. I would like the house deeded to Lucy."

Robert stood up and walked around his desk. "Katie Ann, are you sure?" He paused, brows narrowed.

"Lucy has a baby now. Ivan's child. And Ivan probably would have left her and the child the same way he left me."

"You're being very generous."

Katie Ann didn't feel generous. In addition to wanting to do the right thing on Ivan's behalf— since Ivan had earned all the money for the house while with Lucy—she was hoping to never hear from the woman again, to finally have closure on all this.

But then she recalled the way Lucy was at Ivan's funeral months ago and the way she was when she came to Katie Ann's house, still stricken with grief.

"He built the house with money he made while he was with Lucy. It only seems fair that she should have it."

"It doesn't seem fair—to you." Robert folded his arms across his chest. "There's a considerable amount of money owed on that mortgage. I'm not sure why you would do this, but all right."

"Thank you."

"I'll let Lucy know what you've done, and—"

"No. Please don't."

Robert locked eyes with her. "Don't you think it's odd that Ivan would build a house without any electrical outlets or fixtures?" He rubbed his chin. "Everything is fueled with gas or propane too." Robert paused again, the hint of a smile in his expression. "Certainly resembles a lot of Amish homes I've seen. And Ivan wasn't Amish anymore."

Katie Ann pulled her eyes from his and shrugged. "Do you think you can make arrangements to have the electricity hooked up before you make mention of this to Lucy? I don't want her to have any doubt in her mind that Ivan built the house for her."

There was no reason for Lucy ever to know the betrayal that Ivan had planned for her. And as for Katie Ann, she just wanted to go home. To Colorado. Her life here was behind her. Now she just wondered what God had in store for her future. But one thing was for certain. There was no room in her heart for more heartbreak.

As she walked out of Robert's building toward the driver's car, she wadded up Ivan's letter and tossed it into a nearby trash can.

Good-bye, Ivan.

Now she just needed to say good-bye to Eli.

Chapter Eighteen

Eli sat down at the kitchen table with the package that had arrived in the mail. He stared at it, knowing what it was, but not wanting to admit that his friendship with Katie Ann was over.

Finally he forced himself to open the box and unwrap the cell phone. She hadn't been back in Colorado for twenty-four hours when she called to tell him that she was sending the phone back. Eli wasn't sure what happened in Lancaster County. Maybe she was still grieving for her husband, and being back there made her feel like she was betraying Ivan by being friends with Eli.

But who were they fooling? Katie Ann knew that they were much more than friends, just as Eli did. He had tried to talk her out of sending the phone back, but she was insistent that it was a luxury she shouldn't have. When he asked to visit her, she declined.

Over the next few weeks, he left several messages on the barn phone. She never called him back. He stayed busy planting the fields, but as the seasons began to change, Eli's feelings began to change too. His hurt turned to resentment. Before Katie Ann, he'd been a happy fellow with his entire life planned out. Now he was lonely and bitter. He didn't even want to travel anymore. He missed her so much he could hardly stand it.

It was the first of April when all his daughters once again came to see him. He was out on the plow when he saw their buggies pulling in. He was tempted to stay right where he was, but his strong-willed daughters would only wait him out.

As he walked across the fields, he pulled off his hat and wiped sweat from his brow. Four of his six grandchildren scurried about in the yard among their mothers, and Eli smiled, feeling angry at himself for his bitterness about Katie Ann. He knew that he was blessed more than most men. He'd loved two women with all his heart, and he had a wonderful family and these beautiful grandchildren. He told himself that he would enjoy the Lord's blessings, and he would joyfully endure another intervention from his daughters. Wondering what it would be this time, he recalled the girls' many attempts to cheer him up over the past month. There had been several conversations about Katie Ann. His daughters were convinced he should travel to Canaan and tell her how he felt.

But it was Jake who convinced him otherwise. "If she wanted to be with you, *Daed*, wouldn't she be?" he'd said.

As he got closer, he hesitated for a moment. Jake was sitting on the porch. All of his children were here, and by their expressions, Eli knew this wasn't just a social call or a planned visit to boost his spirits.

Katie Ann added another pot holder to her pile. Her days were long, spent tending to Jonas and working on her handmade items. Turning out lap quilts, pot holders, and knitted items kept her hands busy, if not always her mind. So often her thoughts would drift to Eli, but in her effort to guard her heart, she focused on being a good mother to Jonas and on more tangible goals that had nothing to do with Eli.

Vera paid a visit to Katie Ann every time she heard from him. Katie Ann looked forward to hearing what Eli was doing and how he was, although that same evening she would usually cry herself to sleep. The past two weeks had been better, though, because someone else's love life was the focus of everyone's attention. Martha and Arnold were getting married the first of May.

She smiled as Jonas pulled himself up in the playpen; she couldn't believe he was seven months old already. An April breeze filled the house with the scent of spring, and Katie Ann was looking forward to Martha coming for supper, the way she always did on Saturday night. Katie Ann had said repeatedly that Martha should bring Arnold, but Martha always said this night was reserved for just the girls, which now included Danielle. The teenager was always pleasant, but a bit guarded. Martha said she was just the opposite at home, always rambling on about something. But apparently "Amish folks" made Danielle nervous.

Danielle had finally talked to Martha about her mother, a troubled woman with a drinking problem. Evidently that was not the first time her mother had hit her, but it was the worst. Katie Ann couldn't believe they had not heard one word from the woman since the day she left Danielle there.

And Danielle was a handful for Martha. Twice Martha had awakened during the night to find that Danielle wasn't home. She'd gone for a walk—or so she said. Then there was the loud music, the need for a cell phone, arguments about clothes. And Danielle still didn't have a job, something Martha insisted upon when she agreed to let her stay.

"Where's my baby?" Martha said when she arrived later that afternoon. She handed Katie Ann the casserole dish she was carrying before she marched to the playpen, leaned down, and smothered Jonas with kisses. "Oh, and by the way, I didn't cook that. There was a woman in Monte Vista selling tamales out of a little shack. There was a long line, so I figured they must be good."

Jonas raised his arms, always excited to see Granny, as Martha was now calling herself.

Katie Ann nodded. She'd never had tamales before, but she knew there was a big Latino influence in the area, and she was eager to try something new. "Where's Danielle?" she asked as she peeled back the foil and breathed in the scent of pork and spicy seasonings.

Martha stood up, put her hands on her hips, and huffed. "You know that girl is as smart as a whip. Graduated from high school early before she ended up on my doorstep. But I'm not always sure her choices are as smart. She seemed to think that going to the movies with Angie was more important than our girls' night out."

"Who is Angie?"

"A girl she met in town when I sent her shopping for me. And Angie has a *car.*" Martha rolled her eyes. "I wish she could get friendly with some of the Amish young people around here. I'd feel a lot better. Her new friend's nose is pierced, for goodness' sake." Martha threw her hands in the air. "What kind of girl pierces her nose?" She plopped down on the couch. "And I've told Danielle that she needs a job before we kill each other."

Katie Ann smiled. "You care for her a lot, no?"

"I guess," Martha said with a pout. "But I wouldn't want to have three or four more just like her."

"Tell me about the wedding. Is everything ready?" Katie Ann sat down beside her.

"Everything is ready except for confirmation from Bishop Esh. I visit him regularly, even though I'm not Amish. I figure he can bless our union and stand right up there next to Father Jim, who I also visit often, even though I'm not a Catholic."

Katie Ann grinned every time she pictured Bishop Esh standing next to the priest from Arnold's church—both presiding over a wedding that was neither Amish nor Catholic. She didn't think their bishop from Lancaster County, Bishop Ebersol, ever would have done such a thing, but Bishop Esh was a bit more liberal.

Katie Ann used to think that maybe Martha was considering conversion to their faith, but Arnold was a devout Catholic, so that seemed unlikely now. Martha had a good relationship with both the bishop and the priest. She said it didn't matter what religion you were as long as you were fully committed to the Lord.

"Someone's here," Martha said as she sat taller. "It's a buggy. I can hear it coming up the driveway."

"It's Vera." Katie Ann peered out the window, surprised that Vera was coming so close to the supper hour.

A few minutes later Vera walked into Katie Ann's living room. Her expression was strained, and she didn't even bother with polite small talk or come more than a few feet into the room. "I'm sorry to come this time of the evening, Katie Ann, but I got a phone call from Eli a while ago."

"What is it, Vera?" Martha asked.

"It's his daughter Hannah, his oldest girl. She had the cancer awhile back, and they just found out it's back." She hung her head, then looked back up. "I thought you'd want to know, Katie Ann."

"*Ya, ya. Danki*, Vera." Katie Ann touched her on the arm. "Do you want to stay?"

"No. I have to get home and feed everyone, but I just wanted you to know."

Katie Ann swallowed back the lump in her throat. She forced a smile.

Vera wasn't even around the corner in her buggy when Martha reached into her purse and handed Katie Ann her cell phone. She took it, walked outside, and sat down on the porch step. She dialed his number, and he answered on the first ring.

"Eli?" She hoped she had dialed correctly. It had been so long since she'd heard his voice, she wasn't sure it was Eli who answered.

"Katie Ann?"

"*Ya*, it's me. I—I just wanted to call and tell you how sorry I am to hear about Hannah. I'm so very sorry." She struggled not to cry, knowing how hard this must be for him.

"*Danki*, Katie Ann. The doctor said they caught it early, so we are very hopeful. How are you? It's *gut* to hear your voice."

It took everything in her power not to break down and tell him how much she missed him, but now was not the time. "It's *gut* to hear your voice too." She sat taller and took a deep breath. "Please tell me if there is anything that I can do for you or your family. I will be praying for all of you."

"I pray for you and Jonas every night. I miss you, Katie Ann." His voice was soft and sounded so sad.

She felt a tear roll down her cheek. "I pray for you too." She covered her eyes with one hand.

"Do you miss me?"

"I—I don't think this is—is the time to be…" Her voice cracked as she trailed off.

"It is the time, Katie Ann. I need…I need my friend more than ever right now."

A faucet of tears trailed down her cheeks. "I will always be your friend, Eli. Always."

"Really? Because it hasn't felt like that."

She could hear the anger in his voice, and while part of her wanted to lash out at him for breaking her heart in the first place, she knew his pain was great, and she wasn't going to do anything to add to it. "I'm sorry, Eli. It was just—just getting too hard."

There was silence, and Katie Ann assumed that Eli knew exactly what she was talking about. "Long-distance relationships." He let out a light-hearted chuckle. "Hard work, no?"

She was glad to hear his voice a bit brighter. "*Ya*. Hard work."

They stayed on the phone for another thirty minutes, not saying much, but not wanting to hang up either. Katie Ann offered to pray quietly with Eli before they said good-bye, and as was always the case, she cried for quite a while after they hung up.

"That's just terrible," Martha said about the call, shaking her head as they ate supper later.

Katie Ann placed some peas and ham on Jonas's high chair tray, having decided the tamales were too spicy for him. "*Ya*. It is." Despite her resolve, she was starting to cry again.

"Honey, I don't know why you don't tell that man how you feel about him."

"I'm not going to push him into a life he didn't plan for, Martha."

"Vera said Eli hasn't traveled anywhere. If that was the life he wanted, then why isn't he living it?"

"I don't know, but I'm not going back to how things were. Being so far away from each other was too hard." She shook her head.

"Well, I say life is too short."

Katie Ann was quiet. She didn't know what else to say.

Over the next couple of weeks, Katie Ann slipped into a comfortable routine. After she had Jonas in bed, she'd go out to the barn and call Eli.

After their first conversation about Hannah, he'd asked her to call him the next night, and at the end of each call, Eli would make the same request, for her to please call the following night. She carried the baby monitor to the barn so she could hear if Jonas woke up. Both she and Eli avoided any more mention about their own relationship, and in some ways, it was like old times. Hannah had a good prognosis, and the doctors had removed the small lump in her breast and anticipated a full recovery without Hannah needing to have chemotherapy or radiation. Eli returned to his old self, laughing and being positive.

Katie Ann had to admit, she was happier talking to him than she was not talking to him. Twice he'd mentioned seeing her, but she sidestepped the idea. Besides, he couldn't leave his family right now, and Katie Ann was much too busy keeping Martha on an even keel with the wedding only a week away. But there was a huge part of her that longed to feel his lips against hers, the feel of his arms around her. So much so that she was almost willing to endure another good-bye just to have him hold her one more time.

Martha sat on the edge of her bed eyeing her wedding dress on a hanger across the room. It was a beautiful ivory-colored gown that the lady at the bridal boutique said was tasteful and elegant. Danielle said it looked like an old lady dress, so Martha reminded her that she was an old lady. Martha and Danielle were starting to adjust to each other's ways, but she worried how Arnold would fit into their routine. In a week, they would vow to love each other forever, and he would move into her house, since his was only a rental. She loved that man with all her heart, but she was having some prewedding jitters on this Tuesday afternoon when Danielle knocked on her door.

"Come in."

Danielle walked in, her long blond hair in a ponytail and wearing her usual blue jeans and a T-shirt. "I have some news for you."

Martha crossed herself and looked up. "Please, Lord, let it be good news."

Danielle smiled. "I got a job."

Martha crossed herself again, brought her hands together in prayer, and looked up again. "Thank You, God."

"I'm going to be a waitress at the Mountain View Restaurant in Monte Vista."

Martha smiled. "That's a nice place. They have the best burgers on the planet."

Danielle tucked her chin as she raised an eyebrow. Martha knew what was coming next.

"I'll be working at night, and you'd have to take me there, and I know you don't like to drive at night, so…" She raised her shoulders, then let them fall slowly.

"Yeah, I knew this would be coming. You want a car."

Danielle sat down beside Martha on the bed. "It seems weird to say that. I mean, you're not my mom or anything. And you've already done so much for me."

It wasn't often that Danielle acknowledged Martha's generosity, so it always touched Martha when she did. "Still no word from your mother?"

"No." Danielle stared off into space the way she usually did at the mention of her mother.

They were quiet for a while, then Danielle turned to face Martha. "You're not going to wear that butterfly clip in your hair when you get married, are you?"

Martha frowned, twisting to face her. "Yes, I am. It matches my dress perfectly."

"I don't think so. It's pink." Danielle shook her head, smiling, but she stopped and tipped her head to one side. "Do you think it's okay with Arnold that I'm living here?"

"You two seem to get along well." Martha grinned. "And he knew we were a package deal."

"Arnold *gets* me. He's a good guy." She reached up and pulled her hair tight within the ponytail. "You don't *get* me sometimes."

Martha glared at her, but Danielle just chuckled and did the unexpected. She reached over and hugged Martha. At first Martha just sat there. After a moment, she put her arms around Danielle and they held each other for a while.

"I guess I'll go take a bath." Danielle eased away and started toward the door. Then she laughed. "I wonder when Arnold's allocated bath time will be."

The sound of the girl's laughter warmed Martha's heart, so she decided to ignore her reference to Martha's most-reasonable rules. "I'll tell you what…" Martha reached up and tightened her butterfly clip as Danielle turned around at the doorway. "I have a deal to make with you."

"Really?" She eyed Martha, squinting one eye. "And what's that?"

"You go to worship with me every other week, and I'll buy you a car."

"To that *Amish* church?" Her eyes grew round. *You'd think I just asked her to make a deal with the devil himself.*

"Yes, to that Amish church." She pointed a finger at Danielle. "It's either my church people, or you can go to church with Arnold, but he goes every Sunday, and they don't have food afterward."

"But his church is only an hour long. You're gone like half the day when you go to the Amish church."

"Well, Arnold's church is almost thirty minutes away. So let's see…thirty minutes there, thirty minutes back, an hour for Mass, no meal, gotta go every Sunday…"

"Fine! I'll go with you." She folded her arms across her chest. "That doesn't mean I'll change my mind about God. Besides, you said it's mostly in German anyway. I won't even understand anything."

"The Lord has a way of getting through to us when it counts." Martha smiled, glad she remembered some German from her college days to combine with the Lord's efforts.

"What kind of car?"

Martha cackled. "An old clunker, just like I had for my first car."

"What?"

"Take it or leave it."

Danielle sighed. "Fine. I'll take it."

Martha smiled as Danielle headed out the door and down the hall. The three of them were going to be a family.

Now she just had to figure out what to do about Katie Ann, who would always be like her daughter—but the girl deserved happiness. The kind of happiness that comes from a family who

lives together under the same roof—loving, argu-
ing, and growing together.

Hmm… She could feel the wheels spinning in
her head.

Chapter Nineteen

Katie Ann didn't think God could have blessed Martha and Arnold with a better day to get married.

Their wedding was a conglomeration of compromises. Arnold thought they should get married indoors, and Martha wanted an outdoor wedding. Arnold wanted a small gathering, just family and closest friends. Martha wanted to invite every single person she knew.

"It's not like I get dressed up like this every day," she'd told Katie Ann. "Seems everyone I know should see me at my best."

Arnold wanted the priest to preside over the entire ceremony. Martha insisted the job be shared with Bishop Esh, who had agreed with some reluctance. Katie Ann figured the bishop went along with Martha's request because Martha was as close to being Amish as any *Englischer* they'd all ever known—with regard to her faith only. Her flashy ways hadn't diminished in the least.

Martha's husband-to-be didn't see the need for attendants, but Martha was clear about having Katie Ann by her side. Arnold wanted an evening wedding, but Martha said it would be an all-day affair beginning at eight o'clock in the morning.

"That way we get two meals out of the deal," she'd said. "Like the Amish."

In the end Martha won out on every detail, and Arnold had just smiled. "Whatever my Martha wants," he'd said.

Emily and David offered to host the wedding. They'd recently moved into their new home, and they said they wanted to do this for Martha and Arnold. Martha had played matchmaker between them, and they both wanted to do something special for her. The newlyweds lived on property that Samuel and Lillian had given to their son, and the spacious house was high on a hill with the Sangre de Cristo Mountains to the east and the San Juan Mountains to the west.

Katie Ann tethered her horse amid the other buggies and cars. They'd invited over a hundred people. She took Jonas from his car seat and gazed across the field dotted with the occasional burst of color from the earliest of the wildflowers, an orange glow lingering behind the mountains. Not far into the field, white chairs were lined up on either side of a white runner that led up to an archway that David had built for the occasion. Martha had asked David to walk her down the aisle, and Bishop Esh had agreed to Martha's request.

Katie Ann moved toward the house, and the smell of *roascht* filled her nostrils. That was another tradition Martha wanted for her special day. The chicken and stuffing were always served at Amish weddings. People were scurrying about, and Katie Ann spoke to those she passed as she made her way into the kitchen.

It was nearing eight o'clock when everyone gathered outside for the wedding. Emily took Jonas, and Katie Ann stayed behind, as did David. Martha didn't want Arnold to see her before the wedding, so she'd been hiding upstairs in Emily and David's bedroom. Katie Ann walked upstairs to get her.

"It's time, Martha." Katie Ann walked toward her, surprised to see Martha's hands trembling. Katie Ann picked up the bouquet of flowers on the bed and handed them to her friend. "Here you go."

Martha took the flowers, bit her bottom lip, and blinked a few times. "Katie Ann..." She let out a deep breath. "I don't know why the good Lord saw fit to bless me with Arnold this late in life, but I feel like the luckiest woman in the world. Do you think I deserve all this?"

Katie Ann swallowed hard, thinking Martha had never looked more beautiful, or more vulnerable.

She touched her on the arm. "You deserve all this and more, Martha. And you look beautiful."

Martha reached up and touched the butterfly clip. "Danielle said this doesn't match, but I don't go anywhere without it. What do you think?"

"I think it's lovely."

Martha held the flowers with one hand and reached for Katie Ann's hand with the other. "The wonder of the Lord's love is an amazing thing, isn't it?"

"*Ya*. It is." Katie Ann blinked back tears.

Martha cleared her lungs of the breath she'd been holding. "Well then…let's get this show on the road."

Once they were downstairs, Katie Ann gave Martha a final hug and told David to watch for their cue from their spot on the front porch. Then she went and found her place on the front row. As was customary for Amish weddings, the men were on one side, the women on the other, even though here folks were facing forward instead of toward each other. It was the strangest setup for a wedding that Katie Ann had ever seen. She smiled, knowing she wouldn't have expected anything less from Martha.

Katie Ann's own marriage to Ivan flashed in her mind and, refusing to let anything put a damper on this day, she was able to recall her wedding day with fondness. She'd been so in love. It was a shame that over the years so many bad memories had stamped out many of the good ones.

Then she thought of Eli. They'd continued to talk every night until the past two. Katie Ann had called from the barn phone, but there hadn't been an answer either night. When they talked in the evenings, the conversations ranged from light-hearted to intense, especially when things like Hannah's cancer came up. But they steered clear of any talk about their relationship. Eli ended each call with, "Sleep with the angels," and Katie Ann said the same to him.

Someone Katie Ann didn't know, a woman about her age, was in charge of the music, and Katie Ann watched her get up from her place on the back row and walk a few steps to a CD player. She pushed a button, and as Martha had instructed a hundred times, Katie Ann rose and went to stand beside Bishop Esh, then motioned for David to walk Martha across the field to the white runner.

Bishop Esh had agreed to recite some prayers at the wedding, but he'd drawn the line when it came to officiating the ceremony. Katie Ann was shocked that he'd agreed to as much as he had already. She turned her eyes to Martha as she and David stood ready to walk down the makeshift aisle, then she scanned the crowd for Jonas, expecting him to be in Emily's lap. When she didn't see Jonas, her heart pounded and her eyes started going row to row until she spotted him. In Eli's lap near the back. *Eli's* lap?

When their eyes locked, he smiled and lifted Jonas's arm like he was waving to Katie Ann. As if the sight of Eli didn't warm her heart enough, the vision of him holding her son filled her with so much joy she went weak in the knees. Why hadn't anyone told her Eli was coming? She bit her lip to keep from grinning, and she forced her eyes back to Martha, who glided down the aisle with the dignity of someone entitled, her chin raised slightly, bowing her head to the attendees on either side. Any other behavior simply wouldn't have been Martha, Katie Ann surmised as she struggled to keep her grin from growing to a large smile.

What a wonderful day this is.

Most of the ceremony seemed to Katie Ann to be Catholic, but then occasionally Bishop Esh would interject prayers. The ceremony seemed to fit both Martha and Arnold perfectly. It was shorter than an Amish wedding. Arnold and Martha took their vows after the Catholic folks took Communion, about forty-five minutes into the ceremony. As Martha had instructed, Katie Ann stood up and joined Martha at the front. As Arnold and Martha vowed to love, honor, and cherish each other for the rest of their lives, Katie Ann's eyes involuntarily drifted to Eli. He was still holding Jonas on his lap, and his gaze met hers. Then his mouth silently formed words, but Katie Ann could make them out quite clearly. *I love you.* She held her breath for a moment, then forced herself to release it for fear she might pass out.

She pulled her eyes away and focused on Martha, who was now crying buckets. She kept her attention on the new couple. Next thing she knew, Martha and Arnold were walking back down the aisle and everyone was clapping. She looked at Eli, and this time he just smiled, his eyes bright, and he was standing with Jonas on his hip. She didn't know an Amish man alive who would tend to a youngster during a wedding, or any other time for that matter. She watched as everyone made their way across the grass toward the tents set up in the front yard. A dozen women were already setting out food. She watched Eli hand Jonas to Emily as she walked by. Katie Ann's feet were rooted to the ground beneath her. A few minutes later, everyone was in the front yard, and Eli and Katie Ann stood alone. She knew he wouldn't kiss her with so many eyes nearby, but she'd never wanted anything more in her life. He hugged her, though, then just eased away and stared at her.

As the sun warmed her cheeks and the smells of spring swirled around them, Eli took her hand in his and squeezed, smiling tenderly. "I love you, Katie Ann." He shook his head and looked down for a moment, then back up at her. "I've wanted to tell you that a hundred times. I love you." He gazed into her eyes, and she could feel the sincerity behind his words. Letting him go this time would surely leave her with little room to ever recover, but she knew that she had to tell him what was in her heart.

"I love you too, Eli."

"I know." Then he chuckled, and Katie Ann smiled, filled with love, but so many questions. "We have a predicament." He kept hold of one of her hands tightly, as if he feared she might flee. He stroked his beard. "I can't leave my family."

Tiny cracks in her heart spread like vines, but she knew this was coming. "I know," she said softly, knowing he was going to ask her to leave Canaan, a place that had become home. And her family was here. She lowered her head and waited.

Martha moved through the crowd, making sure that every person here had an opportunity to hug her, but if anyone thought she wasn't watching the events around her—they were wrong. Everyone had gathered outside after the meal, and she'd already spotted Danielle and Levi underneath the big oak tree on the west side of the house. The two young people were deep in conversation, and Martha was thrilled. But when she saw Vera standing a few feet away from what Martha hoped was a blossoming new friendship, Vera stood with her mouth turned down and her arms folded across her chest, pretending to listen to Lillian but staring at Danielle and her son.

Hmm... Martha had wanted nothing more than for Danielle to find some nice Amish friends, mostly because the kids were just good folk, with a strong faith in the Lord. And none of them had their body parts pierced. But she felt a little protective of Danielle. Was Vera thinking that Danielle wasn't good enough to be friends with her son? True, Danielle was a work in progress, but the girl had gone through a tough time.

Martha didn't care if it was her wedding reception, she was going to find out if maybe she was wrong. She waited until Lillian walked away before she approached Vera.

"Glad to see Danielle is making some friends." Martha nodded toward Danielle and Levi.

Vera smiled. *"Ya, ya."* She paused and raised a brow, her voice unusually hopeful. "Has she made any friends with her own kind?"

Never before had Martha felt the invisible lines that divided them as strongly as she did in this moment. A taut reminder that, no matter the love and friendships—Martha and her people were not Amish. And for a group so dedicated to not passing judgment, Vera's eyes were expressively judging Danielle for the Amish person she was not.

"She's made a few friends," Martha said casually. "But I was hoping she'd make friends with some of the Amish folks. You people raise good kids." She grinned, hoping the compliment would make Vera lighten up a bit.

"We believe in hard work and discipline." Vera pressed her lips together as she glanced over at Danielle and Levi.

"Danielle got a job at the Mountain View Restaurant." Martha felt defensive, a place she didn't like to be. "She'll work hard, I'm sure."

Vera smiled. "I'm sure."

Martha wanted to give Vera a little shove and tell her to quit being so judgmental, that Danielle was just as good as Levi. But today was her wedding day, so she wasn't going to let Vera spoil it.

"Where're Eli and Katie Ann?" Martha scanned the crowd around her and didn't see them. She looked back at Vera, who was now grinning from ear to ear.

"It was a wonderful idea for you to invite Eli. And with Hannah doing so well, he was thrilled to come." She pointed toward the field where Katie Ann and Eli were still standing. "There they are."

It warmed Martha's heart to see them together. It was a picturesque setting as an orange glow rose into a deep blue sky, mountains in every direction. She took another look. *Is Katie Ann crying?*

* * *

Katie Ann searched her heart, and she knew that she would travel to Ohio to be with Eli if he asked her to do so. It would break her heart to leave Canaan, to leave Lillian, Samuel, and the children. They were her family. And what about Martha?

"I can't keep doing this, Eli." She lowered her head as a tear trailed down her cheek. Eli lifted her chin and brushed away the tear with his thumb, keeping his hand on her cheek.

"I don't want to be without you either, Katie Ann."

She was surprised when he leaned in and kissed her, but time stopped for a moment as she allowed herself a few moments in his arms. He kissed her again, then kissed her on the cheek, cupping her face in his hands.

"I love you, Katie Ann. I don't want to be without you, but I'm not going to ask you to leave your family here. I wouldn't do that."

The tiny webs in her heart thickened and spread wider, enough so that she was sure she would never survive what was coming. She stared out into the open field toward the majestic mountains and silently prayed for strength. Eli smoothed back a strand of hair that had fallen forward and kissed her again.

"Marry me, Katie Ann. Spend the rest of your

life with me." Eli smiled. "Let me be a *gut* husband to you and a father to Jonas."

She was confused. "But how can that be, Eli? What about your plans—"

Eli gently put a finger to her lips. "*Mei lieb*, God had other plans for me. I have spent my entire life taking care of others. And it's not a burden, but a blessing. I want to take care of you and Jonas. God's plan was for me to fall in love with you, Katie Ann. And nothing would make me happier than living out my life with you and the two of us raising Jonas together."

She looked deep into his eyes, silently begging for the Holy Spirit to guide her. Then she knew. "I will go anywhere to be with you, Eli. I love you."

He smiled. "You don't have to go anywhere, Katie Ann. I'm staying here."

"But…I don't understand. You said you could never leave your family."

"It would hurt me deeply to have to leave all of them."

She shook her head. "I would never ask you to do that, Eli, but I don't understand."

"Do you know how much an acre of land costs here compared to Middlefield?" He stroked his chin. "Much cheaper here." He paused again. "And have you ever noticed how there isn't a camera in your face everywhere you go here? Not nearly as many tourists. And there is plenty of room."

Katie Ann's eyes widened.

"You'll be meeting most of your extended family this fall when they move to Canaan, a decision they made on their own. They want the freedom to spread out and grow here in Canaan—with us."

Katie Ann threw her arms around him. "Eli! I love you so much. This is wonderful news! I can't wait to meet everyone—Jake, Hannah, Ida Mae, Karen, Frieda, Maureen, and all their families and—"

Eli eased her away for a moment. He pushed back a strand of loose hair that had fallen across her face, then cupped her cheek. "They aren't *all* coming."

Katie Ann didn't understand. "What do you mean?"

"Maureen…" Eli lowered his eyes for a moment. "Maureen won't be coming. Her husband has taken over his father's blacksmith business, and he said they will be staying in Middlefield."

She knew that Eli held a special place in his heart for his youngest daughter. "*Ach*, Eli, I—I don't know what to say."

"Say that you love me." He pulled her close.

"I do. And we will visit Maureen often." She pulled out of his embrace slowly. "Are you sure this is what you want, Eli?"

Then Eli did the unthinkable. He picked her up around the waist and swung her around until all the wildflowers molded into a blurred rainbow of sheer beauty. "I've never wanted anything more in my life."

Katie Ann saw Martha stomping across the meadow, lifting her white heels high as she walked. She wiggled free of Eli's hold but could hardly contain herself as tears of joy poured down her cheeks.

"What in the world is going on out here?" Martha put her hands on her hips. "First I saw you crying, and now..." She grinned. "Are those happy tears?"

"Eli and I are getting married!" Katie Ann bounced on her toes.

Martha threw back her head and laughed. "Just had to go and steal my glory today, didn'tcha, honey?" Then she pulled Katie Ann into a tight hug. "I don't know how I'm going to live without you here, though."

Katie Ann had to pry herself from Martha's embrace. "You don't have to. Eli is staying here, and..." She smiled at Eli. "His family—all but his youngest daughter—are moving here."

Martha looked at Eli, her eyes wide. Then she laughed. "That's the best wedding present I could have asked for. This makes me very happy!" She kissed Katie Ann on the cheek and hugged Eli. "Now I have to go find my new husband before he starts missing me." She turned to leave but then turned back around. "Just think of all the fun we're going to have here in Canaan with such a big family."

Katie Ann closed her eyes and thanked God for the wonder of His love. Then she kissed Eli on the mouth—right in front of Martha.

Martha shook her head, mumbling as she turned to head back toward the house. "Good grief. *My* wedding day, and I can't even hold on to the spotlight." She twisted her head around and winked at Katie Ann. "But you go, girl!"

* * * * *

Acknowledgments

There is always a mild level of anxiety when I write my acknowledgments, for fear of forgetting someone. With each book, more and more people are involved in the process, and getting the book on the shelves is a huge combined effort.

I'll start by thanking God, who continues to bless me with stories to tell. Without Him, there would be no books. Thank You, Lord, for guiding my hand in my effort to deliver stories that both entertain and bring folks closer to You.

To my husband, Patrick—you are the constant in my life that keeps me on an even keel despite the chaos sometimes. Thank you for making me laugh, for loving me, and for reading every single book I write, like you promised…ha ha. ☺ I love you with all my heart.

Sherry Gregg, it is an honor to dedicate the book to someone whom I admire in so many ways. I've always said that sometimes God drops people in our paths for a reason. He sure knew what He was doing when He introduced us. Okay, I better mention your husband, too, since I've known him since

I was a kid…ha ha. Tim, you're the best! Thank you both for your hospitality and your friendship. Despite the many places Patrick and I have traveled, we often recall our trip to Colorado as one of our very best vacations. Love you both!

To my very best friend and kindred spirit, Renee' Bissmeyer. You are a walking journal of my life, the one who knows the me I sometimes don't even know. All these books later, your encouragement and love still keeps me going even when I doubt myself. You continue to be the wind beneath my wings. PEACE and love always.

Janet Murphy, you rock! We make a great team. Thank you for walking one step ahead of me and keeping me on track. You're an awesome assistant, publicity coordinator, listener, encourager, and friend. Cheers to an ongoing journey!

To my editor, Natalie Hanemann, and my Thomas Nelson family—I am incredibly blessed to be traveling this road with you all on my team. Thank you for everything, both professionally and personally. You guys and gals are the best!

Mary Sue Seymour, my friend, my agent—thank you for guiding my career and for the friendship we share.

Barbie Beiler, I sure do miss you, and I hope to visit soon! Your input—based on your own Amish background—continues to strengthen my books, keeping them authentic. Sending you big hugs, my friend.

To my line editor, LB Norton— Wow! You jumped in at the 11th hour on this book, and what a fantastic job you did. Thank you for all your hard work and willingness to push a step further to make the book a better read. Hope to meet you in person soon. Blessings to you.

To friends and family not mentioned here, please know that they only give me so much space to write acknowledgments, or otherwise, I could go on forever and ever about how much each and every one of you means to me and how much I appreciate your encouragement, support, and love.

And last, but certainly not least—to my readers. A huge thank you for reading my books. If one of my stories brought you a step closer to God, or perhaps got you off of the fence where He is concerned, possibly gave you hope or a better understanding of His grace—please let me know by sending me an email at author@bethwiseman.net.

The Wonder of Your Love

READING GROUP GUIDE

1. In the beginning of the story, Katie Ann doesn't think Eli is her type. Why? What are some of Eli's characteristics that Katie Ann ultimately finds charming and is attracted to?

2. Katie Ann struggles to forgive Ivan for his infidelities. How does her inability to forgive set roadblocks along her own life path? Who are we really hurting when we can't forgive?

3. Eli has his life planned out, and he feels as though he's earned some time off. When do his big plans to travel start to fall apart and lose the allure? Why do you think that happened?

4. Katie Ann admits to herself that her relationship with God is not what it used to be. What happens when Katie Ann finally accepts that God is in charge and submits to His will without second-guessing His plan for her?

5. As in real life, there are several "gray" areas mentioned in the book, things or a way of life that aren't traditionally part of Amish living.

One of those is the use of cell phones. What are two more instances where rules are bent?

6. Eli notices early on that Katie Ann and Martha's friendship is special, if not unlikely. But despite their many differences, Katie Ann and Martha are more alike than they may seem. How so?

7. What do you think will happen to Lucy? Do you think that she and Katie Ann will cross paths again someday? Will Jonas and Benjamin ever meet each other? If so, how do you think that will go?

8. Martha is a large presence in the book, and her heart is as big as her outspoken personality, which explains why she took Danielle in. As Martha begins to take on a parental role, how do you see her changing with regard to Danielle?

9. Early on, Katie Ann and Eli agree to just be friends. Have you or anyone you've known fallen in love with their best friend? How did it turn out?

10. Katie Ann and Eli share one similar quality. They are both unselfish. What are several instances when this shines through for each of

them, and when does this endearing quality sometimes block God's efforts for their future together?

11. Danielle tells several lies—to her mother on the phone in the hospital, to the nurse and others about not knowing who hit her, and to Martha when she tells Martha that her parents are dead. Is it ever justifiable to tell a lie? How might things have turned out differently if Danielle had always told the truth? Would things have turned out better or worse for her?

12. Often God has a plan for us that we can't see or understand, putting us on the right course for the life He wants us to live. What are some examples of this in your own life? Have you ever unknowingly blocked His efforts? Or do you believe that it was always God's will for things to have happened exactly the way that they did?

Amish Recipes

PEANUT BLOSSOMS

1 cup sugar
1 cup brown sugar
1 cup butter or oleo
2 eggs
1 cup peanut butter
¼ cup milk
2 teaspoon vanilla
3½ cup flour
2 teaspoon baking soda
1 teaspoon salt
2 (10 ounce) packages chocolate kisses or
miniature peanut butter cups

Cream sugars, butter, and peanut butter. Beat in eggs, milk, and vanilla. Stir in dry ingredients. Shape into balls and roll into additional sugar.

Bake at 375 degrees for 10 to 12 minutes. Immediately press a chocolate candy into each cookie.

Yield: about 7 dozen.

CHICKEN AND RICE CASSEROLE

1 cup rice, uncooked
¼ cup onions, minced
2 tablespoon parsley flakes
½ teaspoon salt and pepper
1 whole chicken, cut up
1 can cream of chicken soup
¾ cup salad dressing
1¼ cup water

Put rice in greased casserole. Add onions and seasonings; mix well. Combine soup, salad dressing, and water; beat. Pour half of soup mixture over rice, top with chicken and remaining soup mixture.

Bake at 350 degrees for 1½ hours.

Sprinkle with paprika, if desired.

LAZY WIFE'S DINNER

1 can cream of celery soup
(or cream of mushroom soup)
1 cup macaroni, uncooked
1½ cup milk
1½ cup frozen vegetable of your choice

½ pound Velveeta
(or American cheese)
1 cup diced potatoes
1 cup diced carrots
1 cup meat of your choice, cooked and
chopped into bite-size pieces
3 tablespoon chopped onion

Mix all the ingredients together and pour into 9" x 13" baking pan.

Bake at 350 degrees for 1½ hours.

Thanks to Amish friends in Lancaster County, Pennsylvania and Westcliffe, Colorado.

About the Author

Beth Wiseman is hailed as a top voice in Amish fiction. She is the author of numerous bestsellers, including the Daughters of the Promise series and the Land of Canaan series. She and her family live in Texas.

Visit BethWiseman.com

HEARTWARMING INSPIRATIONAL ROMANCE

Contemporary,
inspirational romances
with Christian characters
facing the challenges
of life and love
in today's world.

**AVAILABLE IN REGULAR
AND LARGER-PRINT FORMATS.**

For exciting stories that reflect traditional values,
visit:
www.ReaderService.com